ACCLAIM FOR

ROBIN LEE HATCHER

"Whenever I want to fall in love again, I pick up a Robin Lee Hatcher novel."

—FRANCINE RIVERS, *NEW YORK TIMES* BESTSELLING AUTHOR

"Hatcher's richly layered novels pull me in like a warm embrace, and I never want to leave. I own and love every one of this master storyteller's novels. Highly recommended!"

—COLLEEN COBLE, *USA TODAY* BESTSELLING AUTHOR

"*You're Gonna Love Me* is a gentle romance that offers hope for second chances. Author Robin Lee Hatcher has a gift for welcoming readers into fictional close-knit communities fortified with love and trust. With each turn of the page, I relaxed into the quiet rhythm of Hatcher's storytelling, where she deftly examines the heart's desires of her characters set against the richly-detailed Idaho setting."

—BETH K. VOGT, CHRISTY AWARD-WINNING AUTHOR

"*You're Gonna Love Me* nourished my spirit as I read about a hero and heroine with realistic struggles, human responses, and honest growth. Robin Lee Hatcher makes me truly want to drive to Idaho and mingle with the locals."

—HANNAH ALEXANDER, AUTHOR OF *THE WEDDING KISS*

"I didn't think *You'll Think of Me*, the first book in Robin Lee Hatcher's Thunder Creek, Idaho series, could be beat. But she did it again . . . This second chance story will melt your heart and

serve as a parable for finding redemption through life's lessons and God's grace. Thunder Creek will always hold a special place in my heart."

—LENORA WORTH, AUTHOR OF *HER LAKESIDE FAMILY*, ON *YOU'RE GONNA LOVE ME*

"With two strong, genuine characters that readers will feel compassion for and a heartwarming modern-day plot that inspires, Hatcher's romance is a wonderfully satisfying read."

—*RT BOOK REVIEWS*, 4 STARS, ON *YOU'LL THINK OF ME*

"A heart-warming story of love, acceptance, and challenge. Highly recommended."

—*CBA MARKET* ON *YOU'LL THINK OF ME*

"*You'll Think of Me* is like a vacation to small town Idaho where the present collides with the past and it's not clear which will win. The shadows of the past threaten to trap Brooklyn in the past. Can she break free into the freedom to love and find love? The story kept me coming back for just one more page. A perfect read for those who love a romance that is much more as it explores important themes."

—CARA PUTMAN, AWARD-WINNING AUTHOR *SHADOWED BY GRACE* AND *BEYOND JUSTICE*

"Hatcher is able to unravel emotions within her characters so brilliantly that we sense the transformation taking place within ourselves . . . readers will relish the warmth of . . . the ranchland."

—*RT BOOK REVIEWS* ON *KEEPER OF THE STARS*

"Hatcher fans will be left smiling and eagerly awaiting her next novel."

—*CBA RETAILERS + RESOURCES* ON *KEEPER OF THE STARS*

"True to the contemporary romance genre, Robin Lee Hatcher's *Keeper of the Stars* will satisfy romance fans and give them a joy ride as they travel the road of pain and forgiveness to reach the happily-ever-after."

—BOOKTALK AT FICTION 411

"Robin Lee Hatcher weaves a romance with heart that grabs readers and won't let go. *Whenever You Come Around* pulled me in from the get-go. Charity Anderson, a beautiful, successful author with a deadline and a painful secret, runs into Buck Malone, a handsome, confirmed-bachelor cowboy from her past, and he needs her help. I was captivated, and I guarantee you'll be rooting for them too."

—SUNNI JEFFERS, AWARD-WINNING AUTHOR OF *HEAVEN'S STRAIN*

"A heartwarming and engaging romance, *Whenever You Come Around* is a splendid read from start to finish!"

—TAMERA ALEXANDER, *USA TODAY* BESTSELLING AUTHOR OF *TO WHISPER HER NAME* AND *FROM A DISTANCE*

"A handsome cowboy, horses, and a hurting heroine make for a winning combination in this newest poignant story by Robin Lee Hatcher. A gently paced but delightful ride, *Whenever You Come Around* will take readers on a journey of healing right along with the characters. Readers will feel at home in Kings Meadow and won't want to leave."

—JODY HEDLUND, BESTSELLING AUTHOR OF *LOVE UNEXPECTED*

"First loves find sweet second chances in Kings Meadow. Heartwarming, romantic, and filled with hope and faith, this is Hatcher at her best!"

—LISA WINGATE, NATIONAL BESTSELLING AUTHOR OF *THE STORY KEEPER* AND *THE PRAYER BOX* ON *WHENEVER YOU COME AROUND*

"In *Whenever You Come Around* Hatcher takes a look at the pain of secrets that kill the heart. But love indeed conquers all. Robin Lee Hatcher is the go-to classic romance author."

—RACHEL HAUCK, AWARD-WINNING, *NEW YORK TIMES*
BESTSELLING AUTHOR OF *THE WEDDING DRESS*

"Robin Lee Hatcher has created an emotionally engaging romance, a story of healing and self-forgiveness wrapped up in a package about small-town life and a cowboy who lives a life honoring God. I want to live in Kings Meadow."

—SHARON DUNN, AUTHOR OF COLD *CASE JUSTICE* AND
WILDERNESS TARGET ON *WHENEVER YOU COME AROUND*

"*Whenever You Come Around* draws you into the beauty and history of the horse country of Kings Meadow, Idaho. With every turn of the page, Robin Lee Hatcher woos readers with a love story of a modern-day cowboy and a city girl. Buck and Charity rescue each other from the lives they had planned—lives limited by fear. Instead, they discover their unexpected God-ordained happily ever after. A discerning writer, Hatcher handles Charity's past heartbreak with sensitivity and grace."

—BETH K. VOGT, AUTHOR OF *SOMEBODY LIKE YOU*, ONE OF
PUBLISHERS WEEKLY'S BEST BOOKS OF 2014

"*Whenever You Come Around* is one of Robin Lee Hatcher's pure-romance best, with a heroine waiting for total redemption and a strong hero of great worth. I find myself still smiling long after the final page has been read."

—HANNAH ALEXANDER, AUTHOR OF THE HALLOWED HALLS SERIES

"*Whenever You Come Around* is a slow dance of letting go of the past and its very real pain to step into the light of love. It's a story that will wrap around your soul with the hope that no past is so dark and haunted that it can't be forgiven and overcome. It's a love story filled with sweetness, tension, and slow fireworks. Bottom line, it was a romance I couldn't—and didn't want to—put down."

—CARA PUTMAN, AWARD-WINNING AUTHOR OF
SHADOWED BY GRACE AND WHERE TREETOPS GLISTEN

"In *Love Without End*, Robin Lee Hatcher once again takes us to Kings Meadow, Idaho, in a sweeping love story that captures the heart and soul of romance between two people who have every reason not to fall in love. With an interesting backstory interspersed among the contemporary chapters, and well-drawn, relatable secondary characters, Hatcher hits the mark with her warm and inviting love story."

—MARTHA ROGERS, AUTHOR OF THE SERIES
WINDS ACROSS THE PRAIRIE AND THE HOMEWARD JOURNEY

"*Love Without End*, the first book in the new Kings Meadow Romance series, again intertwines two beautiful and heartfelt romances. One in the past and one in the future together make this a special read. I'm so glad Robin wrote a love story for Chet who suffered so much in *A Promise Kept* (January 2014). Kimberly, so wrong for him, becomes so right. Not your run-of-the-mill cowboy romance—enriched with deft writing and deep emotion."

—LYN COTE, AUTHOR OF *HONOR*, QUAKER BRIDES, BOOK ONE

"No one writes about the joys and challenges of family life better than Robin Lee Hatcher, and she's at the top of her game with *Love Without End*. This beautiful and deeply moving story will capture your heart as it captured mine."

—MARGARET BROWNLEY, *NEW YORK TIMES* BESTSELLING AUTHOR

"*Love Without End*, Book One in Robin Lee Hatcher's new Kings Meadow series, is a delight from start to finish. The author's skill at depicting the love and challenges of family has never been more evident as she deftly combines two love stories—past and present—to capture readers' hearts and lift their spirits."

—MARTA PERRY, AUTHOR OF *THE FORGIVEN*, KEEPERS OF THE PROMISE, BOOK ONE

"I always expect excellence when I open a Robin Lee Hatcher novel. She never disappoints. The story here reminds me of a circle without end as Robin takes us through a modern-day romance while looping one character through a WWII tale of love and loss and the resurrection of hope and purpose. *Love Without End* touched my heart and guided me to some wonderful truths of how God's love is a gift and a treasure."

—DONITA K. PAUL, BESTSELLING AUTHOR

"A beautiful, heart-touching story of God's amazing grace, and how He can restore and make new that which was lost."

—FRANCINE RIVERS, *NEW YORK TIMES* BESTSELLING AUTHOR, ON *A PROMISE KEPT*

You're Gonna Love Me

ALSO BY ROBIN LEE HATCHER

You'll Think of Me

The Heart's Pursuit

A Promise Kept

Heart of Gold

Autumn's Angel, a novella found in *A Bride for All Seasons*

KINGS MEADOW ROMANCE SERIES

Love Without End

Whenever You Come Around

Keeper of the Stars

WHERE THE HEART LIVES SERIES

Belonging

Betrayal

Beloved

THE SISTERS OF BETHLEHEM SPRINGS SERIES

A Vote of Confidence

Fit to Be Tied

A Matter of Character

You're Gonna Love Me

Robin Lee Hatcher

THOMAS NELSON
Since 1798

Published in Nashville, Tennessee, by Thomas Nelson. Thomas Nelson is a registered trademark of HarperCollins Christian Publishing, Inc.

Thomas Nelson titles may be purchased in bulk for educational, business, fund-raising, or sales promotional use. For information, please e-mail SpecialMarkets@ThomasNelson.com.

Scripture quotations are taken from New American Standard Bible®, Copyright © 1960, 1962, 1963, 1968, 1971, 1972, 1973, 1975, 1977, 1995 by The Lockman Foundation. Used by permission. (www.Lockman.org)

Publisher's Note: This novel is a work of fiction. Names, characters, places, and incidents are either products of the author's imagination or used fictitiously. All characters are fictional, and any similarity to people living or dead is purely coincidental.

Library of Congress Cataloging-in-Publication Data

CIP data is available upon request.

Printed in the United States of America

17 18 19 20 21 22 /LSC/ 6 5 4 3 2 1

Prologue

Nick Chastain heard the sound of horses' hooves and looked up from the irrigation pipes he'd set on the ground. Two horses cantered along the creek bank, too far away for him to see the faces of the riders, but he was certain one was an adult and the other a young girl. Perhaps a mother and daughter.

He was about to return to his work when one of the horses, a big blue roan, flew sideways, twisting in midair. The adult rider parted ways with the saddle. A moment later, the woman hit the ground. The girl gave a shriek of surprise as she reined in her palomino.

Nick waited a few heartbeats, but the woman on the ground didn't move.

The girl slipped from the saddle and hurried toward her. "Gee-Gee Ruth!" she screamed.

Still no movement.

Nick took off at a run, his long strides eating up the distance. By the time he reached the pair, both horses had trotted away. He ignored them and focused instead on the scene in front of him. The woman on the ground—older than he'd expected—groaned, but her eyes remained closed.

Nick dropped to his knees opposite the girl. "That was a bad fall." He touched the woman's shoulder. "Ma'am?"

Her eyes fluttered briefly. "I think . . . I need . . . an ambulance."

"Right away." He pulled out his cell phone and punched in 911. As soon as his call was answered, he explained the situation to the dispatcher. But when it came time to give the address or directions, he found himself at a loss. His employer had transferred him from Cheyenne, Wyoming, to Caldwell, Idaho, less than three months before, and this was his first installation job in the small town of Thunder Creek. He didn't even remember the name of the road he'd followed to get to Derek Johnson's farm. He clenched his jaw, hating the forgetfulness that continued to dog him.

Wordlessly the girl held out her hand for the phone, and he passed it to her.

"My name's Alycia Johnson," she said, sounding more grown up than she looked. "It's my great-grandma, Ruth

Johnson, who's hurt." There was a pause. "No, my mom and dad aren't here." She looked at Nick. "I think so." Another pause, then she gave detailed driving instructions to the farm.

The wait for the ambulance seemed eternal. At some point Nick found himself holding the woman's hand and speaking words of comfort, although he wasn't sure she heard him. Eyes closed, she gasped more than she breathed, obviously in extreme pain.

Nick knew a thing or two about pain. His thirst for adventure used to get him into trouble all the time. His parents and siblings, doctors and therapists, all hoped he'd had his fill of it at last. But there were times . . .

Grinning all the while, Nick stretched his arm toward the branch above his head. He'd already climbed higher than the last time, and today he planned to go all the way to the top.

From the ground his brother Jeff yelled, "If Mom catches you up that tree again, you're gonna catch it for sure."

"If you shut up, she'll never know."

"Okay. But don't blame me when you fall and bust your stupid neck."

"I'm not gonna fall."

The words were barely out of Nick's mouth when he felt his right foot start to slip. Just in time his hand closed around the limb overhead. His balance soon restored, he dragged in a breath, then laughed, pleasure pulsing through him. His big brother didn't understand what he was missing, staying down there on the ground. There was something . . . *special* about being up this high, looking down on the world. Well, not the world. But his backyard and the neighboring ones.

"That's high enough, Nick."

He ignored Jeff. He wasn't stopping until he could carve his initials up at the top in that gap between the branches, a spot he could see from the ground. Then he could point to it anytime and brag that he'd done it when nobody thought he could. Then he could—

The loud *crack* barely had time to register in Nick's brain before the limb was gone beneath his feet. He flailed his arms as gravity pulled at him. He tried to grab hold of anything he could. But nothing stopped his hurtle toward earth—although the tree itself slowed the descent as he smacked into one branch after another.

"Nick!"

His brother's shout ringing in his ears, he hit the ground. For a second he thought he was okay and started to grin. That's when the pain shot through him. Turning his head, he saw the bone near his left wrist sticking through his skin, blood pouring through the torn flesh. His smile vanished.

Turned out it was only the first time Nick Chastain would break that same arm.

Chapter 1

Samantha Winters parked her car in the Caldwell hospital parking lot. Before opening the door, she pressed her forehead against the steering wheel and drew in a couple of deep breaths. She was bone weary after the seven-hour drive from Beaverton, Oregon. She'd stopped only twice, just long enough to refill the tank and use the restroom, and hadn't bothered to eat anything except the snack foods she'd tossed into the car before leaving home before dawn.

The last report from her cousin Derek was that their grandmother's surgery—performed that morning, twenty-four hours after the fall from the horse—had gone well. Derek expected Gran to be able to leave the hospital tomorrow or the next day.

"But from what I understand," he'd told Samantha a few hours ago, "it's going to be a lengthy recovery. Her right ankle was more or less shattered. Broken in three places. It'll be non-weight-bearing for at least three months. She'll be in a cast and then one of those boots. After three months, they'll put her in a splint—I forget what it's called—and then she'll have to go through physical therapy. Not easy for any-body, but she's seventy-six. As active as she normally is, this is gonna drive her crazy."

"Don't worry about Gran's recovery. I'll stay as long as she needs me. I'm using the vacation days I've saved up over the years, and then I'll be on leave of absence for the rest of the time."

"You don't have to do that, Sam. Between me and Brooklyn and Gran's friends—"

"I *want* to do it. Honest."

What she hadn't told her cousin was that she was glad for an excuse—*any* excuse—to get away from work for a while. And away from Daniel Greyson, her boss. Not to be unkind, but the man was a jerk. He'd made her work life miserable for years. She'd put up with it because . . . well, because it was easier and less confrontational. Her only other option was to look for new employment, and that thought terri-fied her. Job security was important to her. She felt *safe* at Whitewater Business Solutions. And above almost anything else, Samantha liked to feel safe.

Drawing one more breath, she straightened and opened the door. She felt rumpled and looked forward to a long soak in a warm bath. But before she could drive on to Thunder Creek, she wanted to see Gran.

The hospital wasn't large, and it didn't take long to find her grandmother's room. A nurse was coming through the doorway when Samantha arrived. They exchanged brief nods as they passed each other.

Gran looked up, registered who it was, and smiled. "Sam! What on earth are you doing here?" She held out a hand.

Samantha took it before leaning in to kiss her grandmother. "Didn't Derek tell you I was coming? I had to come after I heard you took up flying. Or was it crashing?"

"Both, it would seem." Gran pressed Samantha's hand against her cheek, eyes closed for a moment. "Oh, it is so good to see you," she said as she opened them again and gazed fondly at Samantha.

"Same here."

"But such a long drive."

"It isn't so bad, Gran. And I wanted to be with you. You're going to need help for a while."

Gran's eyes widened. "You're going to stay with me? You're not here just for the weekend?"

"Nope. I'm here for a few months, according to the doctor."

"Oh, sweetheart. What about your job? I can't ask you to—"

But Samantha was already shaking her head. "You didn't ask. Like I told Derek, I want to be with you. And I've made all the necessary arrangements with my job."

"They'll let you be gone that long?"

Samantha squeezed her grandmother's hand again. "You're stuck with me, Gran. Get used to it."

Gran smiled. "Getting used to it won't be a problem. I promise." She breathed out on a sigh, then sank deeper into the pillow beneath her head, her burst of energy spent. Samantha saw pain in the crinkles of her grandmother's face as she closed her eyes and almost instantly drifted off to sleep—aided by drugs, no doubt.

Samantha wouldn't mind a catnap herself. She pulled a visitor's chair close to the side of Gran's bed and settled onto it. Closing her eyes, she drew in a long, deep breath. She was so tired.

Through her weary haze, she heard a male voice ask, "May I come in?"

Startled from near slumber, Samantha straightened and looked toward the drawn curtain in front of the door. "Yes."

She expected to see a doctor or a hospital technician of some sort. Instead, a man in jeans and a denim shirt stepped into view holding a vase of flowers in one hand. He smiled for a moment. But only until his eyes collided with hers. Then the smile was gone.

Samantha barely had time to register this before her world tilted to one side. Ocean-like sounds whirred in her ears as she sucked in a breath. It couldn't be—

"Sam?" Nick said, his voice filled with matching disbelief.

"Nick . . . What on earth . . . ?" Her voice strengthened. "What are you doing here?"

He motioned toward the hospital bed. "I came to see Mrs. Johnson."

"You—" She shook her head, trying to clear her confusion. "Gran? But how do you know—?"

"She's your grandmother?"

Samantha nodded. They both stood staring.

"Small world," Nick finally said. He stood still a moment longer, his jaw working, then set the vase of flowers on the nearby counter. "Tell your grandmother I was by. Okay?" A couple of steps and he disappeared beyond the curtain.

Samantha couldn't move at first. Her legs failed to obey the command from her brain. But a few heartbeats later, she rushed out of the room and down the corridor, catching up with him right outside the automatic doors.

"Nick!"

He stopped, seemed to wait as she struggled for words, then finally turned. She gripped her hands together, holding them close to her waist. "I . . . I never expected to see you again. Certainly not here."

He shrugged. The gesture hurt. It seemed to say he didn't care what she'd expected. And he probably didn't. He'd never bothered to respond to the apologies she'd sent to him over two years ago.

She drew a breath and lifted her chin. "Why did you come to see my grandmother?"

"I was there yesterday when the horse threw her. I was the one who called for the ambulance and stayed with her, along with Alycia."

"*You* were there?" Her confusion returned.

"I'm putting in a new irrigation system for Derek Johnson. I guess he's her grandson." His eyes filled with realization. "So that would make Derek your . . . ?"

"Cousin."

"Ah." He nodded.

Samantha and Nick had dated for close to eight months. Naturally, during that time she'd told him about her mother and stepdad who lived back east and that she had a grandmother and cousin living in Idaho. But had she bothered to mention the name of the little town of Thunder Creek? Doubtful. And even if she had, would he have remembered it? Also doubtful. She'd teased him once that he had selective hearing. He hadn't found it funny.

She shook her head again, trying to focus on a more immediate question: Why was a university professor from Oregon installing an irrigation system on an organic farm in Idaho? Her cousin's farm, of all places.

Without an answer that made sense to her, her thoughts spiraled backward again. Nick had been in her thoughts often since their painful parting. There had been nights she'd dreamed of running into him again, of being able to look him in the eyes and tell him she was sorry for what she'd said on that last night they were together. Not long after their argument, she'd e-mailed him. She'd called too. He'd never answered, so she'd left messages. All had gone unanswered. And still she'd wanted to see him.

Now here he was, just as she'd dreamed of. But the

expression on his face told her he didn't want her to say another word. She took a step back, an old pain tightening her chest. "Well. It was good to see you, Nick." The words tasted like sawdust on her tongue.

"Yeah. Same here."

Taking a quick breath, she turned and hurried back through the hospital doors.

&O

After more than two years since his accident, Nick had grown used to blanks in his memory, to confusion threatening to swallow him whole. It wasn't as bad now as it had been early on, but it could be bad enough. Seeing Samantha Winters had thrown him for an unexpected loop. He felt out of touch, not quite sure what was real and what he'd imagined as a result of the traumatic brain injury he'd been living with.

"Here?" he muttered to himself as he yanked open the truck door and slid behind the wheel. "Her grandmother had to live *here*?"

Settling himself, he lifted his gaze toward the entrance. He avoided hospitals whenever he could. He'd been a patient in one or another for too many months to want to return, even to visit someone else. But, as crazy as it sounded, he'd needed to see Ruth Johnson—a stranger to him until yesterday—to make sure she was doing all right. The last time he'd glimpsed her, the woman had been in a lot of pain.

And now it turned out Ruth was Samantha's grandmother.

What were the odds? Astronomical. No wonder he was having a hard time making sense of it.

He rubbed his forehead with the fingertips of one hand as he took a breath and tried to reason things through. Samantha's mother and stepdad lived in New England. He remembered that for certain. He also remembered her mentioning that her grandmother lived in Idaho. In fact, when Brett Masters had asked him to move to Caldwell to become the lead foreman for the southwest Idaho branch of Masters & Sons Irrigation Systems, Nick had thought of Samantha, remembering sitting across from her at dinner on their first date, listening as she told him about her family and her job and her interests.

She'd been the prettiest woman he'd ever seen. Still was. But then, he'd always been a sucker for girls with red hair and green eyes. But there'd been more to the attraction than her looks. He'd liked the honey-warm tone of her voice. He'd liked the sound of her laughter. He'd liked that she loved music from the seventies and movies from the forties and fifties. He wasn't crazy about any of that, but he'd found the discovery of her passions for those things endeared her to him. All that remained clear in his mind, unimpaired by his accident.

Another thing he remembered: Samantha had wanted to change him, to tie him down, to hold him back, to restrain him. They'd fought about it. Broken up over it. He'd said something cruel to her, too, although he couldn't remember exactly what. But he did remember he'd later wished he'd chosen his words better.

He gave his head a slow shake before turning the key

in the ignition and driving out of the hospital parking lot, headed for home. Since February, that had been a two-bedroom month-to-month rental located a few miles west of Caldwell. Built around the time of the Great Depression, the place needed lots of work. But that was one of the reasons the rent was cheap, which suited Nick's bank account. And he had no need for anything more. His life these days was simple and uncomplicated. He got up in the morning, ate breakfast, went to work, laid pipe or whatever the job called for, completed paperwork, checked inventory, came home, ate dinner, played with his dog, and relaxed or took a bike ride before bedtime. The next day he did it all over again.

Again, simple and uncomplicated, as it needed to be at this point in his recovery. He certainly didn't need—

He broke off his thoughts before they could drift in the direction of Samantha again.

Nick's rental property was surrounded on three sides by cornfields belonging to his landlord. In April there wasn't much but dirt to look at in those fields. But that would soon change. The tall trees on the west side of the house were already a deep green, and flowers planted by a previous tenant bloomed in a bright array of colors near the driveway and country road.

As he pulled his truck up near the house, his border collie, Boomer, greeted him with excited barks. Nick got out of the truck and strode to the kennel, releasing the dog. "Hey, boy. How you doing?"

Boomer received a few pats, then took off in search of a

ball or a Frisbee, eager for some exercise. Nick waited, not in any great hurry to go inside in this fine weather. Besides, his Sunday afternoons were for kicking back, and that included playing with the dog he'd adopted from the shelter soon after relocating to Idaho. The two had become pals from day one, and Boomer went with Nick almost everywhere.

The dog returned. Nick took the ball and threw it as hard and as far as he could. Boomer flew after it, ears flat, mouth open. Nick laughed as he watched. His brother Peter—second of the four Chastain brothers—had told him having a dog around would be good for him. Turned out Peter was right.

"For a change," he said, grinning. Maybe he would call Peter and tell him.

Boomer came barreling back with the ball. Nick threw it again, this time in the opposite direction, and the dog sailed after it, wind in his face, excitement in his eyes. The thrill of the chase. The boundless energy. Nick didn't know whether to laugh or cry when he realized he envied his dog.

"That used to be me," he said to Boomer upon the dog's return, ruffling his ears as he spoke.

Gads, he missed it. He missed going as fast as he could, going as high as he could, dropping as far as he could. He missed the stormy ocean tossing his boat around like a toy. He missed the icy river water. He missed climbing the sheer face of a mountain. He missed his old life, the one he'd been told couldn't be his again.

"Promise me you'll be careful," his mom had said to him again and again since the accident that almost killed him.

He'd promised her. But could he keep that promise without going insane?

"Come on," he said to Boomer. "Let's get us something to eat."

His kitchen was the kind Nick's mom would call a postage stamp. Room enough for a small refrigerator in one corner, an electric stove in another, and about two feet of counter space on each side of the double sink. Part of one wall was taken up by the back door. The refrigerator and stove were separated by an archway leading into a narrow dining room and the connected living room.

In no time at all, Nick had mixed kibble with canned food for Boomer, then made himself a grilled-cheese sandwich and a tossed salad with his favorite dressing. The dog gobbled up his food before Nick could sit down at the table to eat his own, then settled a short distance away, eyes watchful, in case Nick dropped something good.

"You're a bottomless pit, boy."

Boomer swept his tail back and forth in response, not the least bit insulted.

That brought a smile back to Nick.

All things considered, he had a good life. Very different from the one he'd had before the accident, but a good one. God had done more than heal his body. The Lord had begun to heal his emotions and adjust his attitude too. Still a long way to go, he had to admit, but they were working on it, he and God. Including that persistent desire to go faster, higher, farther, and to the devil with his doctors' warnings. He was

15

learning to be grateful for what he had rather than resenting what he'd lost. Not lessons that came easy, but he was getting there. Moving to southwest Idaho had helped a lot. He was free from those who put pressure on him, whether intentional or not. He was living alone, standing on his own two feet, making his own decisions. He didn't need someone else to take care of him. He felt like a man again, instead of a helpless kid.

All in all, Nick had no reason to complain.

Chapter 2

The next morning, still in her pj's and with eyes half closed, Samantha felt her way down the stairs in search of her first cup of coffee. Before she reached the last step, she sniffed the warm, familiar scent and somehow knew it came from Gran's kitchen rather than the connected shop, Sips and Scentimentals.

"Camila," she whispered. "Bless you."

And sure enough, her grandmother's best friend—tall and sturdy, black hair streaked with gray, and a smile that, when directed Samantha's way, made her feel all warm and wonderful on the insides—stood in the kitchen watching the last of the coffee drip into the waiting pot. "Morning, sleepyhead."

"Morning," Samantha mumbled.

"Rough night?"

She held out a hand as Camila poured coffee into a large mug. "More than you know." But she refused to think about the reason why. A reason who had broad shoulders, chocolate-brown eyes, and the shadow of a beard that never quite became one. Someone she had nearly managed to banish from her thoughts . . . up until yesterday.

The woman acknowledged Samantha's words with an "Mmm."

Still trying to rid herself of the image in her mind, Samantha went to the kitchen table, where she doctored the aromatic brew with cream.

"I went to see Ruth last night." Camila sank onto the opposite chair, holding a cup of her own. "You know what she said when I told her she had no business being on a horse at her age? She told me if the Queen of England could still ride at ninety, then Ruth Johnson could still ride at seventy-six."

"Lots of people plenty older than Gran ride horses every day."

Camila grunted. "Never understood the desire to get up on an animal that big."

"Then I feel sorry for you." Samantha smiled and took a sip of her coffee.

Camila did the same before saying, "Your grandmother is overjoyed that you're here."

"Did you know it's for the duration? Until Gran's finished with rehab and fully recovered."

Camila arched an eyebrow.

Samantha answered the unspoken question. "I have vacation coming, and then I'll take advantage of the company leave. I want to be here for as long as Gran needs me. Maybe longer than she wants me." She laughed, making a joke of it.

Camila Diaz was nearly as astute as Samantha's grandmother. "What is it, Sam? What's wrong?"

"Nothing." Then she shook her head. "I don't know. I just feel less and less happy at work. It doesn't make sense, because my goal when I started college was to eventually work for a firm like Whitewater. Although it doesn't help that I've been passed over for a promotion I thought for sure was mine." She frowned as she drew in a slow breath. "More than one, actually. I think my boss has made sure he can keep me working in his department rather than have me move elsewhere."

"Have you spoken up for yourself?"

She thought for a moment, then shook her head again. "No."

"Why not?"

She could have told Camila how nervous it made her to think about standing up for herself or to think about looking for work elsewhere. Both were true and accurate reasons. Only unlike yesterday, they didn't seem . . . enough. Giving herself a few moments to form an honest response, she sipped her coffee, then finally answered, "I don't know why. I'm still trying to figure it out."

"Oh."

"I hope this time with Gran will help me do that."

"Then I hope so too. And nobody's better at helping folks figure things out than your grandmother."

Samantha chuckled, her mood lightening. "True."

Camila looked toward the door that led into the shop. "It sounds like things are getting busy. I'd best go help Gina before the morning rush overwhelms her."

"Do you need me to do anything?"

"Heavens, no." Camila waved a hand dismissively as she stood. "You concentrate on your grandmother, and I'll make sure Sips and Scentimentals is taken care of."

"Okay."

"If you've forgotten where anything is, give a holler."

"I will. Thanks, Camila."

The woman disappeared through the doorway.

Samantha closed her eyes and took another sip of coffee. *Ahhh.* There was something rather amazing about a Monday without commutes into and out of the city, without eight hours of staring at a computer screen or studying numbers on a printout or sitting around a conference room table. She could almost feel her heart rate slow down a good ten beats a minute.

She opened her eyes. It felt wonderful to be in Gran's home again. She'd come to stay here right after graduating from college while she looked for employment. Those summer months remained among her favorite memories ever. After God made Gran, He'd broken the mold. She was the absolute best. Ask anybody in Thunder Creek.

The telephone rang, and she forced herself up from the chair to go answer it. "Ruth Johnson's residence."

"Hey, cuz." Derek's voice was full of a smile. "Got here all right, I see."

"Yes. Yesterday afternoon."

"I talked to Gran this morning. The doctor was in to see her, and they're going to keep her in the hospital one more night. So Brooklyn and I want you to come to dinner at our place. No point you eating alone or living on hospital food. Sound good?"

"Sounds great. I haven't seen the inn since your wedding, and it wasn't even open for business yet. Can you believe that'll be two years come September?"

"Yeah. Time flies. As for the inn, Brooklyn's always full of new ideas. But we aren't living in it anymore. We built a new home on the property, and that's where we'll eat tonight."

"Wow. Why didn't anybody tell me?"

"It was a secret." He laughed. "Come about five and we'll tell you all about it firsthand."

"How do I find your new place?"

"As long as you remember the way to the inn, you won't have any trouble finding us. I promise. See you at five."

"Okay. I know the way. See you soon."

Smiling, she put the handset back in its cradle. Although she would never say it out loud, Derek was her favorite cousin. Being around him and getting to know his wife and her daughter better would be an added benefit of staying in Thunder Creek for a few months.

A glance at the clock told her she'd better get a move on. She might not have a job to go to today, but there were things to do. First, pour herself another cup of coffee, followed by breakfast and a shower, then driving back to the hospital in Caldwell to spend time with Gran.

℘

"Boomer, down." Nick pointed to the ground near the side of his pickup. "Stay."

The border collie lay down, eyes watchful. Whoever had trained the young dog had done an amazing job. And whenever Nick thought of that, it also made him wonder why Boomer had ended up at the humane society. It didn't make sense to him, someone giving away such a great animal.

"Whatever the reason, I'm the lucky recipient." He reached down to stroke Boomer's head.

With a smile Nick started unloading more pipe. But before he could get much done, he heard his name called and turned around to see Derek Johnson striding toward him.

"How's it going?" Derek asked when he arrived.

"Good. And how's your grandmother? I went to see her yesterday, but she was sleeping, so I left." *Not to mention seeing Sam made me want to get out of there.*

"She's doing well, according to her doctor. And thanks to you."

"I didn't do anything but call for the ambulance and hold her hand until it got here."

"Seemed like more than that to all of us."

Nick shrugged.

"She gets to go home tomorrow."

"That's good."

"My cousin's staying with her during her recovery."

"Sam." The name slipped out before he could stop it.

"Yeah." Derek's expression showed his surprise. "How'd you know that?"

"She was at the hospital yesterday when I got there."

"Oh. So you met her then." Derek nodded, as if to confirm that it now made sense.

Nick hesitated a short while before correcting him. "Actually, Sam and I knew each other in Oregon. A couple of years ago."

"You're kidding?" Derek's eyes widened, inviting Nick to say more.

"Some coincidence, huh?" He looked down at the ground. What else could he say? He hadn't told anyone in Idaho about the accident that had changed his life. No one in the area knew he held a PhD in Fisheries and Wildlife. Everyone thought he was an ordinary laborer, the lead foreman for an irrigation company, and that's where he wanted to leave it. He didn't want anybody feeling sorry for him or asking questions that he found hard to answer.

"Some coincidence," Derek echoed. He waited a few heartbeats, as if tempted to ask some of those unwanted questions. Finally, he added, "It's a small world for sure."

"Small world." Nick hoped that would put an end to the subject. Luckily, it did.

Derek motioned to the pipe and equipment on the ground.

"I'd better let you get to work, and I need to get to my own." He turned and took a few strides away before stopping and facing Nick again. "Hey, would you like to have dinner with us tonight? My wife's a great cook. I promise you'll like it."

"That's good of you, but I wouldn't want to—"

"Come on. You told me yourself you know hardly anybody in the area."

That was true. Nick had told Derek the first day on the job that he was new to Caldwell. He usually didn't admit such things to any of the company's clients. It led to invitations like this one. And if he accepted, then there would be questions around the dinner table—the getting-to-know-you kind that made him uncomfortable. Not only because he preferred to keep his former life to himself, but because there were too many facts, dates, and memories that remained fuzzy or had disappeared altogether.

On the other hand, he had a feeling Derek was the kind of guy he would like to call a friend, and it was time Nick made a few of those in Idaho. Unless he royally screwed up as the foreman for Masters & Sons Irrigation Systems, Caldwell was going to be his home for the foreseeable future. Maybe for good.

"All right," Nick said at last. "I'll be glad to come. What time? I'll have to drive home to clean up and put Boomer in his kennel."

"Bring the dog. Miss Trouble will love having some canine company."

"Miss Trouble?"

Humor filled Derek's voice. "Our dog. We can tell you that story tonight. Come at five or five thirty. We'll plan to eat at six."

"Okay. I'll be there."

"Great." Derek turned and began walking away. "Sam's coming, too, so you won't be completely among strangers."

Samantha? Nick's heart thudded. Had she known Derek planned to invite him? He'd bet money she hadn't. He'd also bet she wasn't going to like it. Not after the way she'd looked at him yesterday.

He inhaled slowly and let it out. Was this God's way of getting him to ask Samantha to forgive him for the way he'd ended things with her? It was something that had nagged at him, off and on, after memories had begun to return. Sure, he could have picked up the phone and called her, but he'd never been able to make himself do it. Pride, he supposed. He hadn't wanted her to know what happened to him.

He faced his truck. Boomer lay in the exact same spot, watching his master, waiting for a command. A walk would do them both good. "Come on, boy. Let's have a look at where we are."

Derek and Brooklyn Johnson owned about thirteen acres of prime farming land. A couple of acres were in pasture, and another half acre or so hosted a small, mostly immature, fruit orchard. A bed-and-breakfast, the Inn at Thunder Creek, along with its expansive event gardens and enormous shade trees, took up close to an acre as well. Then there was the main house, smaller outbuildings, greenhouse, and barn. That left just shy of nine acres for growing fruits and vegetables.

Inspired by an organic farmer in northern California where the owners grew more produce with less water, no tilling, and no pesticides of any kind, Derek planned to use the same methods on his farm, including swapping out above-ground irrigation methods for a drip system using thin plastic tubes. Starting tomorrow, Nick would be joined by a larger crew to begin installing the system. Today he continued to map things out.

He knew a few people back in Oregon who believed the knock he'd taken on his head had made him lose his mind along with many memories. Why would a man with his education and experience leave behind the academia he loved to do this kind of labor—setting up, repairing, or replacing irrigation systems on farms both large and small? Of course, he didn't have a lot of choice. Even with improvements in his health, he couldn't go back to his former life. He didn't have the required mental agility for the classroom any longer, and he wasn't physically able for the thing he'd loved most: taking those high-risk excursions with students. Countless doctors had made it clear what another accident could mean to him.

Nick had always loved the outdoors. He'd also been eager for new adventures. Big adventures. Scary adventures. The accident may have put an end to his thrill-seeking ways for good, but the outdoors could still be his. There was something rejuvenating about working out in the sun and the rain, the heat and the cold, the wind and the calm. Thanks to Brett Masters, he had a job that gave him all of that. It had been good for him. It was still good for him.

In fact, Nick liked to think he was a better man today than he'd been two years ago. He liked to think he put others first more often than he used to. He liked to think he listened better than he used to.

Would Samantha see the differences in him, given a chance?

He closed his eyes, remembering the first time he'd seen her. Some memories hadn't returned to him, but this one— from two years and eight months ago, almost to the day—was as clear as if it had happened yesterday.

❧

How in the blue blazes had Nick let himself be talked into coming to this stupid thing? A tax seminar. In August!

The meeting room in the hotel was windowless, but Nick knew an incredible summer evening lay beyond those paneled walls. He could be riding his bike or rollerblading or even rock climbing at the gym. Instead, he was stuck here because he'd made a promise to John Moss, his accountant.

"You're brilliant in a lot of ways, Nick," John had said after informing him about the seminar, "but you're going to find yourself with a stiff fine one of these days if you don't pay attention to a few more bookkeeping details. I'm good, but I'm not a miracle worker."

The lecturer droned on. It seemed like hours already. In reality, maybe fifteen minutes had passed.

Nick happened to look to one side in time to see a woman enter through the door. Moving quickly and hoping not to be noticed, judging by her expression, she took a seat in the row in front of him, to the far right of where he sat next to the center aisle. It afforded him a nice view of her profile.

Man, she was gorgeous. The beautiful shade of her red hair. The pale, clear complexion. The perfect arch of her long neck. And although he couldn't see her eyes, he'd bet money they were green. Her attire said "business professional," but at the same time it said "Feminine" with a capital F.

Nick checked his watch. The program called for a ten-minute break on the next hour. Whatever else happened during those ten minutes, Nick would make certain he met that young woman, learned her name, and, most important, made arrangements for when they would see each other again.

Chapter 3

It's fabulous," Samantha said as Brooklyn led the way to the family room. "The whole house is beautiful. You have a real flare for decorating. A gene I'm sorely lacking."

Brooklyn laughed. "I decorate on a shoestring, I assure you. I've become an expert at shopping garage sales and repurposing items others throw away. The B&B taught me how to do that."

"I'd love to see what you've done over there since the wedding."

"I'll be glad to show you."

Derek stood as the two women reentered the room. His gaze went straight to Brooklyn, and Samantha felt her breath catch at the look in his eyes. The love her cousin felt for his wife was palpable, and a sting of envy shot through her. With it came the image of a man she'd once thought, once hoped—

She forced the unwelcome memories away.

"Honey," Brooklyn said, "is your guest coming?"

He glanced at his watch. "Far as I know."

Another guest? Samantha had thought this was a night for family. She'd wanted to catch up and reminisce. It wouldn't be the same with an outsider present.

As if on cue, the doorbell rang.

"There he is." Derek headed for the front door.

He? Samantha looked toward Brooklyn, but she had already walked out of the family room on her way to the kitchen.

"Come on in," she heard Derek say. "Brooklyn's about ready to put dinner on the table."

Samantha turned in the direction of Derek's voice in time to see him enter the family room. A few steps behind him came his guest.

Nick Chastain.

The very man she didn't want to think about.

For the second time in as many days, Samantha felt her world shift beneath her feet. She expected to see a look of surprise in his eyes to match her own. She didn't find it. Had he known she would be here? Had she been kept in the dark on purpose?

Derek said, "Nick tells me you two knew each other in Oregon, so I invited him to join us. He's only been in the area a couple of months and doesn't know many people yet. I thought it would be nice for him to have a friend here."

A friend. Was that what he'd told her cousin she was to him? A friend?

"Hope you don't mind," Nick said softly.

Well, yes. As a matter of fact, she did mind. Whatever they had once been to each other, they weren't now. Not a couple. Not even friends. In fact, they were little more than strangers as far as she was concerned.

"Of course I don't mind," she lied.

Derek was oblivious to the undercurrent in the room, but something flickered in Nick's eyes, telling Samantha he understood her true feelings.

It shouldn't matter that he was there or that he knew she wished he wasn't. It *didn't* matter. None of it. Two years was a long time. She had moved through all the appropriate stages of getting over a failed romance. It hadn't even taken that long. Not when Nick had both ignored her apologies and seemed to have dropped off the face of the earth. That was the real reason for her surprise: she'd never thought to see him again. Anywhere. Least of all here in her grandmother's hometown.

Brooklyn reappeared from the kitchen. "Hi, Nick. Glad you could join us. You already know Sam, I understand."

"Yes, we know each other."

"Well." Brooklyn motioned them to follow. "Dinner's ready. Come take a seat at the table." Her gaze flicked to Derek. "Tell Alycia to join us please."

"Will do."

Brooklyn went one way and Derek went another, leaving Samantha in the family room with Nick.

"I'm sorry if you don't want me here," he said, voicing her feelings more accurately than she would wish. "I didn't know you were coming until after I'd accepted the invitation. Then it seemed rude to back out."

She shook her head. "No. No, it's all right, Nick. Really." She drew in a quick breath and offered him a fleeting smile.

"Hurry up, you two," Brooklyn called from the other room.

"I should help her." Samantha hurried to do just that.

Unfortunately, there was nothing left to help with. Brooklyn had everything on the table. All Samantha could do was choose which side to sit on—and hope she'd chosen the right chair. She was grateful when it was Alycia who took the one next to her. Host and hostess sat at either end of the table. Nick paused and then settled onto the remaining chair opposite Alycia. Not quite in Samantha's direct line of vision, but still closer than she liked.

As the serving dishes made their way around the table, Samantha glanced at Alycia. "How's school?"

"It's okay."

"What grade are you in? I've forgotten."

"Seventh." Without waiting for the next question, the girl added, "I'm thirteen."

Thirteen. As Samantha recalled, that could be a tough age. No doubt Alycia wasn't fond of being grilled by an older cousin, once removed, whom she'd met only one time before. But Samantha persisted. "Any favorite subjects?"

The girl shrugged. "Not really."

"That's not true," Brooklyn interjected, smiling. "Alycia plans to become a veterinarian. Any subject that can help with that is a favorite."

Alycia seemed to perk up. "Ethan—he's the vet here in Thunder Creek. He lets me help out at his clinic on Saturdays. I love getting to take care of the animals."

Nick said, "It's great to have a goal in mind at your age."

Samantha's stomach tightened. For a few brief moments she'd forgotten he was across the table. *It doesn't matter. It doesn't matter. It doesn't matter.*

"So, Nick," Derek said, breaking into her silent mantra, "tell us more about how you know Sam."

Her gaze darted to Nick, but he was looking at her cousin.

"We met at a lecture."

"A lecture? On what?"

"Something to do with taxes." Nick chuckled. "Trust me, I didn't want to be there. I was forced to attend by my CPA. But then I saw this beautiful redhead sitting one row in front of me, and I decided it wasn't a bad place to be. I remember that I was determined to make her acquaintance at the first opportunity."

Samantha felt Nick's gaze on her, but she stared at her dinner plate, trying her best not to remember the night he spoke of.

❧

"So," a male voice said, "what do you think of the seminar so far?"

She glanced to her right, and her pulse hiccupped.

The stranger smiled, as if he'd sensed her reaction. He was tall and broad shouldered. Even in a suit, there was only one word to describe him: *rugged*. She could almost smell the fresh outdoors on him, and it had nothing to do with his choice of soap or cologne. She usually avoided the type. She was more of an indoor girl.

He cocked an eyebrow, as if to repeat his question.

"It's good," she answered.

"I'm not sure I understand much of it."

She looked at the half-filled paper cup in her hand.

He persisted. "My accountant twisted my arm to come. It's not really my thing."

"What *is* your thing?" The question was asked before she could help herself.

"Sailing. Kayaking. Biking. Deep sea fishing. Rock climbing." He ended with a small shrug.

See. She'd known it. Not her type at all.

"Teaching," he added.

Her gaze snapped to him. "You're a teacher?"

He laughed. "You don't have to sound so surprised."

"I'm sorry." She felt her cheeks grow warm. "What do you teach?"

"I'm a professor at OSU. Fisheries and Wildlife."

A professor? Maybe he was her type after all.

He put out his hand. "Nick Chastain."

"Samantha." She took it—and felt that silly hiccup in her chest again. "Samantha Winters."

❧

Samantha took a slow, deep breath and forced her attention back to the present.

Nick was still speaking. "We struck up a friendship after that night."

"Ah. I see," Derek replied into the silence that followed.

A friendship. Yes, their relationship had begun as friendship—despite them having what seemed so little in common. They hadn't liked the same music. They hadn't liked the same kinds of books or movies. He was an outdoorsman, as she'd first suspected, while she liked her creature comforts. He wanted adventure. She wanted safety and security.

Still, despite their many differences, she'd found herself irresistibly drawn to him. He was sexy, like one of the major stars from the Golden Age of Hollywood. A man's man. He was interesting, even exciting. And—she reminded herself now—he was reckless, frustrating, and sometimes selfish. Which were just a few reasons why, despite how much she'd cared for him back then, their relationship hadn't lasted.

Were those the reasons, Sam?

She gave herself a mental shake as she drew in another deep breath. They'd broken up, and it had been for the best for them both. All she'd regretted was the *way* their relationship had ended.

She leveled her shoulders and glanced up from her plate. While her thoughts had drifted for the second time, the conversation had moved on. Just as well. She resolved she would enjoy the rest of the evening.

∞

Nick sensed the moment when Samantha determined not to let his presence spoil the family dinner. Good. He didn't want to be a problem. Just the opposite. He wanted to mend things. He wanted to ask for her forgiveness—both for things he remembered and things he could only suspect through the fog. He wanted them to be friends. It was the most he could want, but he wanted that much.

"Nick," Brooklyn said, "Derek told me you've been looking for a church to attend."

"Yes, I have. I was a member of a dynamic congregation in Wyoming. That's where I lived before coming to Idaho. The church had lots of different ways to minister in the community, and I'd like to find something similar here."

Across the table, he saw Samantha's eyes widen almost imperceptibly. Was she surprised to learn he'd been living in Wyoming? Or was she surprised to know he'd become a church member? Perhaps both.

"Have you visited Thunder Creek Christian Fellowship?"

He looked at Brooklyn. "Not yet. I've been to a few churches in Nampa and Caldwell. Lots of good preaching, but no place has clicked with me yet. You know, that feeling when you know you've found a home."

"Well, you should come this direction next Sunday. Derek is one of the leaders in the men's ministries. We'd love to see you there."

Nick smiled at Brooklyn, then Derek. "Sure. I'll think about it. It's not much farther to drive into Thunder Creek than it is to go into Caldwell."

"Service starts at ten o'clock," Brooklyn added.

He wondered if Samantha would be at their church on Sunday, but he kept himself from looking her way. He wouldn't want to discourage her from attending, and he was afraid any interest on his part might do that.

The conversation moved on, and Nick was satisfied to eat the delicious food and listen as the others talked about family members and mutual friends and acquaintances in Thunder Creek. He learned how long Derek and Brooklyn had been married—a little over a year and a half—and about Derek's adopting Alycia last year and how Derek had also come to adopt the petite and somewhat prissy papillon named Miss Trouble who was currently, as they could witness through the dining room windows, playing what looked like a game of keep-the-ball-away-from-Boomer in the backyard. It was the most pleasant evening Nick could remember having in a long, long while.

The meal of boneless chicken cutlets with a cherry tomato salsa, roasted sweet potato wedges, and peas with pearl onions—all organic, thanks to Derek's farm—was followed by a dessert of chocolate-raspberry tarts.

"This is amazing," Samantha said after her first bite.

Nick nodded in agreement, but his mouth was full, so all he could manage was an "Mmm."

Leaning toward Samantha, as if in confidence, Alycia said, "Mom tries out all of her new recipes on me and Dad before they serve the same thing at the inn. They don't *all* taste this good."

Samantha laughed, her head tipped slightly back, her eyes narrowed, a hand over her mouth.

Nick loved the sound of her laughter. He always had, although he'd forgotten how much until right then.

A short while later, all the dessert plates empty, Brooklyn said, "Alycia, will you clear the table for me please?"

"Sure, Mom."

Brooklyn stood. "You all go into the living room. I'll bring the coffee. Decaf all right for everybody?"

She was answered by a chorus of yeses.

Before leaving the dining room, Nick walked to the window to check on Boomer. Miss Trouble had dropped the ball and was now bathing Boomer with her tongue. The expression on the border collie's face made Nick grin.

"Patient, isn't he?" Derek said as he stepped to Nick's side.

"Yeah, he is. I got lucky when I found Boomer at the shelter."

"Pets make a home, as far as I'm concerned. Brooklyn would agree now, but she didn't always think so. She didn't grow up around animals the way I did."

Nick looked at Derek. "Gotta confess, I would've guessed

Miss Trouble to be your wife's or your daughter's dog. Never would've figured she was yours first. Not even for a rescue."

Derek laughed as he dropped his hand onto Nick's shoulder. "We never know what or who God will bring into our lives. Do we?"

"I guess not." Nick pictured Samantha, the way she'd looked the night they met, back at the beginning before he'd ruined it all. Then he tried to shove the image away. If God had brought her back into his life, it was so he could apologize for the things he'd said in anger. Nothing more than that.

Chapter 4

Given that hospitals and doctors didn't operate on Ruth Johnson's personal schedule, her return home happened midday rather than first thing in the morning, which she would have preferred. The later release meant she had no choice but to roll her way, on her newly rented knee scooter, through Sips and Scentimentals, the only entrance to the house without steps. The customers applauded when they saw her. It felt both good and embarrassing at the same time.

Samantha stepped around Ruth and opened the door to her home's kitchen, then moved aside to let Ruth go first. Before she made it that far, Camila planted a kiss on her cheek and said, "I'll be in to see you later."

It had been only three days since she'd stood in this kitchen—on both feet—and prepared herself a breakfast of one scrambled egg and a slice of buttered toast. She'd eaten that meal without the slightest notion of what would happen within a few hours, and it felt as if she'd been gone for a year.

"Do you want to go to your bedroom, Gran," Samantha asked, "or would you rather sit in your recliner or on the sofa and watch TV?"

"My bedroom, I think. The pain pills are making me a bit woozy." She didn't wait for her granddaughter, but pushed off with her good foot and sent the scooter rolling toward the hallway, thankful that her bedroom was on the main floor of the house.

Samantha caught up with her. "I picked up some other things at the medical supply place yesterday, along with the scooter. A raised toilet seat with arms to make it easier for you to get up and down and a chair for the shower."

The words made Ruth feel old and decrepit. Which she most certainly was not, despite a few signs to the contrary.

"Keeping your cast dry when you shower will be the trickiest part, the nurse told me, but we can put your leg in a garbage bag and tape it closed above your knee, then let that leg stay mostly outside the stall."

"Sounds like I'll be a lot of bother."

"Gran, you are *not* a bother."

At her bedside Ruth maneuvered into position and lowered herself onto the edge of the mattress. She looked to her left and her right and sighed. She might not be old and decrepit, but she was no spring chicken either. "I think I'm going to need your help today, dear."

Samantha was beside her in a snap, lifting her legs, easing her into position on the bed. Her granddaughter slid several pillows beneath Ruth's cast, getting her leg up above her chest as the nurse had instructed. A few more pillows were placed to support her head and back.

"How's that, Gran?"

"Perfect." She patted the back of Samantha's hand where it rested on the sheet beside her hip.

"I'll bring a bottle of water to keep by your bedside. It's important you stay hydrated."

Ruth closed her eyes. "Yes. But I think I'll rest for a bit." She was asleep before Samantha left the side of the bed.

Nick stared into his refrigerator. He was hungry, but nothing appealed to him. Or maybe it was eating another meal alone that didn't appeal to him. He blamed the previous night's dinner at the Johnson home for that. He'd enjoyed sitting with a family around the table. The laughter. The warmth. The camaraderie. Even the awkwardness of being with Samantha hadn't diminished his enjoyment. Or maybe being near her had increased it.

The thought didn't surprise him as much as he'd expected. More than once during the early months of his recovery he'd allowed himself to imagine being with Samantha again. Not in a romantic sense, of course. Romance wasn't something he could handle now. Maybe not ever. But still . . .

He gave his head a slow shake as he closed the refrigerator door, deciding he would take a quick shower and then drive into Thunder Creek. He'd seen the diner on Main Street and had already been told the food there was good. He'd also been told about Sips and Scentimentals, the beverage and gift shop that belonged to Ruth Johnson. But they didn't serve dinner there. Just pastries to go with the coffees and teas. He would have to give that shop a try one morning on his way to Derek's farm. Or perhaps on a Saturday when he could linger awhile.

Half an hour later, Nick was back in his pickup and driving west.

The very first time he'd driven through Thunder Creek on the way to the Johnson farm to write up an estimate, he'd liked the look of the town. The streets lay in a perfect grid. There were larger Victorian-style homes closer to the center of town and smaller 1950s bungalows in neighborhoods farther out. Brick buildings lined Main Street, and there was a large town park with tall, mature trees and the creek that gave the town its name running through the center of it. Although Nick had lived most of his adult life in large cities, he'd begun to realize he was, at his core, a small-town boy.

There were only a few vehicles in the diner's parking lot, leaving plenty of open spaces. Nick pulled into one and cut the engine. That was another thing he liked about small towns. The silence that often prevailed. Not complete silence, of course. But nothing like a city where traffic clogged streets and freeways twenty-four seven.

He got out of his truck and went into the diner. A waitress in a white blouse and black skirt escorted him to a booth and left him to look over the menu. It didn't take him long to decide what he wanted. Laying down the laminated menu, he looked around the diner. The L-shaped room had plenty of booths and a smaller number of tables and chairs. The current customers ranged in age from their teens to perhaps their seventies. Just about everybody wore jeans, although there was one man in bibbed overalls.

"Have you decided?" the waitress asked when she returned.

He glanced at her name tag. "Yes, Lucca, I have. I'll take the chicken fried steak. Gravy on the side. And a green salad with Thousand Island dressing."

"And to drink?"

"Water's fine. Thanks."

"All right. Have it out to you in a jiffy." Lucca turned away and saw some new customers. "Be right with you," she called out.

Nick looked in the same direction. Not so much out of curiosity as reflex.

"Hey, Nick." Derek grinned at him.

Nick nodded a greeting.

"Mind if we join you?" Beside Derek was a sheriff's deputy.

"Not at all." Nick motioned to the other side of the booth. "Please."

The two men slid onto the bench seat, and Derek introduced his friend. "This is Hank McLean. We worked together when I was with the department."

"You used to be a deputy?"

"Yeah. Was full time for a while. Then part time after I started organic gardening on a larger scale. I resigned last fall so I could focus on the farm and help Brooklyn with the bed-and-breakfast."

The waitress returned with hard plastic tumblers of ice water. Neither Derek nor Hank needed to look at the menu. They ordered their meals, and Lucca grinned, not bothering to write anything down. Nick guessed the two men were creatures of habit when it came to their choices at the Moonlight Diner.

Derek confirmed it. "Hank and I have been eating here one evening a week for four or five years now. We know what we like."

"I hear you might join our men's group at church," Hank said, reaching for his water glass.

Nick nodded but didn't commit. "Derek invited me last night."

"You'll be glad if you do. Great group of men. We've all grown a lot in our faith over the years. Iron sharpening iron."

Nick figured he could use some more sharpening. His faith had been lukewarm for many years. It had taken the many months of recovery after the accident to get himself back on track, to put Christ first in his life again. Or maybe he'd never put Christ first until then. All he knew was that he wanted to continue to grow and deepen his faith. He wanted to be the kind of man others looked up to. Like Derek Johnson.

"Tell me again when the next meeting is," Nick said, his mind made up, "and I'll make it a point to be there."

⚬

Samantha was washing the last dinner dish when Camila knocked on the door, then stepped into the kitchen. "I've closed up for the night," the woman said, wearing her usual smile. "How goes the battle in here?"

"Good, I think." Samantha put the dish in the drainer. "Gran managed to eat a little. She's not showing much of an appetite yet."

"That's normal these first few days after surgery. Just make sure she keeps drinking plenty of water." Camila raised an eyebrow. "How about you? Did you eat?"

"Yes. I promise I did."

"Good." The older woman gave a firm nod. "If you're going to be the caregiver, you've got to keep up your strength. Won't do to have you give out."

"I won't. I'm stronger than I look."

"That may be, but I think we need a plan. Let's make sure you get out of the house for two or three hours every day. Ruth's got more friends than she can shake a stick at. We'll organize and take turns staying with her while you're out. The gals in our Bible study are working on meals to bring over that can go in the freezer, and then you can just pop them in the microwave and serve. You won't need to be cooking all the time you're here."

Samantha laughed. "I'm beginning to wonder if I'm needed at all."

"Sam, your grandmother needs you more than even she knows. Don't you doubt it for a minute."

Samantha went over and gave her a tight embrace. "Camila Diaz, I love you almost as much as Gran does."

"I love you, too, *niña*." Camila squeezed her back, then stepped away. "Need anything before I go home?"

"No, thanks. I'm going to relax for the rest of the evening. Watch a little TV. Read a book. Catch up on e-mail." She ended with a shrug.

"All right. See you in the morning."

"See you."

Camila slipped back through the doorway, closing the door behind her.

Samantha left the kitchen, going first to her grandmother's bedroom. Gran was sound asleep, so Samantha quietly turned and walked to the living room.

The decor of the house had changed quite a bit since she'd lived there after college graduation. The walls had received a fresh coat of paint, and Gran hadn't held back on the use of color. The rooms were like Joseph's famous coat—all different. The sofa and chairs were new, except for Pappy's favorite recliner. Gran would never part with it. Samantha knew that without being told.

47

She felt a sting of sadness, remembering her grand-father seated in that chair. It had been six years since Walter Johnson, MD, had passed away, but the missing hadn't eased inside her at all. There was something comforting in know-ing a beloved grandparent was only a phone call away. For advice. For wisdom. For love and unconditional acceptance. She still had that with Gran, thank heaven, but she wished she could still have it with Pappy too. Her grandfather had been a special man and had adored his wife to his dying breath.

"I want that," she whispered. "I want to be loved by a man the way Pappy loved Gran."

And just like that, she thought of Nick Chastain . . .

Samantha opened her front door to find Nick on the apartment landing, his face reddened from a day in the sun and wind. "You should have been there, Sam," he said without greeting. His eyes sparked with excitement. "It was amazing."

"I can tell." She took a step back, widening the opening so he could enter.

He did so, repeating, "You should have been there."

"I've told you, I'm not into spectator sports much."

"You wouldn't have to be a spectator. I could teach you to windsurf."

A shudder moved through her, and memories of her dad threatened to intrude. "No, thanks."

"If it's the cold water you don't like, a wetsuit would help with that."

"It's not the cold water."

"It doesn't matter if you're not a strong swimmer because we wear jackets."

"I can swim just fine, Nick."

Frustration momentarily flashed in his eyes. "Then what are you afraid of?"

"I'm not afraid." It was a bald-faced lie. She *was* afraid. She was petrified. Not only of participating but of watching, of seeing some horrid accident happen right before her eyes. Yet she couldn't bear for him to know that about her. She didn't want this brave, exciting man who made her pulse quicken and her blood run hot to know she was terrified to her core.

And besides, there was one thing she was more afraid of than his recklessness. She was afraid that if he knew how she really felt about his attraction to all manner of dangerous activities, he wouldn't want to be with her any longer. That he would realize how wrong she was for him. That he would see their differences were too immense to overcome.

That he would never learn to love her the way she'd come to love him.

"Sam." His voice was low as he took a step toward her. "You'd have fun if you'd come with me."

She took him by the hand and drew him toward the sofa. "Ask me again next summer when the weather is warm and dry. Maybe I'll think differently by then." She tasted that lie on her tongue, same as she'd tasted the first.

His gaze locked on her mouth, he didn't guess the truth. Instead, he drew her into his embrace and kissed her.

Don't let me lose him. Don't let him get hurt. And please, don't let him break my heart.

Samantha sucked in a quick breath, driving away the memory. It served no good purpose to dwell in the past. She'd moved on with her life. She'd survived that unwanted broken heart.

And Nick? How had he changed, beyond his unusual change in careers? She didn't understand that and wished to know the reason why—even if it would be better to leave things as they were.

Chapter 5

*S*amantha hadn't lived in Thunder Creek when she was little, and she'd been only four when her dad's job transferred the family away from Idaho. But the summer she'd stayed with Gran after college had been among the best months of her life. She'd loved the slower pace. She'd loved the friendliness of people, acquaintances and strangers alike.

Stepping into the narthex of Thunder Creek Christian Fellowship on her first full Sunday in town was like coming home. Even those who'd talked with Samantha when they'd visited Gran during the week welcomed her as if they hadn't seen her in a decade. She was still standing there, talking with others, when Derek and his family entered through the front doors.

"Hey, cuz." He leaned in to kiss her cheek.

That was just one of the things she appreciated about Derek. Like Gran and Pappy, her oldest cousin never had been afraid to show his affection. Samantha wasn't as demonstrative. She kept her feelings trapped inside so much of the time. Her mom was the same way. Why, she wondered, hadn't that expressive trait come down through her branch of the family?

"Sit with us," Brooklyn said, stepping to her other side.

"Sure."

Alycia told her parents she would see them later and hurried to join her friends in the youth group.

"How's Gran?" Derek asked once Alycia was out of sight.

"Still pretty groggy from the pain meds. But she's becoming an expert with that scooter. She doesn't even call for me when she gets out of bed now." Samantha smiled. "And she practically kicked me out of the house this morning. Wouldn't hear of me staying home from church. Her friend Sandra is with her, just in case. Says she'll come over every Sunday if needed."

They walked together into the sanctuary and straight to the second pew from the front on the right. It might as well have had a placard on it that read "The Johnson Family Pew." No one else ever sat there as far as Samantha knew. Not even in Gran's absence.

When the hour-and-a-half service was over, Samantha received several invitations to Sunday dinner before she made it out of the sanctuary. Of course she declined them all, saying, "I need to get home to Gran, but thanks. Maybe another time." As welcome as the invitations made her feel, they also felt overwhelming, and she was glad for the excuse not to accept any.

She was about to say good-bye to Derek and Brooklyn when Nick stepped into her line of sight. She felt an unexpected flutter in her chest as he approached.

"Nick," Derek said. "I didn't know you were here. You could have sat with us."

"I was running on the late side, so I slipped into the back pew. But I'm glad I came. Good sermon." Nick's gaze shifted to Samantha. "Morning, Sam." His smile was brief but seemed genuine, although not as confident as the ones in her memories.

"Morning."

Brooklyn took hold of her husband's arm. "Derek, come say hi to Mrs. Peterson. Excuse us, Sam. Nick." She drew Derek away before he could say anything.

Samantha felt a second flutter of nerves as her gaze returned to Nick.

He cleared his throat. "I was wondering. Do you suppose we could get together some time to talk? There are some things I . . . some things I need to tell you."

Curiosity overcame her nerves. Hadn't she wanted to know more about what brought him to Idaho, to know what he'd been doing the past couple of years and why he'd never responded to her attempts to contact him? Perhaps this was her chance to have better closure on their relationship, because despite telling herself that she'd moved on, she obviously—based on her reactions—hadn't. "Sure. If you want."

"Could we have lunch today?"

"Today?"

His eyes pleaded with her, and the uncertainty she saw there seemed so unlike him that it unsettled her. Nick's rock-solid self-confidence had both impressed and frustrated her when they'd dated.

"I need to get home to Gran." True. But she never had been able to resist those chocolate-brown eyes of his. "You could join me there if you want. We have a freezer full of individual meals that the women of Thunder Creek prepared."

Nick's expression relaxed. "Sounds good. How do I find the house?"

"It's one block east of here, down Sharp Street." She pointed in that direction. "You can't miss it. It's the house with the Sips and Scentimentals shop attached. You'll see the sign."

"Right. I know it. I just forgot it was your grandmother's place."

Forgetting anything was also unlike Nick. He had the sharpest mind of any man she'd ever known. It was like a steel trap. He knew every detail of every movie he'd watched, every article or book he'd read, every news report he'd heard. Then again, he was new to the area and Derek's was the first installation he'd done in Thunder Creek, according to her cousin. Perhaps it wasn't that strange.

Nick motioned with his head toward the exit. "I'll drive home and take care of Boomer, then come back to town. Won't take me longer than twenty, twenty-five minutes tops."

This was good. This was really good. A chance to talk with Samantha. To tell her he was sorry he'd been such a . . . a bonehead. Or whatever noun would best describe his behavior two years ago. There were bound to be a rather large number of choice descriptions he deserved. Even if he couldn't always remember why.

He drove home and let Boomer out to chase his ball a half dozen times. Then, with a few pats and several apologies, he put the border collie into the kennel again and drove back to town. It was easy enough to find Ruth Johnson's home. Sips and Scentimentals, the attached shop on the west side of the house, was closed on Sundays, so Nick felt free to park in the lot before walking around to the front. He didn't have to wait long after ringing the bell before Samantha opened the door.

Her smile was tentative. "That didn't take you long." She widened the opening all the way. "Come on in."

"Thanks." He moved into the living room and stopped, not sure if he should sit.

"Let's go into the kitchen," she said, answering his unspoken question.

"Will your grandmother join us?"

"No. She's had her lunch already."

"Would it be all right if I said hello to her? I didn't get to—" He broke off, not wanting to remind her of how their encounter at the hospital had gone down.

She understood anyway. "You didn't get to say hello to her last Sunday after running into me."

"No, I didn't."

"Come on. I imagine she's still awake." She bypassed the stairs and led the way to a room at the end of the hall on the main floor. At the open doorway she put up a hand so he would know to wait while she looked in. "Gran, do you mind some company? You have a guest."

"I would love company," came the woman's voice. "Bring them in."

Samantha gave a nod to Nick.

"Thanks." He moved past her, taking several steps into the room. "Hello, Mrs. Johnson. Do you remember—?"

"Nick Chastain." Smiling, she held out a hand toward him. He went to the bedside and took it. "Oh, it's good to see you, young man. I wanted to thank you. Not just for the lovely flowers you brought me while I was in the hospital, but for all you did for me the day of the accident."

"Thanks aren't necessary, ma'am."

She raised her eyebrows. "Heavens. That sounds stuffy. Call me Ruth."

"All right."

"Sit down and tell me about yourself. We met under rather unusual circumstances, after all."

He obeyed about sitting, but wasn't sure what to tell her. Not with Samantha standing somewhere behind him. He gave a shrug. "Nothing very interesting about me. I've been in Idaho about two months or so. I came here from Wyoming to manage an irrigation company located in Caldwell, and I was doing some work on Derek's land when I saw you fall from the horse." He stopped and shrugged a second time.

"And? I want details, young man."

Despite his discomfort, he grinned. "I'm single, never married, and I live with a border collie named Boomer. My parents have been married for almost forty years, and I've got three brothers, two older and one younger." Again he wondered what Samantha would want him to say about the months they were a couple in Oregon. Unsure, he played it safe and said nothing. "That's about it."

"No. There is something else. You prayed for me while we waited for the ambulance."

"You heard me?"

"I heard you." She reached for his hand again, and when he complied, she gave it a light squeeze. "God bless you, Nick. Your prayers made a great difference." She squeezed his hand one more time before releasing it. "Samantha tells me she invited you to have lunch so I won't keep you sitting here any longer." She looked beyond Nick's shoulder. "You two enjoy yourselves. I'm going to take a nap." And with that, she closed her eyes.

He stood, waited a few moments, then turned away from the woman on the bed. Samantha gave him another of those nods, her expression revealing nothing, before leading the way out of the bedroom and down the hall to the kitchen.

Nick had felt good about coming here, about talking to Samantha, clearing the air, and seeking her forgiveness, but all of a sudden he felt awkward, unsure how or when to begin. Samantha took care of that for him.

"You didn't tell Gran we knew each other before this."

"I didn't know if you'd want me to tell her."

"Why not? Derek and Brooklyn know. At least a little bit."

Nick ran the fingers of one hand through his hair, his thoughts growing fuzzy. Stress did that to him. Or was it that he felt stress *because* his thoughts grew fuzzy?

Samantha turned toward the cupboard and took out two plates and two glasses and set them on the counter.

"Sam?"

"What?"

"Could we sit down and talk first? I need you to listen. And to be patient with me while I say what I came here to say."

Albeit reluctantly, she did as he'd asked.

He took a deep breath and released it before sitting on the chair opposite her. "First, Sam, I need to tell you I'm sorry for the way things ended between us. As I recall, we were both angry and said things that hurt the other. I don't remember what was said exactly, but I want to ask for your forgiveness for my part in the argument and for my words, both intentional and otherwise."

"My forgiveness," she repeated softly. There was a lengthy

silence before she added, "You weren't so eager to forgive me when I apologized."

He frowned, not understanding.

"My e-mails." Frustration laced the words. "I asked you to forgive me in my e-mails. And in the phone messages I left."

"I don't . . . I don't remember any e-mails or phone messages." He drew another deep breath.

The look in her eyes called him a liar.

"When was that, Sam? When did you try to contact me?"

"I don't know." She looked angry now rather than frustrated. Angry and hurt.

His memory might be poor at times, but he remembered that hurt expression. "Please. Help me out here. When was it?"

"I don't remember exactly. A few weeks after we broke up."

Nick nodded. "I'm sorry, Sam. I don't know what happened to your messages. Honest. But there is a reason for it."

"It must be a doozy."

"It is, I guess. If you're right about when, then I was in the hospital. Maybe I was still in a coma. I can't say for sure. But that's my guess."

A hospital? Samantha's anger turned to stunned confusion. A coma?

"Do you remember that kayaking trip you and I fought about before I went?" Nick continued.

"Of course I do."

"Well, you were right. I got hurt. I about cracked my head open on a boulder, among other injuries." He hesitated, as if considering whether or not to detail what those injuries had been. "It was bad enough that they weren't sure I was going to pull through."

"Nick," she whispered, cold seeping throughout her body.

"I was a long time in a hospital in Colorado and then months in rehab. After I was released, I went to Wyoming to stay with my parents. It was a long recovery." He shrugged, as if to deny the seriousness of his words.

She stood and went to the window, not sure what to do with the tumble of new emotions swirling in her chest. She couldn't even define them. Anger? Self-pity? Self-righteousness? The need to say, "I told you so"?

Another impression intruded. Perhaps Nick's accident explained why he was no longer teaching. Getting a position at Oregon State had been his goal long before she'd known him. He'd loved teaching every bit as much as he'd loved the thrill of white-water rafting the roughest rivers or fishing for sharks in the ocean or sky diving or any other dangerous sport he could think of. His injuries must have been extensive for him to give it up. Sadness swept over her.

Behind her, she heard a chair slide against the floor and turned to see Nick standing.

"I'm sorry, Sam. Lunch probably wasn't a great idea. I just wanted you to know that I'm sorry for whatever I said that hurt you, especially that last time we were together. My memory isn't perfect—about a lot of things—but I remember enough to know I could be a class-A jerk. You deserved better than I gave in those months we were together, and I'm sorry."

She shook her head, even though she agreed with him, at least in part. He'd been stubborn and independent and opinionated. He'd been an adrenaline junkie. But there had been so much about Nick that she'd been crazy about too. His humor. His warmth. The way a certain look in his eyes had made her insides melt like butter.

"I'd like us to be friends." He took a step back from the table.

Her heart skittered, realizing he was about to leave. Not that she could blame him. Her continued silence must have made it appear she wasn't interested in his apology.

"If you think that's possible," he added. "For us to be friends."

"Yes." The word came out, barely more than a whisper. Louder, she said, "Yes, I'd like us to be friends too."

He took another step back. "We'll do lunch another time. If you want to."

As his gaze held hers for a few moments more, something old and familiar coiled inside of her. A tug of attraction. A wanting. A missing. The sensations surprised her. Even more surprising, something in his eyes told her he might feel the same.

Then he gave her a fleeting smile, turned, and walked out of the kitchen, leaving her wondering if she'd seen anything in his eyes at all.

❧

Nick and Samantha sat on the leather sofa in the family room of his home, a half-empty bowl of popcorn on the coffee table near their knees, while the movie *Notorious* played on the big-screen television opposite them. Samantha watched the movie while Nick watched her.

Ingrid Bergman's character was in danger, and worry and tension played across Samantha's face in reaction to the storyline. She took Nick's hand and held on tightly. He suspected she didn't know she'd even reached for him.

Adorable. She was simply adorable.

It surprised him that he was enjoying this movie night. Watching old films wasn't high on his list of things he liked to do. But Samantha's enthusiasm had drawn him in before he could find a reason to refuse her suggestion.

"You haven't ever seen *Notorious*?" she'd asked a few days ago, her tone incredulous. "But you must see it. It's so intense. Bergman is amazing, as she always is. And who doesn't love Cary Grant?" And then she'd continued to give him a summary about Nazis and spies and narrow escapes. Not to mention romance.

Now Samantha glanced over at him and her eyes widened a little. "You're not watching the movie."

"Yes, I am."

A tiny smile tugged at the corners of her mouth. "Liar."

"Okay, I was watching you."

This made her smile grow.

"You really are more entertaining to me than any black-and-white film."

With her free hand, she lightly slapped his thigh. "There is more to life than what you can find in the wild outdoors, Mr. Chastain."

"Hmm." He brushed a lock of her hair back, hooking it behind her ear. "I believe you're right about that, Miss Winters," he whispered as he drew close and kissed the newly exposed spot on her neck.

She gave a soft gasp.

The sound lit a fire inside of him, and he took hold of her shoulders, turning her toward him, meaning to kiss her more thoroughly. She stopped him with a hand flattened against his chest while her eyes pleaded with him to hear her.

"We'd better watch the movie," she said hoarsely.

He drew a breath to cool his desire, knowing she was right. Samantha wasn't the type for a casual fling. She wanted more from a relationship than that.

Trouble was, he didn't know if he was the sort of man who could give her what she wanted.

Chapter 6

The Men's Group met on Tuesday evenings in the fellowship hall of the church. Nick arrived fifteen minutes early on his first time to join them. There was only one other vehicle in the parking lot when he got there, so he decided to wait in the truck. He turned off the engine but let the radio keep playing. During his recovery, contemporary Christian music had come to mean a lot to him. Listening to it calmed his more anxious moments. Whenever he went through one of his dark patches, the melody and lyrics brought him back to a place of serenity.

He closed his eyes and leaned against the headrest. Before long, his thoughts drifted to the previous Sunday and his short time with Samantha at her grandmother's home. It wasn't the first time they'd drifted in her direction. She'd said she was willing for them to be friends. He assumed that meant she'd forgiven him, although she hadn't said so exactly. Then again, maybe the friendship she'd offered was only out of pity.

A thump on the door of his truck startled Nick from his deep reverie. Looking out the open window, he saw Derek.

"Coming in or taking a nap?" His friend grinned.

Smiling back, Nick answered, "Coming in." He turned the key in the ignition the rest of the way off and removed it, grabbed his Bible, and opened the truck door. The two men walked into the church together.

The pastor, Adrian Vinton, had arranged folding chairs in a circle near the stage of the fellowship hall and was attending to the large coffeemaker as they entered the room. "Evening," he called to them.

"Evening." Derek motioned with his head. "You remember Nick."

"Of course. I met him on Sunday. Glad you could join us."

"Glad to be here."

"Coffee should be ready soon." Adrian stepped away from the table.

Derek gestured toward the setup. "Need help with anything?"

"Nope. Everything's done."

The three of them headed for the circle of chairs. A worn Bible, a small notebook, and a pen lay on the seat of one of them, and the pastor went to it. But before any of them could sit, other men began filing into the large room. Derek made it a point to introduce Nick to each. His head swam with names before those first minutes were over. Hopefully, he'd be able to remember most of them in an hour or two. Although he couldn't count on it.

Nick's memory had once been as sharp as a tack. He'd never forgotten names. He'd had a knack for meeting someone, looking in their eyes, repeating their name in his head, and never forgetting it again. Remembering wasn't as guaranteed these days. But it could have been worse. It could have been much worse. And in those times when he grew frustrated with himself, he tried to remember that.

Once all the men were seated, Derek opened their time together with a prayer. Afterward, Justin Mathers—a math professor at Boise State, Nick had learned earlier—led a time of worship on his guitar.

"Amen," Derek said softly at the end of the final song. Then he looked around at the group. "As most of you know, tonight we're kicking off a new eight-week study. The video study guides are here—" Adrian got up and began to pass out the guides while Derek continued to talk. "—and if you haven't read the book the video series is based on, I would encourage you to do that too. We've got a few extra on hand, just in case. See Adrian if you want one. All right, let's dive in."

An hour and a half later, Derek closed the evening with another prayer and the men began moving from their chairs toward the table with the coffeemaker. Several of them made sure to talk with Nick, to draw him into other conversations.

It was obvious they didn't want him to feel like an outsider, and he appreciated their efforts.

It was one more reason he believed God's hand had been on his move to Idaho. At first it had seemed nothing more than an opportunity to continue working and to be out on his own again rather than living with his parents at the age of thirty-five. While he loved and appreciated his mom and dad and all they had done for him, especially after his accident, as his health improved he'd begun to chafe under their care. He'd needed to feel like himself again, as much as that was possible. Transferring to Idaho with Masters & Sons had provided that fresh start for him.

As for Samantha, so often in his thoughts—she seemed one more reason to believe God had orchestrated the move. How could Nick have imagined that she would also be in Idaho at this precise time in this very same small town? Only God could have made that happen.

Samantha was in the kitchen, enjoying her first cup of coffee on Wednesday morning, when Camila rapped on, then opened the shop's door wide enough to poke her head in. "Oh, good. You're up."

"Morning, Camila. You're here early."

The woman stepped into the kitchen and closed the door, her expression worried. "Is there any chance you could help me with something?"

"I'll try. What is it?"

"The recordkeeping for Sips and Scentimentals. From the day Ruth opened the shop, she's taken care of all the bookkeeping herself. I am completely lost in that accounting software, even though I know the ID and password and all of that. I don't know how the cash registers hook up to the software, but I think they do. There are the receipts and the deposits, and I know I must be missing something important. Can you look at it for me? I don't want to trouble your grandmother. She needs to rest."

Samantha almost laughed. She'd been half afraid Camila was going to ask her for help with something difficult. But accounting had been her life's work since she graduated from the university. She lived with numbers and ledgers every day at work. Sometimes she dreamed about them. She almost breathed them.

"I would love to help you. Let me fix Gran's breakfast. Then I'll shower and dress and come find you."

Relief washed across Camila's face. "Thank you."

A short while later, Samantha carried a breakfast tray into her grandmother's bedroom. Gran was sitting upright, back braced by pillows. Her hair was arranged and she wore a bit of mascara, telling Samantha that she'd been up long enough to wheel herself into the bathroom to prepare for the day.

Gran smiled a greeting. "Good morning, dear."

"Morning, Gran." She put the bed tray over her grandmother's lap, then kissed her cheek before straightening. "You're looking chipper this morning."

"I'm feeling much better today."

"I can tell."

"Did I hear Camila's voice a while ago?" Gran reached for the fork and speared a cube of cantaloupe in a bowl of mixed fruit.

"Yes. She asked if I could give her some help with the bookkeeping in the shop. You don't mind, do you?"

Gran's eyes widened. "Mind? Good gracious! I would be thrilled. I'll wager I've been doing something wrong from the get-go."

Samantha laughed. "I doubt that."

"Well, be on the lookout anyway."

"Okay. I will." She turned toward the door. "While you eat, I'm going to shower. I won't be long."

"Take your time. I'm fine."

Samantha hurried up the stairs. In her room, she gathered clean clothes and took them with her into the bathroom. Half an hour later, she was all set. She'd always been what her friends called "low maintenance." She liked to believe that was true. Still, the last glimpse at her reflection reminded her she needed to make an appointment for a haircut. That was where the low-maintenance label failed her. She was very particular about her hair. Would the local hairstylist know how to give her the cut she wanted? Or would she have to venture farther afield?

With a shake of her head, she left the bathroom and made her way down the stairs. In her grandmother's bedroom she retrieved the breakfast tray and, as usual, asked

Gran if she would like to spend some time in the living room. She'd grown used to a refusal, but this time her grandmother answered in the affirmative.

After getting Gran settled in Pappy's recliner—pillows beneath the broken ankle, water glass on the side table, a half-read novel beside the glass, and an extra throw draped over the chair's arm—Samantha made her way out to the shop. The place was busy this early in the day. Most of the tables had customers, and several teenagers stood in line for their beverage orders. They had to be cutting it close for getting to school before the bell. Or maybe they had a late start on Wednesdays.

The small business office of Sips and Scentimentals had been one of Pappy's examination rooms, back when he was running his clinic in this addition to the house. With a desk and chair, computer, printer, and other equipment, it felt cramped, but it served its purpose, leaving the majority of the former clinic for the coffee-and-gift shop.

Samantha sat in the rolling chair and clicked the keyboard to awaken the iMac screen. She poked around for a while, looking at the installed applications and figuring out the filing system. It wasn't difficult. Unlike her computers at work or at home, this one was used for little besides the business. At least it was connected to the Internet in case she needed to check the accounts via online banking. She was about to rise from the chair, in need of IDs and passwords, when Camila appeared in the office doorway.

"You probably have everything in order already," the woman said.

"Not quite. I need the login information for the software and for the bank."

Camila came around one side of the desk and opened a drawer. "We keep that information right here in this notebook."

"Not exactly secure," Samantha said with a slow shake of her head.

"That's what Derek told your grandmother."

"She should have listened to him." Her brow furrowed in a frown. "What sort of security do you have on your Internet?"

Camila straightened. "I haven't a clue."

"Do your customers have access to your Wi-Fi out in the shop?"

Camila nodded. "Yes. But it's separate somehow. Public. No password required."

Samantha leaned back in the chair. "I hope it's all right if I do more than look at the accounting."

"Sam, I can say without hesitation that Ruth would be delighted with whatever you choose to do to get things running the way they should."

Chapter 7

On his way to the jobsite Thursday morning, Nick parked his truck on the street outside Sips and Scentimentals. He might not have the sharpest brain in the world, but he was still smart enough to know what he was doing there. It had little to do with food and beverages. Instead, he was there in the hopes of seeing Samantha again, of spending a little more time with her, of hearing her laugh and seeing her smile. Which meant he wasn't smart enough after all. Because, while forgiveness was a good thing, wanting anything more than that wouldn't be fair to Samantha. Her stay in Thunder Creek was temporary. She was there to take care of her grandmother, not to renew a relationship with him.

And yet he couldn't shake the memory of that moment

on Sunday when something had flickered between them. There'd been a connection of sorts, and it had surprised him, coming as it had on the heels of her seeming disinterest in what he'd tried to tell her.

He got out of the truck and went into the shop, greeted by pleasant odors that made his stomach growl in anticipation. Good thing he'd skipped breakfast, because he was going to treat himself and his crew to something sweet and gooey, along with their coffees.

He recognized the woman behind the counter from the previous Sunday at church. At least he thought that's where he'd seen her. Some details escaped him. He got into the queue and waited, looking around the interior with interest.

The front side of the shop held small tables and feminine-looking chairs. Windows lined the entire length of that outside wall, allowing muted sunlight to spill into the room. A gift shop took up lots of space to the left of the entrance. One large display in the center of the area held all sizes and shapes of scented candles. Scents. He would bet that explained the odd spelling of the shop's name. He felt proud of himself for figuring it out.

"What can I get for you?"

While he'd been distracted, Nick had somehow moved to the front of the line. He hesitated a few moments to collect his thoughts, then placed his order.

"You're the young man who helped Ruth after her accident," the woman said. Without waiting for his reply, she turned toward the coffee machines.

Small towns were like that. It was hard to remain a stranger, and news always traveled fast. He'd learned that from his childhood in Wyoming.

After a lengthy period of time, while the machines hissed and whirred as they filled to-go cups with coffee, the woman faced him again. "I'm Camila Diaz. Ruth and I go way, way back. She's my very best friend. And I heard you know Sam too."

"Yeah. I do." He took his wallet from the back pocket of his jeans.

Camila moved to the display case and retrieved the cinnamon buns he'd ordered. When she placed the box on the counter next to the tray of coffees, she waved her hand at his wallet. "Put your money away. This order's on me."

"I can't let you—"

"Of course you can. After what you did for my dear friend, I'd like to do a lot more."

"But I—"

A smile lit her face even as she scolded. "Young man, don't argue with me."

Obediently, he pressed his lips together.

A sound off to the right, barely audible above the din of the shop, drew Nick's gaze in time to see Samantha step through a connecting doorway. From his visit on Sunday, he figured it must lead into the house's kitchen. She glanced up, saw him, and stopped, as if uncertain what to do next. He gave her a quick smile, hoping it would help her make up her mind.

It must have worked, for she returned the smile with a brief one of her own and proceeded toward him. "Hi, Nick. I see you decided to give Gran's coffee and pastries a try."

"It seems like it's the thing to do in Thunder Creek." He motioned toward Camila. "Can I buy you a cup?"

Samantha smiled again—as if he'd suggested something silly. Which he supposed was true. Undoubtedly she could have as much coffee as she wanted for free, whether out here in the shop or beyond that door in her grandmother's kitchen.

What he wanted to do next was invite her to sit down. After all, he'd come here in hopes of seeing her. But now that the moment presented itself, it seemed a dumb suggestion. He didn't imagine she'd come out to the shop to join one of the customers at a table. Any of the customers, let alone him.

He saw Camila glance between him and Samantha, a look of curiosity in her eyes.

"I guess I'd better get to the jobsite," he said, taking the tray in one hand and the pastry box in the other. "Have a great day." He included both women with his parting words and headed outside. "Coward," he muttered as he put the containers of coffees and pastries on the passenger seat of his truck.

No, not a coward. Despite his traitorous hopes, he'd been smart. He'd done the right thing. He'd been friendly and courteous but had kept the proper distance.

Only it didn't feel as if he'd done the right thing. It didn't feel right at all.

Samantha stared at the screen of the desktop computer, but what she saw in her mind was thick, wavy dark hair, brown eyes, and a smile that made her chest feel funny.

"No, no, no, no, no," she whispered, trying to drive the image away. She inhaled slowly and deeply, then released the breath the same way. It helped. A little.

She had effectively kept thoughts of Nick at bay ever since he'd walked out of Gran's kitchen on Sunday. But seeing him in the coffee shop this morning had changed all that. Now she couldn't seem to stop thinking about him. Imagining what had happened to him on that kayaking trip, conjuring up the full extent of his injuries. She wished he'd told her more. Then again, she wished he hadn't told her anything at all.

"And none of it is my business."

She leaned her head back against the rest, considering. Maybe that wasn't true. Didn't being his friend mean they should talk about their lives? Wouldn't it give her the right to ask those kinds of questions?

"Not necessarily," she answered herself.

With a sigh of disgust, she rose from the chair and left the office. The early-morning coffee rush was over. The remaining customers were those who wanted to linger. A few had laptops open on tables. Others were in pairs, visiting as they sipped hot beverages.

Samantha gave a brief wave to Camila as she made her way to the connecting door to the house. Once it was closed behind her, she went to check on her grandmother and found her in the recliner. *Napping*, she thought.

"I'm not asleep," Gran said without opening her eyes, proving Samantha wrong.

"Sorry. I didn't want to disturb."

Now her grandmother looked at her. "You didn't disturb me."

"I need some fresh air. I thought I might go for a walk in the park."

Gran lowered the footrest of the recliner. "Great idea. I'll go with you."

Samantha's eyes widened. "You must be joking."

"I'm not joking in the least. I've mastered the scooter. I think a brief outing would be good for me."

"Gran . . ."

"I was married to a physician, my dear. I know a thing or two about recovering from an accident. The best plan includes exercise and fresh air."

Samantha gave her head a slow shake, not to argue further but in resignation. Gran would have her way. She might as well accept it.

Once Gran was out of the chair, her knee firmly planted on the scooter, Samantha helped her into a sweater to protect her against the early-morning chill. Then the pair of them headed outside. Samantha let her grandmother set the pace.

The house and shop were surrounded on three sides by

the town park. The pair followed a sidewalk toward the creek that ran through the center of it. At this time of day in the middle of the work week, they had the park all to themselves. Not even the playground was in use by children too young to be in school.

The soft sounds of nature—a breeze through the limbs of the trees, a songbird announcing its presence, the tumble and gurgle of the creek—and the whir of the scooter wheels surrounded them.

"This is lovely," Gran said. "Just what I needed. I hate being cooped up day after day."

Samantha glanced over at her grandmother. "That's great, but we don't want to go too far. You shouldn't overdo things."

"Then let's sit on that bench near the bridge. I'm not ready to go back inside yet."

"All right." Again, she knew it was useless to argue.

Once they were settled, the morning sun caressing their faces, Gran took hold of Samantha's hand. "Now why don't you tell me what's troubling you."

"Troubling me?"

"Oh, Sam. I broke my ankle, but my ability to observe wasn't affected. I've tried to be patient, to wait for you to tell me what's wrong." She shook her head. "If you really don't want to talk about it, of course I will not press you. But maybe telling me will help."

Denial rose in Samantha's chest. An instinctive reaction, an urge to keep her life in order and under control.

Admitting her confusion aloud to another person, especially to her beloved grandmother, felt like failure.

Her grandmother closed her eyes and tilted her face toward the sun, the image of patience.

"It's complicated, Gran."

"What is?"

"For starters, my job. I don't like my boss, and I can't seem to get anywhere. You know how much I dislike change. But even so, I feel stuck. I'm restless. Restless with everything." She looked at the trees on the other side of the creek. "Including my personal life. It feels like an utter disaster. I haven't had a serious relationship in my life since—" She broke off abruptly.

Gran waited several moments before asking, "Since?"

Samantha released a breath, needing to be honest. "Since Nick."

"Do you mean . . . ? Oh, good gracious."

She laughed, a humorless sound, and repeated her grandmother. "Good gracious."

"Well, well."

Softly, "Well, well."

Another silence, this one lengthy. Finally, Gran asked, "Do you want to tell me about it?"

"I don't know what to say. We were together about eight months. When he wasn't working or off wind surfing or sailing or hiking, we spent time together." She drew in a breath, her thoughts flittering from memory to memory. "We liked such very different things. I don't suppose it ever could have worked. And yet I liked him so much. I loved those times we spent together." She felt Gran's gaze on her but refused to look in the older woman's direction. "One day the differences became too much. We argued and broke up, and that was it. It ended just like that."

"Are you sure?"

She met her grandmother's gaze. "What do you mean?"

"Are you sure it ended . . . for you? Because there is something in your voice that makes me think that might not be so."

"Of course I'm sure." She sat straighter on the bench, looking toward the creek, hating that her grandmother had seen something Samantha had managed to keep hidden even from herself. "I never spoke to him again. Not until he walked into the hospital and found me with you."

Gran released a soft breath. "Were you in love with Nick?"

Unexpectedly, tears welled up. She was horrified by their presence but was unable to stop them from falling.

"Oh, sweetheart." Gran put an arm around her and drew her close. "Oh, my dear."

Samantha turned her face into her grandmother's shoulder and let herself cry.

She hadn't meant to pry when she entered Nick's spacious home office. She'd wanted a sticky note, and she'd known there was a dispenser on his desk. But as she removed the sticky note, her eyes fell on the printed sheet of paper in the center of the desk. The word *ITINERARY* was typed boldly across the top, easy to read even though it was upside down. Without considering her action, she turned the sheet of paper to face her.

Her stomach fluttered when she saw the dates at the top of the page. Was this part of Nick's surprise? He'd been so evasive about what he planned to do during the university's spring break that she'd convinced herself his secrecy included something special to do with her.

The flutter stopped, then hardened and sank like a rock as she took in more of the information on the page. Colorado. Kayaking. Almost a whole week of white-water rafting and camping.

"Sam?"

She turned toward the office doorway.

"I wondered where you went," Nick said. "I've got the movie in the player and the popcorn's ready."

"I wanted to make a note for myself." She held up the yellow Post-it. "Why didn't you tell me?"

Nick gave her a quizzical look.

"About your spring break plans."

He was silent a short while, then answered, "Because I didn't want to argue with you about my trips again. I'm tired of it. We've been over it ad nauseam."

"I wouldn't have argued with—"

"Yes, you would have, Sam. You don't like what I do for fun. Even when all I do is go mountain biking for an afternoon. You've made that plenty clear. And this is one trip I didn't plan to pass up because of your fears."

"What if you get hurt again? Remember how you dislodged your shoulder blade when you fell rock climbing last month?"

Nick moved into the room. His mouth seemed hard. "You worry too much."

"With good reason."

"Sam, I'm not your dad."

She sucked in a breath.

"His death was an accident. You told me so yourself."

Yes, she'd told him about the skiing accident that had killed her dad. But she hadn't expected him to turn the tragedy against her like this.

"His death has turned you into a coward."

She drew back, as if struck. "That's a little harsh."

Regret flickered in his eyes. It seemed he might reach for her, might say he was sorry for his word choice, if nothing else. Then the moment passed, and with firm resolve in his voice he added, "It's not harsh. It's the truth. You're afraid of your own shadow."

"That's not true," she whispered.

His expression softened a little. "Sam, you need to accept it." He spread his arms. "This is who I am."

"It isn't who you have to be."

"I can't let your fears change the way I live my life."

"It isn't fear. It's being sensible. Sensible people don't risk their lives just for the thrill of it." Her voice rose sharply. "Nick, sometimes you are reckless with yourself and thoughtless with others. Sometimes I think you're a highly educated idiot. You even take unnecessary risks with your students."

"Is that what you think?" All emotion bled from his voice, leaving it flat and cold.

Her own hurt gave way to anger. Tilting her chin in a show of strength, she answered, "Yes, that's what I think."

The air seemed to be sucked out of the room. They stared at each other, unblinking, unmoving.

After what seemed an eternity, Nick said in that same flat, cold voice, "Then we have a bigger problem than where I plan to spend spring break."

"Maybe you're right."

He spun on his heel. "A movie wasn't such a good idea."

"No." She turned and slapped the sticky note onto the edge of his desk. "It wasn't." As she left the office, she flipped the light switch off, wanting the action to make a statement of some sort, though she knew not what.

It wouldn't have mattered if it did. Nick didn't see her do it. Didn't care either, from the look of it. He awaited her by the front door, her sweater held in one hand. Obviously all he wanted was for her to leave. Now.

Her anger continued to rage as she took the sweater from him. She wished she could slap his face. Hard. And not for this argument alone. Not even for him calling her a coward or bringing up her dad. No, for all the little disagreements that had happened before tonight. For his stubbornness. For his inability to see her side of the issue. For the way he refused to understand that her concern was because she cared for him so much.

Since it wasn't in her nature to slap another human being, the best she could do was clench her teeth and say, "Good night, Nick." She stepped through the open doorway.

"Good-bye, Sam."

His choice of farewell felt like a shaft in her heart. It sounded so . . . final. She spun around on the stoop, hoping to see another glimmer of regret in his eyes. It wasn't there. A shudder ran through her. "Nick . . ."

"It's over, Sam. It has to be."

He couldn't mean it. Surely he couldn't. They'd had a disagreement. They'd both lost their tempers. But he couldn't want to break up with her over it.

"I'm not the guy you're looking for," he said, the anger gone, even the coldness gone. "I'm sorry. I thought maybe we could make it work, but I don't think so anymore. You need somebody . . . safe. I hope you find him. I really do."

Anger welled again, although even at that moment, she understood it was a reaction meant to protect her shattering heart. "Fine. Have a fun spring break. Maybe you'll drown in that white water you crave so much. I won't care if you do."

Hateful, stupid words. Words she was immediately sorry for but couldn't take back.

"I'm sorry it had to end this way, Sam."

He didn't close the door on her. Not the one she could see. But she felt an invisible door slam closed.

She turned and hurried to her car.

Chapter 8

In the days that followed her granddaughter's revelation about her former relationship with Nick Chastain, Ruth spent a great deal of her time pondering ways that she might be of help to Samantha. She prayed and she plotted. What else was there to do when she was confined most of the time to her bedroom or the living room?

First thing she wished to know was more about Nick. Was he a man worthy of her granddaughter's affections? Some investigation seemed to be in order. Careful investigation, of course. She wouldn't want Samantha to feel she was prying.

Which, of course, she was.

Her granddaughter hadn't said she had once loved Nick. But she'd burst into tears at the question, which Ruth thought was a good indication of her answer. Ruth also suspected the past two years hadn't erased Samantha's old feelings. If Nick *was* a man worthy of Samantha's devotion, a man who could be trusted with her granddaughter's future, then Ruth wanted to do her utmost to see if he, perhaps, might feel the same way.

Seated in the recliner, she glared at the ugly cast encasing her broken ankle. If not for that blasted thing, she could be up and about and seeing to what needed seeing to. Of course, without it, Samantha wouldn't be in Thunder Creek. But that was neither here nor there. Samantha *was* here, and she needed her grandmother's help.

"I'll have to recruit some assistants," she said to herself. And Camila would be the place to start. Perhaps she should—

"What?" Samantha stepped from the hallway, her hands behind her head as she caught her gorgeous red hair in a ponytail. "Did you say something, Gran?"

"Nothing, dear. You caught me talking to myself." She tapped her temple with an index finger. "A sure sign of old age."

"I hope not. I talk to myself all the time." Samantha stopped a short distance away. "Are you ready to go?"

Ruth lowered the foot rest. "I can't wait."

"You like your doctor that much?" Her granddaughter grinned.

"I do like him, but that isn't why I can't wait. I'm dying

to get out of the house again. I'm missing far too much of spring. Summer will be here before we know it."

Ruth's eagerness had her on the scooter and out the door in no time. She felt the warmth of the May sun on her head and shoulders as she rolled toward Samantha's car. She delighted in the brightly colored flowers now in bloom around the borders of her house and stopped long enough to admire them.

"Not a weed anywhere." She looked over her shoulder at Samantha. "You've been busy."

"Camila and Sandra have both helped."

"God bless you all."

Getting settled into the car took some maneuvering, but it wasn't nearly as bad as the day Ruth had come home from the hospital, still weak and somewhat woozy.

"You doing all right, Gran?" Samantha asked as she lifted the scooter with both hands.

"I'm good."

Her granddaughter carried the scooter and put it into the back of the vehicle, then came around to get behind the wheel.

"I should have broken my left ankle," Ruth said. "Maybe then I could have driven myself to my doctor appointments."

Samantha shot her a questioning look.

Ruth patted the center console that went from car seat to dashboard. "Nowhere to put my right leg. Even if I was coordinated enough to drive with my left foot, my right leg would be in the way. But I think I could have managed if it was my left leg in a cast."

"Gran, you're too independent for your own good."

She chuckled. "You may be right about that, Sam."

It hadn't always been that way. Ruth had been a woman of her generation, the babies born during WWII. She married Walter when she was eighteen and set up her first home before the sweeping cultural changes of the 1960s. She had allowed her husband to manage their lives without ever asking a question. Not that she'd minded. Walter had been a generous, kind, and godly man. So she hadn't had any reason to chafe beneath his control.

She smiled as she remembered those early years of their marriage, Walter busy with his medical clinic and her busy with the children that had come along. Life had changed both Walter and Ruth, but Ruth most of all. Somewhere along the way she'd come into her own, and her loving husband had supported her as her interests had grown and changed.

"Gran?" Samantha's voice snapped her out of her memories.

"I'm sorry, dear. I was daydreaming. What did you say?"

"I asked if you've been to this doctor's office before."

"No. He was the surgeon on call the day of my accident."

Samantha reached into the console and then handed a piece of paper to Ruth. "I googled the address. Can you read me the directions? I don't know my way around Caldwell without a map, and sometimes the GPS on my phone doesn't give me the next turn soon enough for me to change lanes if I need to."

"Of course. Between the pair of us, we'll do fine."

⨀

Nick knocked on the back door of the Johnson home, but he wasn't surprised when no one answered. He'd noticed Derek's truck was missing from the driveway. He pulled his cell phone from his pocket, scrolled to *Johnson*, and tapped the number on the screen.

"This is Derek."

"Hey, Derek. It's Nick. Sorry to bother you."

"No trouble. What do you need? I'm in Caldwell right now but should be back in an hour or so."

"No need to rush. Just wanted you to know that the crew and I have called it a day. We're waiting for some supplies to be delivered on Monday. But it looks like we'll have the job finished by the middle or end of next week."

"That's great, Nick. You've all done a great job. I couldn't be more pleased with how it's turned out."

Nick grinned. It felt good to have his work praised. There'd been a period of time when he'd wondered if he'd be able to work at anything again. In any field. He was thankful to God for the progress that had been made, physically, mentally, and spiritually.

Derek said, "I'll see you at church."

"I'll be there."

He tapped the screen to end the call, then slipped the phone into his pocket. As he turned, Miss Trouble appeared through the doggy door. She barked at Boomer, who waited obediently near the trunk of a tall tree. Boomer shivered with excitement, his tail sweeping the ground, but he didn't move until Nick said, "Free." Then Boomer darted across the barnyard to the white picket fence, and the two dogs pressed their noses together through the slats. Like old friends, the two of them.

Nick smiled again. That's how he felt too. His time in the area had been brief, but he already felt at home in this small town. He'd made good friends—perhaps lifelong friends—Derek Johnson being one of them.

"Let's go, Boomer."

He walked toward his truck. The dog ran on ahead of him, sailing up onto the lowered tailgate and to his favorite spot near the cab. Once Nick was behind the wheel, he stopped to wonder what to do with the rest of his Friday afternoon. He wasn't ready to head back to his rental house. There wasn't anything awaiting him there. Not even breakfast dishes to wash. He was still trying to decide when his phone rang. When he looked at it, his mom smiled back at him from the screen.

"Hey, Mom."

"Hi, hon. Have I caught you at a bad time?"

"No. I've finished work early and was about to leave the jobsite."

"That's good. How are you feeling? You aren't working too hard, are you?"

He smiled. "I'm fine, Mom. I'm feeling great and taking care of myself. I promise." He paused before asking, "What's on your mind?"

"It's about Rudy."

Rudy was Nick's youngest brother. "What about him?"

"He's getting married."

"What?"

"Rudy's getting married. In Boise."

Nick felt rising confusion threatening to overwhelm him, and he gripped the steering wheel with his free hand. His mom's words weren't making sense. Rudy didn't live in Idaho. He lived in Denver. Why would he get married in Boise? And to whom?

"Honey, it's one of those whirlwind romances. We haven't even met the girl yet."

That made him feel a little less confused. No wonder it didn't make sense to him.

"Rudy and Chelsea—that's her name: Chelsea Lord—met in Las Vegas at a convention about a month ago. She lives in the Phoenix area, but her parents live in Boise, so that's where they're having the wedding."

"When?" He asked the question with a niggle of foreboding.

"Next Saturday. A week from tomorrow."

"He's only known her a month," he said softly. "And they're getting married next week?"

"I know, but he won't listen to anything your father or I have to say. Anyway, he intends to ask you to be his best man since you're there in Caldwell and can easily drive to Boise. I thought you should know so it wouldn't come as a complete surprise when he calls you."

Most of the time Nick didn't like his mother to hover

over him, even from a distance. In this case he was thankful for the heads-up. "I'm glad you told me, Mom. I take it you're coming to the wedding."

"Yes, if they go through with it, we'll be there. We're still hoping they'll come to their senses and put it off for another six months at least. We have no reason to object to them getting married. Just to them doing it so soon."

They chatted for a few more minutes before saying goodbye. After ending the call, Nick stared through the windshield, mulling over the news about his kid brother. Rudy . . . getting married. He couldn't wrap his head around it. That would make Nick the only bachelor in the family.

And just like that, he thought of Samantha. Again. Over a week had passed since he'd seen her at Sips and Scentimentals. He'd looked for her at church a few days later—his second Sunday to attend Thunder Creek Community—but she hadn't been there as she had been the week before. His disappointment had been keen. Unreasonable, even.

Unreasonable. That was a good word for him to remember. He gave his head a shake, then reached for the key in the ignition.

Samantha followed her grandmother through the open automatic doors of the medical building. Once outside, Gran stopped her scooter and looked up at the sky. "Thank You, Jesus," she said with a grin.

Samantha didn't have to ask what Gran meant. The cast had been removed by the surgeon, and Dr. Smith had opted not to put on a second cast as Gran had expected. Instead, her grandmother was in a large, black boot. One she would have to wear for another ten weeks at least. The ankle couldn't bear weight, even with the boot, but at least Gran could scratch when something itched, as she'd said in the examination room.

"Why don't you wait here and I'll drive the car over," Samantha suggested.

Before Gran could answer, the doors opened behind them. Samantha glanced over her shoulder, thinking they might be in the way. Her eyes widened when she saw who was exiting the building.

"Hey, there." Derek sounded as surprised as Samantha felt. His arm, already around Brooklyn's shoulders, tightened, slight but noticeable, as his gaze shifted to their grandmother. "Look who's not wearing a cast." He grinned. "How does it feel, Gran?"

"Heavenly. And what a nice surprise to run into you. Or were you looking for us?"

"No." Derek glanced at Brooklyn, who nodded. "We were here to see a doctor ourselves."

Gran's smile faded. "Everything all right?"

"Everything's perfect. And it'll be even better in about six and a half months." His eyes twinkled. "We're about to make you a great-grandmother again, come December."

Gran released a squeal of joy. Samantha gasped in surprise.

Then everybody was laughing and hugging and talking over each other.

When things quieted down, Gran said, "Do you have to go home right away, or can we celebrate? There's a restaurant down the street that has great pies. I'll buy."

"How can we pass that up?" Derek looked at Brooklyn for confirmation.

"I'd love to," she said.

As Samantha followed Gran toward the car, she realized that her happiness for her cousin and his wife, although real, was mingled with envy. She was ashamed of the feeling. She didn't begrudge her favorite cousin this additional joy in his life, but Derek and Brooklyn's happiness left her feeling more alone and unloved than she cared to admit.

Of course, she was neither of those things, but the feeling persisted all the same.

Chapter 9

*N*ick was drying Boomer after a bath when he got the anticipated call from his younger brother. He dropped the towel on the bathroom floor and picked up his cell phone from the counter. "Hey, Rudy."

"Hey, Nick."

"What's up?"

Rudy laughed. "You aren't going to pretend that Mom hasn't called you already."

"No. You're right. That would be a waste of time."

"Yeah. That's what I thought too."

Nick motioned for Boomer to come and led the way outside to the kennel so the dog could finish drying in the sun.

"Will you do it, bro?" Rudy asked, not bothering to add any details.

"Do you mean be your best man?"

"Yes."

"Next Saturday?"

"Yes."

He opened the gate to the kennel. "I guess you're going through with the wedding. Mom and Dad haven't changed your mind."

"Not even for a second. I love Chelsea. I know she's the girl for me."

Nick was eight years older than Rudy. He remembered the day their folks had brought the baby boy home from the hospital—a red-faced, squalling infant wrapped in a pink, blue, and white-striped blanket, a tiny blue knitted cap on his head. He remembered the toddler he'd pushed into a pile of snow beside the driveway, making him laugh. He remembered giving Rudy, a young teenager by then, advice about girls. Despite the near decade that separated their ages and the miles that had physically separated them later, they were best friends. And one thing Nick knew for certain about his best friend: Rudy could be as stubborn as the day was long. Good sense be hanged.

"What do you need me to do?" he asked as he walked back to the house.

"There's a rehearsal on Friday at five o'clock, followed by dinner at six thirty. You'll need to be there for both of those. Mom and Dad will be there too. At least in time for dinner on Friday. They're driving over."

"Yeah. Mom said they'd be there."

"Hey, bring a date if you know somebody."

He thought of Samantha. It no longer surprised him that he did so.

"The ceremony's going to be on Saturday. Late morning. You'll need to be at the church by nine, I think. I'm hoping Jeff and Peter will make it for the wedding. It would be great if all us brothers could be there."

Nick wondered if that was likely. Jeff lived in North Carolina. Peter lived in Connecticut. And they hadn't had a lot of warning.

Rudy continued, "I haven't talked to either of them yet. Maybe Mom has, like she did you. Either way, not much notice for them to make flight reservations."

Just what Nick had thought. "What am I supposed to wear for the wedding?"

"That part's easy. Nice pair of jeans and some good boots. I'll have your shirt for you. We're going with a casual western theme, all the way. No time or desire to wear morning suits or tuxes or whatever. But dress up a bit for the dinner on Friday. You know, a regular suit. Nothing more."

Inside the house, Nick grabbed paper and pen and sat down at the kitchen table.

"Bring a date to the wedding too," Rudy added. "Not just the rehearsal dinner. There's gonna be dancing at the reception."

Samantha's image filled Nick's thoughts a second time since the call had begun. "Tell me where I'm supposed to go and the times I need to be there. I need specifics."

Rudy rattled off the information.

"Okay. I've got it."

"Hey, Nick." Rudy's voice was softer now. "How are you doing? Really. I haven't seen you since Thanksgiving."

"I'm doing good, bro."

"I wish there was going to be time to get together, but my future in-laws have us booked from the moment the plane touches down."

"It's okay. It's gotta be crazy, trying to organize a wedding this fast."

Rudy didn't rise to the bait.

The call ended a short while later. None of the four brothers in the Chastain family were good communicators when it came to the telephone. They definitely didn't go in for small talk. Their calls were mostly about checking in: I'm good. You good? Fine. Glad to hear it. Bye.

As Nick set the phone on the table next to the paper of written directions, Rudy's voice echoed once more in his head. *"Bring a date."* Nick hadn't been on a date in over two years. He could go alone, of course. Nothing said he had to have a date. And yet having one appealed to him on several levels. First, it would make his mom happy and might stop her from worrying about him. But he didn't want to ask just any girl to go with him. In the end there was only one he could imagine taking to his brother's wedding. Would Samantha be his date if he asked her?

Determination stiffened his jaw. He got up from the chair, grabbed the keys to his truck, and headed out the door.

〰

Samantha opened the back door and entered the house, carrying a bouquet of cut roses from the garden. She soon had them arranged in a vase, then took them into the living room.

"Look what I brought you, Gran."

"Oh, sweetheart. How beautiful."

Samantha set the vase on the coffee table where her grandmother would have easy view of the flowers.

"I miss being in the garden. Summer will be nearly over by the time I'm able to move about the yard."

Samantha was about to comment when her phone announced a text message. A glance told her it was from Daniel Greyson. It was the third one today. Didn't the man know it was Saturday? For that matter, didn't he know she was on leave?

"Is something wrong?" Gran asked.

Samantha shook her head.

"Then why are you frowning?"

"Am I?" Samantha rubbed the furrow between her brows. "I guess I am. But it's nothing urgent. My boss is looking for some information." She slipped her phone back into her pocket. "I'll get back to him in a bit."

"Dear, may I ask you something?"

"Sure. What?"

But before her grandmother could pose her question, the doorbell rang. "Hold that thought, Gran." She went to answer it, expecting it to be one of Gran's friends. Perhaps someone bringing another casserole hot from the oven or a knitted prayer shawl or—

"Hi, Sam." Nick stood on the front porch.

She'd missed him over the last week. Without hardly realizing it, the missing had been there. "Nick."

"Is that Nick Chastain?" Gran called. "Bring him in, dear. Don't leave him standing on the porch."

Samantha stepped back, opening the door wide.

He gave her a nod before moving past her. Once inside, he went straight to the living room and toward Gran's chair. "You're looking good, Mrs. Johnson."

"I thought we'd settled that. I'm Ruth to my friends."

Samantha couldn't see his expression, but something told her Nick's smile widened at her grandmother's words.

He took Gran's proffered hand. "Look at that. You don't have a cast."

"It came off yesterday, and I'm so relieved. The boot's a little more comfortable than the cast." She motioned to the nearest easy chair. "Derek tells me you've joined the men's group at church."

Nick nodded as he sat on the indicated chair.

"That means you'll spend more time in Thunder Creek than in Caldwell. Good for us."

Samantha's heart fluttered at the news.

"I suppose it does," Nick answered. "I prefer small towns. Not that Caldwell is a metropolis, but it doesn't compare to Thunder Creek."

Gran's eyes twinkled with civic pride. "Nothing compares to *my* town, young man." She turned her gaze toward Samantha. "Come in and join us, Sam."

She did so, settling on the far end of the sofa.

For the next fifteen minutes or so, Gran plied Nick with friendly questions about his hometown and his family and his work. Samantha listened, too, in some ways feeling as if this was the first time she'd heard his answers. But maybe it wasn't the answers but the listening that was different. Her eyes narrowed as she mulled that uncomfortable thought around in her head. Hadn't she listened to him before?

"Sam?" Her grandmother's voice pulled her back to the present.

"Yes?"

"Nick says he's here to ask you a favor."

Her gaze moved from Gran to Nick. "What's that?"

"Turns out my kid brother, Rudy, is getting married in Boise next weekend, and I need a date for both Friday night and a good portion of Saturday."

A date? Her pulse skittered. "I didn't know your brother lived in Boise."

"He doesn't. His fiancée's parents live there."

A date? Would that be wise? She glanced at her grandmother again. "I don't know if I should go. You—"

"Nonsense," Gran interrupted. "About the only thing I can't do for myself now is drive or maneuver steps. I'll be fine. And you know Camila is never far away."

Nick stood. "You would be doing me a favor, Sam. I'd

like to go with a friend instead of stag. I won't know anybody there other than my parents and my brother."

Friends. So not really a date. Her pulse settled back to normal. Not a date. That was good to know and better for both of them. It was what she'd wanted, to move from forgiveness to friendship.

Gran said, "Weddings are wonderful occasions. Go with him, Sam. You'll have a good time."

Two years ago she'd longed to meet his family. And even though the reason had been different back then, it would still be nice to know the people who had raised him. "All right. I'll go with you. What time?"

Ruth shifted from the chair to the knee scooter and then rolled to the living room window, observing her granddaughter as she said good-bye to Nick. She had a good feeling about that young man, especially after their brief visit this afternoon. And from the expression that had flashed across Samantha's face when Nick had asked her to be his date for the wedding, her granddaughter's feelings for him were definitely not a thing of the past.

Samantha was walking back toward the house when Ruth saw Nick open his pickup door again and get out. She thought for a moment he meant to say something more to her granddaughter. But instead, he rounded the cab of his truck and went across the street. That's when she noticed a young woman, toddler in arms, standing beside a car. Nick spoke to the woman, then reached through the open window.

What on earth was he doing? She had her answer a short while later after he used the keys to retrieve a spare tire from the trunk of the automobile.

Ruth hadn't noticed at first that Samantha had stopped and turned. Now her granddaughter was the one who watched Nick as he helped out a stranger in need. He jacked up the car, removed the flat, replaced it, and then lowered the car again. Samantha's profile and posture spoke volumes to her grandmother.

No, Ruth thought with conviction, *Samantha's feelings for Nick aren't a thing of the past*. But what, if anything, should she try to do about it?

Chapter 10

*B*rooklyn insisted on taking Samantha shopping. "It might be casual, but it's still a wedding," Brooklyn had replied when Samantha tried to say a trip to the mall wasn't necessary. Once they were in Brooklyn's car on the way to Boise, Samantha realized she was glad she'd agreed to go with her. She didn't want to wear any old thing when she met Nick's parents and younger brother.

The passing freeway hummed beneath the wheels of the SUV as they drove east. Ahead of them, the Boise foothills, brushed with the green of spring, rose from the valley floor until they became pine-tree-covered mountain peaks, the tallest of them a mile above sea level. Samantha thought they were like beautiful sentinels, protecting the Boise River and all that lay in the valley. How amazing it must have been for those early explorers and settlers to see those mountains and trees for the first time after so much time crossing the high desert.

"Hey, Sam. Where'd you go?"

She blinked as she looked toward Brooklyn.

"You were thinking hard about something."

"Sorry." She gazed out the front windshield again. "I was thinking about the pioneers who first came to the valley."

Brooklyn laughed. "Now that was *not* what I expected you to say."

"I know. But I've always been fascinated by the history of this valley. I think I was ten when Gran took me to see parts of the Oregon Trail where it drops down to the Boise River. I remember being amazed that I could stand in ruts made by those wagon wheels after more than a hundred and fifty years. Gran told me how the wagon trains could travel only about ten to fifteen miles in a day. It took them four or five days to get to Boise from what's now Mountain Home. We can cross that same ground on the freeway in half an hour or so." She gave her head a slow shake. "I would never have had the kind of courage needed to be a pioneer. You know, to leave everything you know behind, understanding you'd probably never be able to return. No matter how much you might want to."

"Goodness, you *were* deep in thought."

Samantha chuckled in agreement.

"Tell me something. If you love history so much—and

I know you do because I can hear it in your voice—why on earth are you an accountant? The two interests don't seem to go together. Or am I wrong about that?"

She shrugged. "Accounting seemed like a more sensible and secure way to make a good living. And when I was in college, that's what I wanted most."

"Security?"

"Yes."

"Hmm."

Samantha echoed, "Hmm," and then deftly changed the subject.

They arrived at the mall about ten minutes later. Brooklyn chose a parking spot on the south side of the building, and they entered through the main doors. Three senior-citizen mall-walkers, arms in brisk motion, moved past them as Brooklyn studied the directory.

"What Gran wouldn't give to be able to do that," Samantha said, her gaze following the gray-haired ladies in pastel warm-up suits.

Brooklyn looked at Samantha, then in the direction of her gaze. "She will be before she knows it. Ruth never shies away from a challenge."

"You're right. She's always been like that."

Brooklyn nodded, then pointed to a shop name on the directory. "Let's start there. They've got lots of cute dresses. And there's a shoe store right next door with some to-die-for heels."

Samantha had been to the Boise mall in the past, but not

often enough to be familiar with its layout. She was content to let Brooklyn lead the way. It turned out her cousin's wife not only knew where to go but was as good as any personal shopper could have been. And the bonus was she knew how to buy stylish clothes without spending a small fortune.

When Samantha said as much to Brooklyn, the other woman laughed. "I was a single mom working as a waitress for a decade. I was always broke and scraping by, so I learned how to shop on the cheap. I don't have to be as careful these days, but I still hate to waste money."

By the time they left the mall, after lunch in the food court and another hour of shopping, Samantha carried several bags. One contained a gorgeous emerald-green dress. It had a scooped neck, capped sleeves, and an asymmetrical hem with soft fringed lace along the edge of both hem and sleeves. The skirt was short but not too short. Elegant, yet subtle. Another bag held a pair of green satin heels that matched the lace of the dress exactly. Those were for the Friday rehearsal dinner.

For the wedding she'd chosen a dress of black, white, and wine-colored fabric. The flowing skirt, again asymmetrical, fell to just below her knees. Brooklyn had insisted—given the attire of the wedding party—that Samantha buy a pair of Western boots to wear with the dress. And that was where the cost-cutting measures had ended. The boots cost Samantha more than the two dresses and the pair of heels added together.

But she could not care less about the expense. Because when she'd put on those boots with that dress, she'd felt beyond fabulous. She'd even imagined what Nick might think when he first saw her in the outfit, and it had made her stomach and heart react in those fluttering, quickening ways. All too familiar reactions. Perhaps dangerous reactions.

When they reached Brooklyn's automobile, Samantha tossed her packages into the back and closed the hatch. "I've never enjoyed shopping much. The difference must be your company."

Brooklyn laughed. "I'm sure that's it."

"Seriously. You made this a lot of fun."

"You too." Brooklyn's expression was earnest now. "It's been great getting to know you better, Sam. I would envy Derek his wonderful extended family, only now you're all my family too." Her smile returned.

Was it contentment that flowed over Samantha? Serenity? Peace? Whatever it was, it was something she hadn't felt in so long she couldn't name it. But she liked it.

Ruth glanced at her cell phone and read the text on the screen. "That was from Brooklyn," she said to the three women—Camila Diaz, Tracy Vinton, and Lucca Phillips—seated with her at the kitchen table. "They're on their way home. But I think we're done. We all know the plan for Thursday."

"Don't you worry," Camila said. "We know what to do." She rose from her chair. "We'll take care of everything. All you have to do is look innocent and pretend you've forgotten what day it is. Sam will never suspect a thing."

Ruth frowned. "Do you think she'll believe it? I've never forgotten her birthday before."

"When you get up on Thursday," Tracy said, "act like your ankle is extra painful and that you had to take a pain pill. Then stay in bed and pretend to be asleep whenever she checks on you. That should do it."

Lucca chuckled. "You're awfully devious for a pastor's wife."

"You have no idea." Tracy's smile was full of mischief.

Everyone laughed at that.

Doubt began to swirl inside of Ruth after her friends departed, each with their own assignment for the surprise birthday party. Perhaps it wasn't a good idea. Samantha's feelings might be hurt when Ruth didn't wish her a happy birthday, let alone have a gift or a card for her. And what if Bianca called to wish Samantha happy birthday and then wanted to talk to Ruth too? She hadn't considered that. It would surely spoil the surprise. She'd better let her daughter in on the plan. She reached for the phone.

"Mom?" Bianca said instead of hello. "Is everything all right?"

"Everything's fine, dear."

"Is Sam taking good care of you?"

"You know she is."

"Yes." The tension melted from Bianca's voice. "I do know that. Sam would do anything to take care of her gran. She loves you to the moon and back."

Ruth smiled at the familiar phrase. "I love her the same

way. And you too." She paused. "But listen, dear. I'm calling about Sam's birthday." She quickly told her daughter the plans for the surprise party on Thursday night, ending with, "So if you could hold off calling her until evening, it would help."

"Of course I'll hold off. Oh, I wish I could be there too. Tell you what: I'll send her a text first thing in the morning, wishing her a happy birthday and promising to call in the evening. That way she won't be suspicious."

"Perfect."

When they ended the call ten minutes later, Ruth leaned back on the kitchen chair, her booted leg braced on the scooter and her eyes closed as her thoughts drifted to other birthdays celebrated in this house. Walter had been the mastermind behind more than one surprise, for Ruth and for their children and grandchildren. Oh, that man. She'd been such a sucker for his dry sense of humor. Time and again, she'd fallen for it, becoming part of the joke. Even when she'd expected he was up to something, he'd been able to fool her.

"I miss you, Walter," she whispered to the empty room. "But we're all in God's hands, and we're well because of it."

Derek put a hand on Nick's shoulder as the two men looked over the land. "This new system is going to make our farm even more successful. You and your crew did a great job, and I'll make sure to let your company's owner know how pleased I am."

"I appreciate it. They've never done an installation quite like this one, according to Brett. Maybe now they'll do it more often."

"I'm thinking they couldn't have done it without you. Your suggestions made a big difference, even if I did have my ideas mapped out in advance." Derek looked at Nick. "Come on up to the house. We'll get something to drink before you take off. I think there's Dr. Pepper and Diet Coke in the fridge."

"Sounds good."

As they walked, Boomer following close behind Nick, Derek said, "Before I forget, I'm supposed to tell you there's a surprise birthday party in the works for Sam. You're invited."

Samantha's birthday. He hadn't known. Or if he had known once, he'd forgotten it since. "When?"

"Thursday evening. We're supposed to be at Gran's house by five thirty. They've devised a plan to have Sam out of the house until about six. Presents are optional. It's the people Gran wants there."

"I'll be there."

He wouldn't have refused under any circumstance. After all, Samantha was helping him out by being his plus-one for Rudy's wedding. No, that wasn't the reason. He *wanted* to be at her party. He was glad for any reason to spend more time with her. Her party and Rudy's wedding were good starts.

Good starts to what? he wondered. Then he answered his own bothersome question with, *To friendship.* But did he believe that was enough for him any longer?

Even as he shoved away the question, another one occurred

to him. This one he gave voice to. "Any chance Brooklyn could find out what Sam plans to wear to the wedding?"

Derek cocked an eyebrow.

"I thought my birthday gift could be a necklace or bracelet or something to go with whatever she's wearing on Saturday."

"Ah. I see. And you're in luck. Brooklyn should know what Sam's wearing. That's where she and Sam are now. Shopping for clothes to wear this weekend. I'll tell Brooklyn what you need when she gets home and have her call you. She'll be able to give you a few ideas."

"Thanks."

At the house Derek got cold bottles of pop and brought them to the back porch. Miss Trouble came out of the house with her master and joined Boomer in the shade of a tree. The two dogs began to chase each other, the smaller, older dog delighting in tormenting the larger, younger one. It never failed to amuse Nick. Boomer always seemed confused around Miss Trouble.

"So, where's your next job?" Derek settled onto a chair.

"Not too far from here. The Riverside Vineyard is expanding, and we're handling the new irrigation system for them."

"That's great. I love to hear about a place doing well enough to expand. And you can be sure that I'll be recommending you to plenty of other area farmers."

Nick grinned before taking a long swig from the bottle of Diet Coke. It felt good to receive Derek's praise. It felt good to know that his work was appreciated. Sometimes, during his recovery, it had seemed an impossibility that he would even be able to hold down any job, let alone excel at it. But if succeeding in his job wasn't impossible, what else might not be impossible?

"Hey, Derek."

"Hmm?"

"I've heard that there's some great white-water rafting in Idaho. Any idea where I could go see some?"

Derek, like Samantha and Ruth, now knew a little about what had happened to him on a kayaking trip in Colorado. Not everything, but enough to make him give Nick a questioning look.

"I'd just like to look," he answered.

"Well, the Middle Fork of the Salmon River is probably the most famous for white-water rafting trips. But you probably know that."

Nick tried to remember. It sounded familiar to him, so he nodded.

"But the Salmon's more than an easy day trip away. If you want something closer, you should look at the south fork of the Payette up near Banks. It's maybe forty miles or so north of here. I'm not very knowledgeable about rafting, but I've heard the south fork has Class IV rapids."

Excitement coiled inside of Nick. It made him feel more alive than he'd felt in a long while. He was going to take that drive, just as soon as he could manage it.

Chapter 11

On Thursday morning Samantha opened the door to The Clip Job, Thunder Creek's one and only hair salon. Taking a quick breath for fortification, she walked inside. Gran had insisted that Georgia Hanover, the owner, was just the person to trim and style her hair. She hoped her grandmother was right, because tomorrow night was the rehearsal dinner for Nick's brother.

"Sam!" Georgia greeted her on sight. "Welcome!"

Since Samantha was a young girl, she'd known Georgia as one of Gran's close circle of friends—which had always puzzled her. They were such an unlikely pair. Her grandmother was traditional to her core. On the other hand, Georgia's bohemian nature showed in the visible tattoos on her arms, the hippie style of her clothing, and the bright-purple stripe in her slightly bird's-nest-looking hairdo. The latter didn't instill much confidence in Samantha as she settled into the styling chair.

"Ruth says you have some special events this weekend and want to look your best." Georgia swiveled Samantha around to face a full-length mirror.

"Yes." Nerves tumbled in her stomach again. Were those nerves about her hair or those special events?

"Well, we'll get you all fixed up."

Samantha started to wish she'd flown home to Portland to her regular stylist. She could have done it all in one day with an early enough start and a rental car. That would have been one expensive haircut, to be sure, but at least she would have known what she was getting.

"All right." Georgia met Samantha's gaze in the mirror, at the same time fastening a cape around her neck. "Tell me what we're doing for you today."

She explained her preferences, hoping she made herself clear. Then, to make sure, she pulled out a page she'd torn from an old *People* magazine. It was a photo of the actress Emma Stone. "I want it to look like this."

"Sweetheart, it already does." Georgia laughed. "I guess what you're telling me is just give you a trim and keep the shape. Maybe an inch off the ends, I'm guessing."

Samantha nodded as the tension eased from her shoulders.

Georgia escorted her to the wash bowl. When they

returned to the styling chair, a towel wrapped around Samantha's head, her cell phone chirped, notifying her of a text message. She drew it from her pocket beneath the cape. The text was from her mom.

Happy birthday, it read. *I have a crazy busy day ahead of me and will call you tonight. Do you have special plans?*

No, as a matter of fact, she didn't have plans, special or otherwise. Gran seemed to have forgotten that today was her birthday. No surprise there, especially considering that Gran's pain level seemed to have increased overnight. And really, what was one more birthday in the scheme of things?

"Hold your head up, Sam." Georgia removed the towel. "My, my, my. You do have such beautiful hair. You can't get that color of red from a bottle, although plenty of people have tried."

The compliment made her smile. As a kid, she'd hated being a redhead. She'd felt too different from the other girls, especially from the cute blonds in her class. But somewhere along the way, she'd begun to like the way she looked, including her hair color. Nick had once told her it was her hair that had made him come over to talk to her at the seminar where they'd met. Perhaps that's when she'd begun to truly like the color.

She felt that all too familiar sense of pleasure roll inside of her at the memory.

Georgia began to chatter about other people in Thunder Creek as she took a comb in one hand and scissors in the other. She didn't stop talking until she set down the scissors and picked up the blow dryer. When she was done, she spun the chair toward the mirror once again. "Ta-da!"

It was, Samantha realized at once, the perfect haircut, and she told Georgia so. The woman beamed with pride.

"What do I owe you?" Samantha asked as the cape was removed.

Georgia waved dismissively. "Not a thing. Hap—" She broke off and turned away with a cough. "Hap . . . happens that I owe your grandmother a haircut and she told me to use it for you."

"She didn't say anything to me about that."

Georgia waved again. "Maybe she forgot."

"At least let me give you a tip."

"Nope. Not a cent." She looked at Samantha. "Now you go and have a great day. I mean, a great weekend. The wedding and all. Is that what I heard? That it's a wedding? I love to go to weddings myself."

Samantha frowned. "So do I," she agreed slowly. Why did she feel as if she were being manipulated? She couldn't put her finger on it, but something wasn't quite right. "Thanks again for the great cut."

"You're welcome, sweetheart. You're surely welcome."

⸎

Nick pulled his truck to the curb on the far side of the park from Ruth's home. He was right on schedule, according to the time on his phone. Walking briskly, he followed the sidewalk to Ruth's backyard gate. His knock on the kitchen door was answered by Adrian Vinton.

"Hey, Nick," the pastor said. "Come on in."

"I take it someone got the birthday girl out of the house as planned."

Adrian nodded. "Brooklyn said she needed help with the set for a play at Alycia's school, and Samantha went to her aid."

Nick followed the pastor to the large living room, where Ruth sat in the recliner. The sofa and several chairs were already occupied by other guests. He recognized many of the faces, which pleased him.

Over the next fifteen minutes, more guests arrived at both the front and back doors. People spilled from the living room and into the large den. Gifts began to pile up on a table near the front door. Nick added a small, gold-wrapped box to an open space at the back of one stack. As the clock ticked closer to six, Camila asked the guests to be quiet, and they soon complied. It felt to Nick as if the entire house held its breath, and anticipation began to build in him.

At last the silence was broken by the soft, almost imperceptible sound of a door opening. Laughter followed from the kitchen. Samantha's laughter. Nick recognized it right away.

"Gran?"

Nick saw Ruth put a hand over her mouth.

"She must be asleep," Samantha said, lowering her voice. "I'll check on her." A heartbeat later, she stepped into view.

"Surprise!" everyone in the room shouted.

Samantha went pale. For a brief moment, Nick thought

she might faint from the shock. But then the color returned to her cheeks and she laughed again, her eyes twinkling. "I don't believe it." She looked around the room. When her gaze fell on Nick, it stopped. If possible, she appeared more surprised than before.

Her reaction bothered him. He didn't want her to be shocked that he'd come to celebrate with her. Surprised by the party, yes. But not by him being present. She turned away and said something to Brooklyn and Alycia, and when she turned back, her gaze avoided Nick.

That bothered him too.

A memory tried to surface. He saw her eyes brimming with tears. He felt a dull ache in his chest, seeing the hurt in their green depths. But before the scene could fully form in his mind, it vanished, like a mist in the morning sun, and he was left to wonder if it had been something real or only his imagination.

"Doesn't Sam look pretty?"

"She sure does." He glanced to his right.

The woman beside him—probably in her late forties or early fifties—had what could only be described as an outlandish sense of style, from her clothes to her hair to her makeup. "I'm Georgia. I own the beauty salon in town. And you're the young man who helped Ruth when she fell off that stupid horse."

He swallowed a chuckle. He'd heard similar words more than once over the last month. He wasn't Nick Chastain to many of the women in this town. He was that guy who'd helped Ruth. And any time the horse was included in a comment, it was a stupid one.

"Well, God bless you," Georgia continued. "None of us would know what to do without her."

He no longer tried to say he hadn't done all that much. Ruth's friends never believed him anyway.

"I hear you're taking Sam to a wedding."

"Uh . . . yes." Small town strikes again.

Georgia grinned. "I gave her a trim this morning in preparation for the weekend. I've always loved her red hair. So pretty."

His gaze swung back toward Samantha. "Beautiful," he said softly, watching her move among the guests. Funny—lots of hazy or missing memories were in this banged-up head of his, but he'd never forgotten her beauty. He'd never forgotten the smile that was both sweet and seductive. He'd never forgotten that fire that could flash in her eyes or the lyrical sound of her laughter.

Samantha's path around the room brought her closer to him and Georgia, and eventually her gaze met his again. "Hi, Nick. Thanks for coming."

"My pleasure. Happy birthday."

A question filled her eyes, but she didn't give it voice.

"Look how loved you are." He motioned with a hand toward the packed living room as a longing tightened his chest. A wish that he could read her every expression. A wish that he could be counted among those who loved her.

"It's more about how loved Gran is," Samantha answered.

Georgia grunted. "Nonsense, sweetheart. We love you in your own right." She patted Nick's arm. "I'd better get into the kitchen. They must be putting out the refreshments by now and might need my help." She hurried away.

There was more than one kind of love, Nick thought, his gaze still on Samantha. He could love her as a friend. That would be enough. It would have to be.

Not since she was a little girl had Samantha had a birthday party with so many guests in attendance. It didn't matter to her that they were more Gran's friends than hers. Their good wishes were genuine, and she loved them all for it.

Samantha sat on the sofa, the house now empty except for her and Gran. The unopened gifts lay at her feet, the opened ones to her right. But her thoughts were on Nick. He'd been among the first to leave the party, and yet his presence had lingered in her mind. She could still see his smile, still smell his woodsy cologne, still hear the warmth of his voice.

"Go on, dear," Gran said, intruding on her thoughts. "Open another one."

"Maybe I ought to wait until morning. It's late and you should be in bed."

Gran sent her a look of disgust. "All I do is rest these days. Now go on and open your gifts. I want to see every single one of them."

Samantha complied without further resistance. She wouldn't win, so there was no point in trying.

The gifts, for the most part, were simple and inexpensive. A knitted tea cozy. Pottery from a local artist. A board game. A framed inspirational saying, hand-printed. Near the last, she came to a small box wrapped in gold foil. A tiny gift card was attached to the ribbon.

Happy birthday, Sam. Nick.

Her pulse quickened at the sight of his distinct handwriting. She freed the tape and removed the wrapping paper, then lifted the lid of the white box. Inside, nestled in a cloud of cotton, was a tennis bracelet. Cubic zirconia rather than diamonds, she was certain, but beautiful nonetheless. It took her breath away, mostly because the Nick she'd known hadn't been a gift giver.

"Who is that from, Sam?"

"Nick."

"Well, for goodness' sake. Isn't that lovely?"

Samantha sensed her grandmother watching her. Lifting the bracelet from the box, she said, "He must be very grateful that I'm going with him to his brother's wedding."

"Hmm. Is that the reason?"

"Don't read more into this than it is, Gran."

"I wouldn't dream of it."

Chapter 12

When Samantha opened the door to Nick late the next afternoon, he was struck speechless. The word *stunning* didn't come close to defining how she looked in that dark-green dress, perfect with her ivory complexion and red hair. He was going to look like a pauper escorting a princess.

"Wow," he managed to say.

Her smile was quick, there and gone. Then she raised her right arm slightly. The tennis bracelet caught the light of the sun that descended in the western sky. "Thank you for your present, Nick. It was . . . unexpected. And thoughtful." She turned away. "Gran, we're leaving now." She took a sweater and small evening bag from the table in the entry.

"Not before I see Nick." Ruth wheeled her scooter into

view. She smiled as she looked at him. "My, don't you clean up well."

He chuckled. "Thanks." He ran his hands over the fabric of his suit coat. "Haven't worn this is more than two years. Glad it still fits."

"It fits very nicely," Ruth assured him. Then she gave Samantha a kiss on the cheek. "You two have a lovely evening."

"We will, Gran. We shouldn't be too late. You're sure you don't want Camila to come stay with you?"

"I'm well past the stage where I need someone with me twenty-four seven, thank you very much." Ruth waved her hand, shooing her granddaughter out the door.

Nick didn't take Samantha's arm, although he was tempted to. Instead, he walked beside her to where his truck awaited them at the curb. Despite her high heels and her short skirt, she managed the step up into the cab with surprising ease. He didn't allow his gaze to linger long on her shapely legs. Well, not *too* long.

After closing her door, he hurried around to the driver side and got in. "Thanks again for going with me, Sam."

"It gave me an excuse to buy a new dress. Brooklyn helped me pick it out."

He almost told her how great she looked but swallowed the words as he started the truck, afraid he might say too much.

"Besides," she said as the vehicle pulled away from the curb, "I haven't been a guest at a wedding in a long while. I'm looking forward to it."

They were silent on the drive out of Thunder Creek, but once they reached the freeway and were headed toward Boise, Samantha said, "Tell me about your family."

"My family?"

"You never really talked about them when we were . . . dating. I knew you had brothers, but not a whole lot more. I always assumed you weren't close with them."

He frowned as he thought back, trying to remember how he had managed to give her that impression. Details escaped him. Was it because he hadn't been ready for a serious relationship, because he hadn't wanted to let her get too close? His gut told him he'd guessed right. His head told him he'd been a fool.

If I had it to do over again, I'd never let you go. The truth of it stole his breath away.

"Tell me about them," she prompted again. "Who am I meeting tonight?"

He shook off his thoughts and tried to sound normal. "You'll meet my mom and dad. Her name's Tricia, and his name's Rocky."

"Tricia and Rocky."

"My two older brothers won't be there tonight, but you'll get to meet Jeff, the oldest, tomorrow at the wedding. Assuming his plane arrives on time. So that just leaves Rudy, my kid brother. He's the groom, of course."

"How much younger is Rudy than you?"

"Eight years. But we're tight. He and I are alike in a lot of ways."

"Only unlike you he's a romantic at heart."

He wanted to protest, to say he could be romantic, too, but she wouldn't have believed him. And with good cause.

"Love at first sight," she continued. "You don't believe in it. You told me so once."

She was right. He remembered that conversation.

They fell into another silence as they completed the drive to Boise. Nick found the church without a problem and parked his truck in the lot across from the older, stately building. Not until they reached the main entrance did he say, "My folks don't know that you and I met in Oregon. I told them I was bringing a date. Nothing else."

Samantha gave him a sharp look. "Don't you want them to know?"

"No, it's fine with me. But I wanted it to be up to you. Be warned, though. My mom will want to know everything about you, no matter what." He yanked open the door. "Be prepared for that."

The entry hall was empty, but the sounds of talking and laughter led them to the sanctuary. They stepped inside the large room and stopped.

At the front of the church, Rudy saw them at once. "Nick!" He rushed down the long center aisle in their direction.

Grinning, Nick shook his brother's hand, followed by a sturdy embrace as they each gave the other some solid pats on the back. When Rudy stepped back, his gaze shifted to Samantha. Frank admiration filled his eyes before they shot back to Nick.

The pauper-with-the-princess feeling returned. "Rudy, this is Samantha Winters. Sam, this is my kid brother, Rudy."

Rudy grinned. "When I told him he could bring a date, I sure didn't expect him to find someone like—"

Nick gave his brother a quick elbow in the ribs.

Although it momentarily shut Rudy up, it didn't stop him from offering Samantha his arm, then escorting her away from Nick. "Come meet my fiancée and the rest of our families."

"Sit with us," Tricia Chastain said as the rehearsal began. The woman led Samantha to the front row, right side of the aisle.

They were silent while the wedding party organized themselves at the rear of the church. Eventually, Rudy, Nick, and another guy about the same age as the groom—a cousin of the bride, Tricia whispered to Samantha—came down the aisle and took up their places in front of the pastor. He began explaining how the ceremony would go, speaking in a low voice that barely carried to the first pew.

"Nick says you live in Thunder Creek," Tricia said softly.

"Yes. Temporarily. I'm staying with my grandmother while she recovers from a fall."

"How did you and Nick meet?" Tricia's gaze returned to her sons.

Not for the first time, Nick had left it up to Samantha

what to tell others, and she made a quick decision. "Actually, we knew each other in Oregon. When he was still teaching at the university. Then we lost track of each other until we met again here."

Tricia looked at her. "It must have been nice for him to see a friendly face when he got here."

Samantha nodded rather than try to explain how unfriendly her face had been that first day.

The organ began to play the "Wedding March," ending the brief conversation. Those seated in the pews swiveled to watch as the bridesmaids came down the aisle. Right after them came the bride and her father. Chelsea made Samantha think of a porcelain doll with her pale complexion, rosy cheeks, bow-shaped mouth, and long blond hair. But it was the adoring way the bride looked at her groom that made Chelsea more than pretty. Her eyes were so full of love it seemed to spill over onto everyone around her.

As the bride passed her, Samantha turned in her seat again, a twinge of envy squeezing her heart. Despite herself, her gaze shifted to the best man. Nick grinned as he leaned forward and whispered something to his brother. The two of them laughed. Chelsea lightly slapped Rudy's upper arm, then laughed with them.

"Behave yourselves, boys," Tricia called to her sons.

Nick looked at his mom and winked.

Samantha wondered again why he had been so close-mouthed about his family. His silence had given her a mistaken impression.

Then again, maybe her impression had more to do with herself than with Nick. She and her mom weren't as close as they'd once been. Not that they didn't love each other. They did, and they both knew it. But Samantha had never warmed to her stepdad, Trent Adams, and that had put emotional distance between her and her mom. No. If she was honest, it wasn't her mom's second husband who was the cause. The fault lay with Samantha. She frowned, wondering if this was another result of her fearful nature.

A collective sigh went up from the observers of the rehearsal. Her attention reverted to the bride and groom in time to see Rudy kiss Chelsea, her back bent over his arm in a romance-novel-worthy pose.

Rudy looked at the pastor. "Good enough?"

The pastor grinned. "Good enough."

Rudy helped Chelsea stand upright before facing his audience. "Let's eat!"

Moments later, Nick arrived at the front row, his gaze moving from his parents to Samantha. "Looks like everybody knows what they're doing tomorrow." He patted his breast pocket. "And I am now in charge of the ring. Make sure I don't lose it, Sam, or Rudy'll kill me." To his mom he said, "Where are we headed for dinner? I'll need directions."

"We're walking there as a group. Just one block from here. Chelsea's parents rented a room in a historic house and are having the rehearsal dinner catered. The groom's parents usually take care of the dinner, but they wouldn't hear of us paying for a thing." She ended with a shrug.

Nick leaned in and kissed his mom's cheek, whispering, "Are you doing okay?"

It was hard to tell by her profile, but Tricia seemed sad as she nodded. Then she smiled again. "If I'd wanted to be in charge of a wedding, I should have had at least one daughter." She patted Nick's cheek, the last one slightly harder than the others.

He laughed, and the sound swept away any hint of melancholy from his mom's expression.

"Come on." He offered Samantha his elbow. "I'm hungry."

He was different around his family, she thought as they walked, her fingers resting in the crook of his arm. Actually, she'd noticed other changes in him in these past weeks in Idaho. He was more laid back than before, less intense. But the difference in him tonight was that he emanated joy.

"What?" he asked when he noticed her watching him.

"Nothing."

"*What?*"

"I like your family. Especially your mom."

He grinned. "Easy to do."

It frightened her a little, this changed man beside her. It frightened her because she thought she could like him even more than she'd liked the old Nick. And that simply would not do.

Chapter 13

*I*n Samantha's opinion, the ceremony on Saturday was every bit as adorable as the bride. Everyone in the wedding party wore western boots, both guys and gals. The bride and her attendants had knee-length skirts, and the groom and his groomsmen wore jeans and long-sleeved black shirts with white piping. Sunflowers were everywhere, including in the bride's bouquet. The service itself was conventional, the couple promising to love and honor each other until death parted them, and when the groom kissed the bride at the end—without bending her over backward as he had at the rehearsal—Samantha had to wipe away a few tears with a tissue.

At the dinner the previous night, she had been able to

stay somewhat in the background, observing the Chastains, listening to their easy banter and their lively laughter, learning a little about the family dynamics. It had made for an enjoyable evening for a confessed introvert.

Today was different.

"Mom tells me you knew Nick in Oregon," Jeff Chastain said. He was seated on Samantha's left at a large round table, both watching while another photograph of the bride and groom, their parents, and the attendants was taken.

"Yes."

"It was rough on him, letting go of the life he used to have there. I thought for a while the loss would leave him bitter."

She turned toward Jeff. He looked the most like Rocky of the three brothers who were present, and he seemed the more serious one too.

"All we cared about was that he would live through it," Jeff added. "We almost lost him a time or two early on."

"Nick and I have never talked about what happened to him on that kayaking trip. Not in any detail. He doesn't seem to like to talk about it, so I haven't asked him to share more." The admission made her wonder if she'd done the right thing. Perhaps it wasn't Nick who was reluctant to talk as much as it was her not wanting to listen.

Jeff's gaze moved back to Nick. "Well, he sure looks happy and healthy now. Coming to Idaho has been good for him." Once more he looked at Samantha. "Maybe it's running into you again."

She felt warmth enter her cheeks. Embarrassment or pleasure? She couldn't be sure. She lowered her eyes to her hands, now folded in her lap.

"What I can't figure out," Jeff continued, his voice louder now, "is why someone as pretty as you is with him. You could do a whole lot better, Ms. Winters."

"Get lost, Jeff," Nick said from somewhere close by.

Surprised by his nearness, Samantha looked up. He was scowling at his older brother from the opposite side of the table, but there was humor in his expression too.

"For some crazy reason, bro," Nick said, "Rudy wants a couple of photos with you in them." He jerked his head toward the photographer.

Laughing, Jeff rose from his chair. His gaze went to Samantha. "Don't go too far. I've got stories about some of this guy's antics that'll curl your hair."

"As if I'll let him do that," Nick muttered as he sat in the chair next to hers. The teasing grin returned. "I prefer your hair straight rather than curled."

"I don't need to hear his stories to do that. I remember what you were like."

Her honesty surprised them both. She saw it in his eyes and felt it in her heart. But perhaps it was good to remember what he'd been like before—and to let him know she remembered. Because a man never strayed too far from who he was at his core. Right? Nick might seem different now, but how long would it last? How long before he reverted to the man he'd been when they were together?

She needed to heed the warning in those questions. Or was it too late for that?

ℂΟ

Nick felt something trying to inch its way in between them, and he knew what that something was. His old self. Her memories of him, the way he used to be. He wanted to tell her that he wasn't the same man, that he would never be the same again.

She wouldn't believe me. I have to prove it to her.

But would God give him the time he needed to do that? The weeks were melting away. Her grandmother was on the mend. All too soon she would go back to Oregon.

Say something, his heart demanded. *Ask her to give you time to prove you're different now.*

Jeff returned to the table, his hand landing on Nick's shoulder. "You're wanted at the mic. Time for the toast."

Samantha glanced away, and the opportunity to speak vanished.

He stood. "I won't be long." He headed toward the small stage, pulling a slip of paper from his shirt pocket as he went. He'd made sure to write down what he wanted to say since he wouldn't have trusted himself to remember more than three words once he was at the microphone.

"Hello."

The mic squealed and he took a step back, wincing. Soft laughter rolled over the room. He stepped forward again.

"I'm Nick. Rudy's brother. And it's my job to give the toast."

He glanced at the sheet of paper.

"I plan on making this short and sweet."

He looked up again, and his gaze went to the newlyweds.

"I don't think it's a secret that Rudy fell in love with Chelsea at first sight. So, when I was looking for something to say today and came across a poem by John Clare, I was convinced Rudy could have written it for his lovely bride."

He drew a breath. "It's titled 'First Love' . . .

I ne'er was struck before that hour
With love so sudden and so sweet,
Her face it bloomed like a sweet flower
And stole my heart away complete.
My face turned pale as deadly pale,
My legs refused to walk away,
And when she looked, what could I ail?
My life and all seemed turned to clay.
And then my blood rushed to my face
And took my eyesight quite away,
The trees and bushes round the place
Seemed midnight at noonday.
I could not see a single thing,
Words from my eyes did start—
They spoke as chords do from the string,
And blood burnt round my heart.
Are flowers the winter's choice?

Is love's bed always snow?
She seemed to hear my silent voice,
Not love's appeals to know.
I never saw so sweet a face
As that I stood before.
My heart has left its dwelling-place
And can return no more.

Pausing at the end of the poem, he looked up. This time his gaze went to Samantha, and the dreamy expression on her face made him long to be more like his younger brother, the romantic. If only . . .

Realizing the entire room was waiting for him to say more, he cleared his throat and checked the paper in his hand again. Quickly, he repeated the words in his head before looking toward the bride and groom.

"And so, in the words of St. Augustine, I say, 'Insomuch as love grows in you, so beauty grows. For love is the beauty of the soul.' And in the words of Lennon and McCartney, I remind you that 'love is all you need.'" He lifted a champagne flute. "To the bride and groom."

"To the bride and groom," voices echoed throughout the room.

As Rudy leaned in to kiss Chelsea, Nick stepped off the stage. At the same time the lead singer invited the bride and groom to the floor for their first dance. Rather than make his way back to his table, Nick stopped to watch the couple.

The band began to play a Chris Young song, "You're

Gonna Love Me." Nick saw Rudy mouthing the lyrics to Chelsea as he turned her around the dance floor, and he felt another tug at his heart. Once again he wished he was more like his brother.

Only he didn't want to be more romantic with just anybody. He wanted it with Samantha. He wanted to take her in his arms, to move with her in time to the music, to ask her to take a chance on him a second time.

But would that be fair to her? He frowned, hating the question he returned to again and again. After all, what could he offer her? The career he'd once had was gone. His life's savings and most of his material possessions had been eaten up by hospital and doctor bills. And the brain injury he'd incurred might continue to impact him for the rest of his life.

He'd tried to tell her that day in Ruth's kitchen how bad things could still be for him, but pride had kept him from being thorough. Maybe he'd hinted at things a time or two since then, but no details.

And yet, what if he *was* over the worst of things? What if he could offer her more than he thought? He didn't want to throw away a chance at happiness with her. Not if one existed.

Movement on the dance floor pulled him from his inner thoughts. The bride now danced with her father while the groom danced with his mom.

I envy them.

Drawing a breath, he made his way toward Samantha. When the ritual of wedding dances was over, he wanted to be ready to ask her to dance with him before someone else could. As he neared the table, she looked his way. A faint smile appeared, as if to say she was glad he'd rejoined her.

Another song began. Nick glanced toward the floor. More couples had joined the newlyweds. He returned his gaze to her and held out his hand. "Shall we?"

Her eyes widened, and he suddenly remembered that she'd once told him she loved to dance. Yet even knowing that, he'd never taken her dancing. Not even just to please her.

I was a lousy boyfriend. What did she see in me back then? Why should she give me another chance now?

He took her in his arms, grateful that their first dance together was a slow one. He wanted an excuse to hold her close. They moved easily in time to the music. He caught a whiff of her fruity-scented shampoo and wanted to bury his face in her hair.

As the melody ended, Samantha drew back and looked at him. "You're a good dancer." There was a hint of a question in the statement.

"Mom made sure her boys all had lessons. But I never cared for dancing much."

"I wouldn't have guessed." Her tone was wry.

"I think I may have been mistaken in my opinion."

That faint smile returned. "Really?"

A different song began. Another slow one.

"Mind helping me be sure?" He held out his arms again.

She stepped into them. He hoped they would keep playing slow dances for hours.

Chapter 14

Ruth was rolling her way back to the living room, a couple of books in the basket of the scooter, when she heard voices from the front porch through an open window.

"I had a wonderful time," Samantha said.

"Me too." That was Nick of course.

"It was fun getting to know your family."

"They're a good bunch. Wish you could have met Peter too. Another time."

Ruth smiled, hearing something more than politeness in those words about the future.

"Yes, another time."

Silence followed. More than a few moments for someone

to think of something else to say. But perhaps less than Ruth would expect if a kiss was involved.

"I'd better go." Nick's voice barely carried through the open window this time. "See you at church tomorrow?"

"Yes. Gran and I will see you there."

Spurred into action, Ruth rolled the scooter backward down the hall, listening for the sound of the opening door. Only when she heard it did she push the scooter forward again.

"Gran?"

"I'm here, dear." She rolled into view, hoping she didn't look guilty for eavesdropping.

Samantha stood in the entry hall, her sweater over one arm, her clutch in the opposite hand.

"Did you have a good time?"

"Yes. The wedding was absolutely perfect. How they put it together in such a short time amazes me."

"I hope I'll get to see pictures."

Samantha set her clutch and sweater on the entry table. "I took some photos with my phone. I'll put them on my laptop so you can see the larger versions."

"I'd like that." She pushed on to the recliner. Before settling into the chair, she removed the books from the basket and set them on the end table within easy reach.

"Did you manage all right while I was gone?"

"I managed fine. Mostly I read and napped. But Camila had lunch with me. By the time I am rid of this boot and scooter, I am going to be spoiled so rotten I won't be able to do a thing for myself."

Samantha laughed. "As if." She walked to the sofa and sat down. "What are you reading?"

"A couple of old favorites by Catherine Marshall."

"I'll bet *Christy* is one of them."

Ruth smiled. "Yes."

"And the other?" Samantha leaned over and pulled off the boots she wore.

"*Adventures in Prayer.*"

Her granddaughter straightened. "I've never read that one."

"It's a classic, in my opinion. Would you like to read it now? I can wait." She lifted the book from the table and held it toward Samantha.

"Thanks." Her granddaughter took the slender paperback. "There's lots I need to pray about."

"Anything you want to tell me?"

"Oh, Gran. I don't know." Samantha leaned her head against the back of the sofa and closed her eyes.

Ruth said nothing more, knowing it was time to wait.

Samantha felt something give inside of her. She sat up straight again. "Gran, you already guessed how I used to feel about Nick."

"Mmm."

"Well, it seems like seeing him has stirred up a lot of old memories." She thought of the way he'd held her on the dance floor, and her pulse quickened. As if to deny the reaction, she added, "I'm not even sure what I'm feeling."

Gran watched her with a tender gaze that said she knew the truth.

"No. You're right. I do know what I feel. I'm attracted to him, and I'm afraid." She took a breath and released it on a sigh. "I'm afraid I'll get hurt again."

"By Nick."

She nodded slowly. "But I shouldn't be afraid of that. After all, I'll be going home in a couple more months."

"Hmm."

Samantha lowered her gaze to her hands, folded in her lap. "He was different in lots of ways when I knew him before. He loved to teach, especially the more adventurous aspects of it. Like taking his students out on the ocean to fish for sharks. Crazy, huh?"

Gran made a soft sound, acknowledging that she was listening.

"We broke up over the trip he had planned for spring break. We were both angry that night, and it ended badly. I tried to apologize not long after, but he never replied to either my e-mails or phone messages." She met Gran's gaze. "I thought he didn't want to hear from me, and that made the pain even worse. But the real reason he didn't reply was because he was in the hospital. He never knew I had tried to contact him."

"Oh. I see."

Samantha rubbed her eyelids with her fingertips, wondering how things might have been different if Nick had known of her attempts to apologize. Then with a sigh, she lowered her hands. "But I was right about that trip. He was reckless. He did get hurt."

"Is it important to you that you were right?"

She sighed. "I guess not." She got up from the sofa and moved to the front window. A car went down the street. A couple holding hands strolled on the sidewalk, headed toward Main Street. "I guess I'm afraid that I'll care too much and then something else will happen to him. I'm afraid that he'll put himself at risk again. I'm afraid because I don't know what my own future looks like, let alone his." *And I'm afraid that I'll love him and he won't love me in return.*

"Sam."

She turned to face her grandmother.

"None of us knows what the future holds. Much of what happens in life will never make sense to our mortal minds. But nothing is random or by accident. Our God still reigns, and He still has a plan for every one of us. All things still work together for good for those who love Him."

Samantha struggled against Gran's words. "Are you saying that your broken ankle was part of God's plan?"

"Perhaps it happened so that you would come to stay with me and discover how *not* to be afraid. Or so that you could see Nick again."

"Couldn't God have arranged that some other way than dumping you off a horse?"

Gran's smile was gentle even as she answered a question with a question. "Will the pot argue with the Potter?"

"And Nick's accident?" Samantha challenged, not ready to give in. "Was that part of God's plans too? He almost died."

Her grandmother's smile disappeared. "I don't have all the answers, Sam. If I did, I wouldn't need faith. And if you had all the answers, you wouldn't need it either."

The urge to argue drained out of Samantha, leaving her spent and frustrated. She wanted those answers from God. She wanted to understand the things that happened to her and to have a good plan for her future. She hated the unknown. She wanted her path to be well defined and as smooth as possible.

She returned to the sofa and picked up the boots she'd left on the floor. "I'm going to change." She took a couple of steps away, then added, "Thanks for the talk, Gran."

Nick had just enough time to change his clothes and feed Boomer before his parents arrived at his house. Like Nick, his dad now wore a dark-colored T-shirt with his Levi's. His mom had on a pair of denim capris with a yellow blouse and light sweater.

"Mom. Dad. This is Boomer." He stroked the dog's head, keeping him at a sit.

His mom smiled. "Hello, Boomer."

Nick released the dog, and Boomer trotted over to meet her.

"What a good boy you are." She ruffled his ears.

His dad's gaze swept the area—the small house, the few outbuildings, the farmland surrounding them. "Lots smaller from the house you owned in Corvallis."

"You think?" Nick laughed at the understatement.

His dad grinned. "This seems to suit you."

"It does. Come on. I'll give you the grand tour. It should take about five minutes, max. Then I'll drive you into Thunder Creek."

It wasn't much longer than those promised five minutes before the Chastain family was on the road into town, Nick's mom in the front seat beside him, his dad in the backseat, and Boomer riding in the truck bed near the cab's rear window.

Nick slowed the truck to twenty miles per hour as they entered Thunder Creek from the east side. As if he'd been a resident for years, he pointed out places he thought might interest his folks, including the church he attended and Ruth Johnson's shop. "I wish I could buy you a coffee or pastry, but they close early on Saturdays."

He drove them out the other side of town and on toward the Snake River. He pointed out the winery where he and his crew had started work earlier in the week. On the return route, he took them past Derek's organic farm. He shared a little of the concept for the new irrigation system his company had installed, and that made his dad, usually the silent type, perk up and ask a few questions.

Back in Thunder Creek, Nick drove to the diner and parked in the lot. Seeing the curious look on his mom's face, he said, "It doesn't look like much, but the food's great. I promise." They got out of the truck and went inside, where the waitress greeted him by name.

"These are my parents, Lucca," he replied. "I'm showing them the sights."

She laughed. "That doesn't take long." Motioning with the menus in her hand, she led the way to an open booth.

Once all three of them were settled, Nick's mom said, "You really have made this town your home, haven't you."

"What do you mean?"

"You know the waitress by name, for one."

"This is the only restaurant in town." Nick shrugged. "Besides, Lucca goes to the same church I do."

His mom reached across the table to take his hand. "I was worried when you agreed to this move to Idaho, but I can see that it's been good for you."

Nick thought about her words for a few moments. "Yeah, it has been good for me. In more ways than one."

"Is Sam one of those ways?"

He didn't hesitate this time. "Maybe."

She raised an eyebrow.

"Okay. Yeah. I'm sure she is one of those ways. But we're just friends."

For now.

Chapter 15

*H*eart hammering, Nick pulled his pickup over to the side of the road. *Think*, he told himself. *Just take a breath and think.*

After taking that recommended deep breath, he let his gaze roam the farmland on both sides of the country highway. Nothing looked familiar. Where had he been headed? A job. He knew that much. He'd driven into Caldwell on this Monday morning to get some documents from the office, but after leaving there, things had grown fuzzy. The longer he'd driven, the more lost he'd felt.

Early in his recovery, he'd become lost frequently. Panic

had overwhelmed him when that happened. But he hadn't gotten lost since moving to Idaho. Despite doctors' warnings to the contrary, he'd begun to believe those episodes were a thing of the past. That he'd been cured of them. Apparently he was wrong and the doctors were right.

He took another deep breath and closed his eyes. "God, I don't know where I am, and I don't remember where I was going. Help me. Please."

With the brief prayer lingering in the air, the panic left him, replaced by a quiet that seemed to enfold him like a warm blanket on a chilly night. It would be okay, he told himself. It would be okay. He could figure this out. He wasn't in the wilderness. He was in the midst of farmland. Even if he couldn't remember his destination, he wasn't alone. He could ask someone for help, if worst came to worst.

He opened his eyes and looked around a second time. That barn up ahead on the left. He'd driven past it before. He was sure of it. Not today but recently. Yesterday? Last week? He couldn't be sure of when, but he recognized it. He wasn't lost. Merely confused. Another deep breath, and he felt brave enough to continue driving west.

"Keep your eyes open. You'll remember where you were headed. You aren't lost. Just forgetful. Keep looking."

He pulled back onto the roadway, waiting, watching. When he came to a fork, he followed it to the right for no reason that he understood—until row upon row of grapevines came into view. And just like that, he knew the vineyard had been his destination all along. The fog lifted from his brain. He released a sigh of relief. Before long, Nick had joined his crew and was giving them new instructions for their installation.

But that evening, when he sat down at the table in his kitchen to eat dinner, his thoughts returned to that morning's episode. It was a stark reminder of how his accident had changed him from the man he used to be. Would he ever be one hundred percent reliable? For himself? For anybody else?

The last silent question caused his imagination to go one step further. What if he was one day responsible for someone else? A little girl, perhaps. A little girl with green eyes and pretty red hair. What if he was supposed to pick that little girl up from school but forgot her? What if the day was cold and snowy and this imaginary child was all alone because he didn't remember her or because he was lost on the side of the road somewhere?

He leaned back in his chair, his meal forgotten.

"I can't put someone else at risk," he whispered, his gaze lowering to Boomer who lay on the floor nearby. "I don't have the right."

Nick had a particular "someone else" in mind, of course. Samantha, with her green eyes and pretty red hair, so like that little girl of his imagination. But he couldn't put Samantha—or her future happiness—at risk.

Almost from the moment he'd seen her in her grandmother's hospital room, hope had taken root in his heart, although he'd done a good job of disguising it, even from himself. But when he'd watched Rudy and Chelsea at their wedding, when he'd seen the love they shared, he couldn't deny he had a longing for more. A longing for more . . . with Samantha. And for a couple of days, he'd let that hope burn bright.

This morning reality had reared its ugly head.

"I was fooling myself, Boomer."

The dog rose to all fours.

"You and me, fella. We do all right the way we are. Right?"

Boomer wagged his tail.

"Yeah. We do all right."

The words tasted like sawdust in his mouth.

The grandfather clock in Gran's entry hall ticked off the seconds, a soft but audible sound that was beginning to drive Samantha crazy. She moved the laptop aside and picked up her phone. The screen brightened. No missed calls. No missed texts.

She'd been so sure Nick would call her today. She'd expected it. She'd waited for it. Whether or not she should *want* him to call was a separate matter.

They had both enjoyed the other's company on Friday and Saturday, and his warm greeting at church yesterday morning had seemed to confirm it. He'd even told her how much his mom and dad liked her—which pleased her a great deal. Perhaps more than it should, given her fears and uncertainty.

She looked at the phone's screen a second time, then tapped through to the messages. Just in case. Nothing. She set down the phone and drew the laptop back to her lap, but she found little there to hold her attention. She liked a few updates in her Facebook feed, but there wasn't anything interesting enough to click through to. Not even one of those silly tests that would tell her the one word that described her—always, she'd noticed, a positive word, like *loyal* or *peaceful* or *trustworthy*.

Once again she set aside the laptop, this time closing the top to put it into sleep mode. Then she got up and strolled into the kitchen. She wasn't hungry, so instead of looking for a snack, she filled a glass with ice and water.

It felt strange to be in the house alone. Gran had gone out to dinner with friends. They had invited Samantha to join them, but she'd declined. Gran didn't need her to tag along everywhere. Now she realized her real reason was the expectation of that call that hadn't come.

She looked out the kitchen window toward the town park, one finger tapping the glass in her hand.

He doesn't owe me a phone call.

They'd been two old friends, dancing at a wedding. That was all. She was making too much of it. But some of the songs replayed in her head, and she could imagine Nick's arms around her as he turned her about the floor. She breathed in, and it was as if she caught the faint scent of the cologne he'd worn.

Her phone sang out her ringtone, jerking her from the

memory. She set down the water glass and dashed to the living room. Instead of Nick's face on the screen, however, she saw Daniel Greyson's image. Disappointment washed over her.

Reluctantly, she answered the call. "Hello?"

"Hey, Samantha. Glad I caught you."

"Hi, Daniel."

"Listen, sorry to bother you again. I know I've been texting a lot. But I'm wondering, is there any chance you could shorten your leave?"

How typically Daniel. No "How is your grandmother?" No "Hope everything is all right."

"Because that gal who's filling in for you is an idiot. She can't do anything the way you do."

Something snapped inside Samantha. Her patience was all dried up. "No, I can't cut it short. And Marti is not an idiot. That's her name, by the way. Marti. If she isn't doing something the way you like, it's because you aren't explaining what you need." Gracious! That might be the most honest thing she'd said to Daniel in years. She'd grown much too adept at swallowing her opinions rather than speaking them aloud.

Perhaps her reply caught him by surprise, too, because he didn't continue right away.

"Was there something else you needed, Daniel?"

"Then you aren't coming back soon?"

She drew a quick breath. "No. I'm not coming back soon."

Another silence, then, "This isn't like you, Samantha."

"You're right about that. It isn't like me. But I'm trying to change that." *And I'm learning not to be afraid, starting with you.* "Try to be nicer to Marti, and I'm sure she'll do a good job for you. Take care, Daniel. I'll see you later this summer. Bye."

She ended the call without waiting for his response and stared at the blank screen while drawing several more breaths.

With a shout, she executed a brief hand-pumping dance, circling around in something akin to a victory lap. Then she released a laugh. Silly, perhaps, but it sure felt good to stop Daniel from pushing her around. And she hadn't been unkind. Simply firm. It seemed a healthy first step. She could hardly wait to tell Gran about it.

After the men's group study was over, Nick tried to slip away without being noticed. He failed.

"Care to tell me about it?" Derek asked, stopping his departure. "You seemed troubled tonight. Am I wrong?"

Nick wanted to shrug off the question, but honesty demanded an answer. "No, you're not wrong."

Derek watched and waited.

How much did Nick want to tell him? About the accident. About the past. About the future that seemed much more unsure than it had a few days ago. Finally he said, "It's a bigger topic than a few minutes and one cup of coffee." He motioned with his head toward the other men who stood in small clusters near the coffeemaker and dessert table.

"Come to my house for lunch tomorrow. Brooklyn has

a seminar to go to in the afternoon, and Alycia's in school. We'll have the place to ourselves. We can take as long as you need and your job allows."

"All right." He almost added, *If I can find your house.* But that would invite more questions. "See you then." With that, he walked out of the church.

One of the things Nick loved about this area of Idaho, situated on the western-most side of the time zone, was how late the sun set. Noticeably later than where he'd grown up or where he'd lived much of his adult life. In mid-May the sun didn't go down until after nine p.m., and it would remain light enough to see until nearly half past the hour. Now, as he walked to his pickup, where Boomer faithfully waited for him in the truck bed, the first stars were beginning to appear in the twilight sky.

He remembered the spectacular brightness of the stars when he'd been in a boat at sea or in a camp in the Rocky Mountains, far from civilization. The vastness of the heavens had filled his heart with awe, but he hadn't thought about the Creator back then, only the creation. He would like to experience some of his old adventures with his new perspective. Would he get to do that? His physicians warned against it.

He'd lost so much when his head slammed into that rock beneath the surface of the river, but it wasn't old adventures that thought recalled. It was Samantha and the future he didn't believe he could have.

"Hey, boy," he greeted Boomer, giving the dog the anticipated pat. "Want to join me in the cab?"

As if understanding the words, the border collie sailed over the tailgate and raced to join his master. Nick gave him another pat on the head, then opened the truck's door, and with a hand motion gave the dog permission to hop inside. Nick got in next, but he didn't start the engine right away. He sat there, in the silence of the gathering night, and waited for that unfruitful sense of despair to pass.

Chapter 16

Come on, Sam. It'll be fun." Brooklyn leaned back in the chair across the desk from Samantha. No sounds from the coffee shop drifted through the closed office door.

"But I don't have an artistic bone in my body," Samantha protested.

"You know what I was told recently? We're made in the image of God and God is *the* Creator. Thus, we are all created to create."

"You didn't see the finger painting I did in first grade."

Brooklyn laughed.

Samantha hadn't meant it to be funny. She was dead serious.

"I *need* you to go with me, Sam. I don't want to be the

only adult with five thirteen-year-old girls." Brooklyn pushed the flyer across the desk so that Samantha could get a better look at it. "Everyone I know who has been to a paint-night event has said it's a blast. These things are sweeping the country. You should experience it."

Samantha stared at the image of daisies in front of what looked to be the side of a red barn. A professional had painted that picture. She couldn't begin to imagine how.

"They provide the acrylic paints and the canvas, and they walk you through each and every step. How hard can it be?"

"There are a number of reasons I became an accountant." Samantha pointed at the flyer. "This is probably one of them."

Brooklyn laughed again as she stood. "I'm not taking no for an answer, so you may as well accept your fate. Besides, if you really hate the idea of trying, you can sit and watch the rest of us have fun."

Hate the idea of trying? Ouch. That hurt. Was it true of her? Was she so set in her ways or so afraid of failing that she wouldn't *try* something new?

"Not trying is worse than trying and failing," she whispered to herself.

"What?"

"Nothing." She shook her head. "And yes, I'll go with you and the girls."

"Great!"

"That remains to be seen." Samantha rose and walked out of the office with Brooklyn.

This late in the morning, the shop had only a few customers, people on their laptops making use of the public Wi-Fi while sipping their coffees or teas. That's why Samantha chose to do the bookkeeping during this lull.

"I'll pick you up on Friday at five thirty." Brooklyn stopped and gave Samantha a hug. "You can eat before or you can order something at the restaurant where the event is held. Or you can eat burgers with us on our way there."

She nodded. "Okay."

"We really are going to have fun."

Samantha planned to keep her wait-and-see attitude about that.

She remained where she was, watching Brooklyn as she left Sips and Scentimentals, got into her car, and pulled out of the parking lot. She smiled to herself, realizing that over the past month she'd gained a special friend. She hadn't expected that to happen when she came to stay with Gran.

Brooklyn always seemed so upbeat too. Remarkable, considering her past. She'd been abandoned by her mother and rejected by her father. After her husband left her, Brooklyn had raised her daughter on a waitress's salary without help from the girl's father. Yet Brooklyn's peace about it all was deep and real. She'd placed her trust in God and hadn't allowed the pain of the past to color her future.

"I'd like to be more like her."

With a sigh, she returned to the office and turned off the computer, done with her work for the day. A short while later, as she entered the house, she discovered Gran in the kitchen baking cookies for that evening's Bible study.

"Gran, I could have done that." Samantha closed the door behind her.

Her grandmother smiled over her shoulder. "But I enjoy doing it, and there is no reason I can't. I'm an expert with this scooter now."

Samantha couldn't argue. Her grandmother zoomed around the house. She didn't need help in and out of bed or in and out of her chair. She didn't need help with showering as she had before the cast was replaced with the boot. In some ways Samantha felt unneeded. Gran could probably take care of herself, except for the need of a driver when she had to go out, and she had plenty of friends who could do that for her.

However, her grandmother had made it clear that she *wanted* Samantha to stay with her. Which felt good. To be wanted.

She closed her eyes, disliking the feeling that had stolen over her. Self-pity wasn't attractive. And she disliked the reason for it even more. Four days, and still no call from Nick. How pathetic she was. How like him to do this.

No, that wasn't fair. She had no reason to expect him to call. He wasn't under any obligation. Only it felt like rejection, and it hurt.

Nick arrived at Derek's house before noon. He'd had a last-minute doctor's appointment in Boise that morning and had driven straight to the Johnson farm from the city.

His host was watching for him. As soon as they were in the kitchen, Derek put cheese sandwiches into a frying pan. "Have a seat." He motioned toward the table, where tall glasses of iced tea awaited them, along with a serving bowl of tossed salad and several types of dressing to choose from.

The two men exchanged a few remarks about the weather and Nick's work at the vineyard. When the sandwiches were ready—the bread toasted and the cheese melted—Derek brought them to the table on a platter, sat opposite Nick, and said a brief blessing. But when it was time to eat, he also seemed to think it was time to talk. "Okay, Nick. Tell me what's up."

Until Samantha had come to Thunder Creek, Nick hadn't told anyone about his accident. But in the weeks since, he'd opened up a little more to a few people like Derek. He hadn't shared many specifics. He'd thought it would be better that way. He still hadn't liked the idea of anybody feeling sorry for him. He'd always been proud of his ability to take care of himself in dangerous situations, so admitting he could be helpless in something as simple as driving to a jobsite was hard.

But he did it. He told Derek everything, ending with what had happened to him two days earlier.

"If there's anything I've learned about traumatic brain injuries," he concluded, "it's that no expert can say for certain what will or won't happen. No doctor can make promises. It isn't like the mending of a broken arm or leg. Each person's TBI experience is unique, including the amount of time it takes to recover." He drew a breath. "*If* they recover."

Derek nodded but made no comment.

"I saw the specialist in Boise this morning. They had a last-minute cancellation and managed to squeeze me in. Like I said, he couldn't promise I won't have more of these episodes. The best he could do was give me a list of things to try. Things I can do to relax or focus or calm down if I get too stressed out. You know, hobbies like bird watching or painting landscapes and fruit bowls."

"Painting, huh? You should talk to Brooklyn. She's taking Alycia and a bunch of her friends to a painting night of some sort. Sam's going too."

"I didn't know Sam liked to paint."

"I don't know that she does, but she's agreed to go along." Derek pushed his empty plate off to one side and leaned forward. "Sorry. I didn't mean to change the subject."

"No problem." In a way he was relieved to have the focus off himself for a few moments.

Derek's gaze was thoughtful as he waited in silence. Finally, he said, "I get the feeling there's something you still want to tell me."

"Yeah." Nick raked the fingers of one hand through his hair. "I guess there is. It's about Sam."

"Sam?"

"Spending time with her last weekend, it got me thinking . . . got me wondering . . . made me wish—" He broke off, not sure how to put his feelings into words. How could he explain what he hardly understood himself? At last he shrugged. "But it wouldn't be fair."

"What wouldn't be fair?"

"Like I told you, I don't know what'll happen with my health. I could go on like I am now for the rest of my life. Or I could take an unexpected turn for the worse. I could forget something critical. I could put someone in danger. It isn't fair to want Sam to share that uncertainty."

"Share?" Derek leaned back in his chair. "The two of you weren't just friends back in Oregon, were you?"

Nick drew a long, slow breath and released it. "No. We've got history." An understatement, he knew. "And not all of that history is good. I'm not sure I'd have any chance with Sam under the best of circumstances, let alone with things the way they are."

Derek folded his hands on the table. "Look, I'm no expert in the romance department, and I don't know much more about head injuries than what you've told me. But it seems to me the only way you can really lose in life is not to try. Maybe Sam won't want you or what you can offer. Maybe there are too many complications for you to overcome. But you'll never know for sure without trying."

At his friend's words Nick felt the hopelessness that had nestled in a dark corner of his heart loosen its grip.

Chapter 17

Brooklyn arrived at Gran's home on Friday promptly at five thirty. The back two rows in the van held the five girls—Alycia along with four of her friends. They were excited and giggly as they talked among themselves, and none of them seemed to notice the addition of Samantha when she entered the vehicle. If she were the gambling sort, she would have bet money the chief topic being whispered about was boys.

Brooklyn said, "See why I needed you to come with me?"

Samantha laughed as she nodded.

Brooklyn put the van in gear and steered it out of town.

"I looked up this paint thing online," Samantha said, intruding on the brief silence. "It may not be as horrible as I feared."

"I'm positive you'll enjoy yourself." Brooklyn glanced her way. "It'll get you out of the left side of your brain. Make you forget all those numbers you deal with all the time."

"Not all the time. It isn't like Gran's shop is all *that* demanding. Not like my regular job."

"Do you enjoy that? Working with numbers and balance sheets and so forth."

"Mmm." Samantha looked out the passenger window at the passing farmland. "I appreciate order. Two and two is always four. That's what I like about what I do. The order of it all."

Brooklyn chuckled. "You know what I pray most mornings?"

Samantha glanced back at her.

"God, bless this mess."

"I don't believe you."

"It's true."

"But you run a successful B&B. You must be analytical for that."

"Not necessarily. I have a head full of creative ideas all the time. New ones show up every morning, it seems like. It's chaotic up here most of the time." Brooklyn tapped her forehead with her right index finger. "But the business part—the spreadsheets and the budgets—I have to force myself to do those. I think I lived with austerity for so many years that once I allowed myself to begin to dream and imagine, I couldn't turn off the tap." She shrugged. "I'm probably mixing metaphors or something."

Dream and *imagine.* The words seemed foreign to Samantha. Oh, she enjoyed an escape into a good novel, and she loved movies that swept her into another place or time, especially old classics. But dreams for herself? Imagining something different for her life? She hadn't done that since . . . She frowned, trying to remember how long ago that had been. Eventually she came up with an answer: not since before her dad died. Not since she was a teenager.

No. That wasn't completely true, she decided. There had been a brief period of time, when she and Nick were together, when she'd begun to imagine marriage and children and Nick and her growing old together, like Gran and Pappy.

"We might see Nick there tonight," Brooklyn said, almost as if she'd guessed the direction of Samantha's thoughts.

"Where? You mean, where we're going? To paint?"

"Yes. Derek told him what we were doing tonight, and he called me to ask for more information. He didn't tell me he was coming for sure, but he did say his doctor thought it would be good for him."

"Good for him?" Samantha said to herself. "Why would a doctor think that?"

Her friend heard her, despite how softly she'd spoken. "I don't know. Nick talked to Derek in confidence a couple of days ago. Something to do with the aftermath of his accident, I think. But Derek couldn't tell me anything without Nick's permission. I'm only guessing." Brooklyn glanced over at her. "You don't *mind* that he might be there, do you?"

Mind? No, she didn't mind. He could do whatever he wanted. It made no difference to her. She had reconciled her hurt over his silence. In fact, she'd come to believe it was all for the best that he hadn't called her all week.

"I thought after last weekend, after going with him to the wedding and all—"

"I don't mind, Brooklyn. I'm just surprised, that's all." She forced the frown from her forehead. "Really." She did everything but point to the corners of her mouth as she smiled.

Nick entered the doors of the Mexican restaurant about fifteen minutes ahead of the appointed time. After inquiring at the register, he made his way through to the banquet room. A surprising number of seats were already filled. Many of the customers—correction: would-be artists—had chips and salsa on the table next to easels and canvases, paint brushes, plastic cups filled with water, and paper plates with pools of different colored paints on them. A few people sipped margaritas, the rims of their glasses coated in salt.

Nick gave his name to the girl in a bright-pink bibbed apron. She checked him off the list, and then he in turn received his own pink apron. He'd worn an older T-shirt and jeans that had seen better days, in case he got sloppy with the paint. Still, he supposed if the other men in the room could wear pink aprons, so could he.

Brooklyn had told him there would be seven coming in her van tonight. Nick would make it eight in the total party. He moved things around, saving three spots for the adults at one table and five spots right behind them for the girls. He didn't know if that's what they would want, but it made sense to him.

A short while later, he saw Brooklyn talking to the gal at the entrance to the room. He stood, and as he did, Samantha stepped into view. Her hair was tucked beneath a black base-ball cap. Like him, she wore a T-shirt and jeans, but her shirt was orange with a black Oregon State University bea-ver emblem on the front. He'd seen her in that same T-shirt before, the time he'd taken her to an OSU football game. It had been early fall, before the weather required a warm coat.

Why hadn't he fully realized back then what he'd found in her? He'd been attracted to her radiant beauty, but she was so much more than her physical appearance. How could he not have known what she could mean to him. If only—

Samantha saw him, hesitated, then acknowledged him with a quick nod. She didn't look surprised to see him. Neither did she seem pleased. He smiled, but she had already turned to look behind her. Moments later, the five girls moved into the room, each of them grabbing a pink apron on their way. Nick waved to Alycia and motioned her toward him.

"Is it okay that I crashed your party?" he asked when the girl arrived with her friends.

"Sure. It's fine."

"Thanks." He indicated the five chairs behind him. "I saved those for you."

"Great."

Brooklyn and Samantha arrived at the table. As with Alycia, he motioned to the seats he'd saved. Brooklyn took a step backward, leaving Samantha to take the center chair. Nick was glad. As much as he'd tried not to care, he had wanted it to work out that way. He'd wanted to be next to her.

He waited as both women donned their aprons, then the three of them sat down. He lowered his eyes to the paper-plate palette. The colors of paint were white, red, black, and yellow. In several places around the room, he saw finished paintings using the same colors, all of them of the same subject, although none looked exactly the same. He guessed that his painting was meant to look like one of those at the end of the evening.

He glanced over at Samantha. "Have you ever done this before?"

"No." Her voice sounded cool, and she didn't meet his gaze. "Have you?"

"Not really. As part of my physical therapy, while I was recovering from the accident, I did some painting. But that was more freestyle than what this looks like it'll be."

"So becoming an artist got into your blood?" Again, the question didn't sound particularly friendly.

He pretended not to notice. "Hardly. No, I saw my specialist in Boise this week, and he thought painting would be a good way to relax my brain."

Now she looked at him. "I didn't know you were seeing a specialist. I thought all that was behind you."

"Sam . . ." He drew in a slow breath. "I don't know if seeing doctors and trying to overcome the . . . things that go with a TBI will ever be behind me."

He watched that information sink in. Then the coolness faded from her eyes. "I'm sorry, Nick. I . . . I didn't realize." Her words sounded genuine.

"That's my fault." He drew another breath, determined to speak the truth, to lay out more facts. "I haven't wanted to talk about it, especially after moving here. Until you arrived, nobody else knew the old me, the guy I used to be, so that made it easier not to talk about the accident or my recovery from it. It changed my life in big ways, maybe in permanent ways. I can't know if there'll be any more improvements. Not until it happens. *If* it happens."

Softly she repeated, "I didn't realize."

Nick decided it was time to change the subject. He didn't want her feeling sorry for him. He was after a much different emotion, and that would take time. He pointed toward the canvas in front of her. "What about your artistic aspirations?"

She laughed. "I have none. Trust me. I was arm-twisted into coming."

Brooklyn leaned forward, looking at Nick. "That isn't true. It was a gracious invitation."

"Want me to show him the bruise you left on my arm?" Samantha challenged.

"Sure," Brooklyn retorted, eyes twinkling.

Samantha turned toward Nick again. She lifted her left arm and feigned a pained expression. "Do you have an aspirin?"

"Sorry." He laughed along with her this time.

Coming tonight had been a good idea, even if he never picked up a paintbrush. He already felt better than he had all week long.

How had Nick managed it? Samantha had entered the restaurant tonight certain that she couldn't care less what he said or did. It no longer bothered her that he hadn't called. She had determined to treat him as no more than an acquaintance. Yet within minutes he had drawn her in, made her sympathize with him, even made her laugh.

It was about five minutes past the hour when the event host called everyone's attention to where she stood. A tall, lithe woman of about twenty-five or so, she introduced herself as Heather and gave a quick rundown of what to expect during the evening.

Could it be as easy to recreate the example painting on the easel as Heather made it sound? If so, perhaps Samantha wouldn't be completely embarrassed.

"I think we can manage this." Nick leaned closer to her. "Don't you?"

Her traitorous heart skipped a beat at his nearness. "Yes, I think so too."

Heather held up a brush. "We're going to begin with the wider brush that's in front of you, and we're going to cover the entire canvas with red paint. Like this." She began applying paint, thinned with a small amount of water, to the blank canvas on an easel near her. "Don't forget to do the sides and top of your canvas as well." She demonstrated.

"That's easy enough." Samantha went to work, glad for something to concentrate on other than the man beside her.

The girls chattered and laughed, clearly enjoying themselves, but the adults were silent as they worked.

"The paint will dry quickly, but do be careful when you paint the sides. It's easy to forget and take hold where you shouldn't."

Samantha quickened her strokes.

"When you're done with that," Heather said, "you're going to take the black paint and the smaller brush and draw lines. Most people find this easier to do with the canvas on its side so that you're drawing the line from side to side rather than up and down. We want the lines to be as straight as possible, but don't try to make them perfect. Relax and enjoy the process."

"Hey, Sam." Nick leaned toward her again. "Did you hear what she said?"

She caught a whiff of his familiar cologne.

"Relax and enjoy." He pointed at her right hand, holding the brush. "You look a little intense."

She followed his gaze. He was right. She was gripping the brush as if to wring the life out of it. "Perfectionist tendencies," she confessed, trying to sound lighthearted. "A line should be a *straight* line, the same way that numbers should add up."

"Without order you're left with chaos. Is that it?"

Strange. She felt a flicker of pleasure that he understood her without need of more explanation.

"Sam, can I tell you something I've been learning over the last couple of years? And I was reminded of it again this week."

"Sure."

"Life is full of chaos, no matter how hard you try to keep it in order. You have to live it the best you can." He gave her a smile, one corner of his mouth lifting slightly higher than the other. "Stop thinking and start painting."

For a second her breath caught, and then she laughed. It seemed the best advice she'd heard in ages.

◊

Nick hadn't expected her to respond with laughter. The sound lit something inside of him. In fact, it brightened the entire room.

Heather gave more instructions to the large group. Tips for shading and for mixing some of the colors on the paper-plate palettes. She reminded them to be careful when reaching for the beverages some had purchased. "You don't want to drink your paint water instead."

As if on cue, a server came down the aisle between the tables to take orders.

"Can we get something to drink, Mom?" Alycia asked.

"Yes."

"Chips and salsa too?"

"You can't be hungry. You had dinner."

"Please."

"Oh, all right."

Nick looked at Samantha. "Do you want something to eat or drink?"

"Some water with lemon would be nice." She seemed more relaxed than she had been earlier.

"And you, sir," the server said.

"I'll have a Diet Coke, and she'll have a glass of water. Both with lemon, please."

The server nodded and moved on to the next person.

Nick's gaze flicked to Samantha's canvas. "That looks really good."

"Do you think so?"

He tipped his head to the side so he could view it as it would look when upright. "It's realistic."

"Really?" She tipped her head, mimicking him. "Maybe I need to stand farther away from it."

"I may need to stand on the opposite side of the room for mine to look good."

Again she laughed.

Suddenly his painting didn't look half bad.

Chapter 18

Seated in the recliner on Saturday afternoon, the quiet house warmed by the sunshine falling against the windows, Ruth felt herself grow drowsy. That was one of the worst things about her broken ankle. It left her sitting too much of the time and taking more than one nap per day.

"Gran."

Her eyes managed to open again. "In here." As if Samantha didn't know where to find her.

Her granddaughter appeared in the doorway, carrying a couple of file folders and a small notebook. "Can I talk to you about something?"

Ruth answered a question with a question. "Have you been working in the office on a Saturday?"

"Yes."

"For heaven's sake, why? There's nothing that's so urgent it can't wait until Monday."

Samantha walked to the sofa. "I felt like working." She sat on the end closest to Ruth. "I was going through past inventory reports, and I wondered if you shouldn't change some of the items you carry in the gift shop."

"Like what?"

"Well, you've given a lot of retail space to those scented candles you like so much. I know they're why you used 'Scentimentals' in the business name and why you spelled the word that particular way. But if you look at the sales from the past two years, the candles aren't your bestsellers. Not even close." She opened one of the folders and passed it to her.

Ruth obediently studied the papers inside, but what interested her wasn't written on them. What intrigued her was a new enthusiasm in her granddaughter's voice. She read for as much time as she felt it required, then closed the folder and lifted her gaze. "So, what are your ideas, Sam?"

"I'm glad you asked." Her granddaughter grinned as she presented another open folder. "You already know that you get lots of customers who are headed for the vineyards and to the Snake River, especially in the summer months. People out for a fun weekend drive. You also get customers from the bed-and-breakfast, thanks to Brooklyn. Instead of what they can buy anywhere, like the candles, you should have more specialty items on your shelves. Made-in-Idaho kinds of things." She pointed at the top paper in the folder. "I pulled some suggestions from the Internet that I think you should consider. Including nonfiction books about Idaho and novels set in Idaho and books by Idaho authors. Did you know that the author who won the Pulitzer Prize for fiction two or three years ago lives in Boise? What if you could get some signed copies in here? Or maybe you could do an author signing on a Saturday."

"Gracious," Ruth whispered.

"You could sell so much more than candles, Gran."

"Have you talked to Camila about any of this?"

Samantha leaned against the back of the sofa. "A little. She said to talk to you, but she likes my suggestions. I'm sure I could get you some catalogs to thumb through. Or I could let you use my laptop so that you wouldn't have to wheel yourself into the office."

"The catalogs would be nice."

Grinning, her granddaughter stood. "I'll get right on it." She took a few steps toward the entrance to the kitchen, then stopped and looked back. "And if you decide to focus on Idaho for your gift items, maybe we could come up with some appropriate Idaho names for your beverages as well. You know. Something more original than a caramel latte or a chai tea. Something like a Bogus Basin Latte or a Gold Rush Chai. That kind of thing."

As Ruth watched Samantha leave the room, she had an idea of her own. For the first time she wondered if, deep down, her granddaughter didn't want to return to Oregon at all. And if that were true, she wondered, how might she help Samantha discover what it was she did want?

ꝏ

Nick stared at the finished canvas he'd brought home with him. He'd set it on the kitchen counter as he came in the door last night, leaning it against the wall beneath the cabinets. Now the afternoon light falling through the window seemed to spotlight it. Which, of course, his artistic endeavor didn't deserve.

He picked up his phone and opened the photo app. There he was, standing between Brooklyn and Samantha in the back row, the five teenaged girls kneeling in front of them. Everyone held their paintings, all of the artwork alike and yet different at the same time.

His doctor had been right. The evening had been good for him, but the positive result had little to do with acrylic paints and a twenty-by-sixteen-inch canvas. Laughter had been his much-needed tonic. Lots and lots of laughter. And the company of the woman who made him feel whole and connected.

He moved closer to the painting, studying it but imagining Samantha. Hope and caution warred within him. Hope wanted him to take out his phone and call her. Caution told him to take it slow, not to rush.

He turned away from the painting, and his gaze swept the small kitchen. He'd long since completed his Saturday housekeeping and laundry chores. The thought of hanging around the house for the remainder of the day left him feeling claustrophobic.

"Come on, Boomer. Let's take a ride."

The dog was waiting at the door before Nick could pick up his keys.

A short while later, when he drove his truck down the driveway, he didn't have a destination in mind, but it seemed natural to turn right onto the road and follow it all the way into Thunder Creek. Once there, he turned onto Orchard Street and drove to the town park. When he got out of his pickup, Frisbee in hand, his gaze flicked to the back of Ruth Johnson's home. Maybe after he and Boomer got some much-needed exercise, he would stroll over to the shop for a coffee or a cold beverage of some sort. He might even run into Samantha while there.

Maybe he'd had an actual destination in mind after all.

Samantha stepped outside, stopping on the back stoop to draw in a deep breath. The weather was perfect. She'd never grown used to the clouds and rain that were common in the Portland area. She much preferred the plentiful sunshine of southwest Idaho.

A sharp bark drew her gaze over the hedge and across the park. She looked just in time to see a dog sail high into the air to catch a Frisbee. "Good boy," the unseen owner called.

But she recognized both dog and voice, and she was instantly drawn out of her grandmother's backyard and onto a path into the park. She crossed the creek on the footbridge. Beneath her, the water was high on its banks, and she felt a coolness rising from its surface as it flowed by. Not long after, Nick and Boomer came into view. She saw Nick toss the Frisbee, and once again the border collie flew after it, catching it with ease. Boomer was twisting toward his master by the time his feet hit the ground. Samantha stopped and applauded. In unison they looked in her direction. Boomer wagged his tail while Nick smiled.

Her heart fluttered erratically. "Boomer's amazing," she said as she continued toward them. But it wasn't the dog that had made her pulse quicken.

"Yeah. He is."

"Have you thought of entering one of those Frisbee contests?"

"Nah. We do it for fun."

She reached the pair and leaned down to stroke the dog's head. When she glanced up, she said, "I haven't seen the two of you in the park before."

"We did this at home in the winter, but I can't throw into the fields now. Crops have been planted. I'd be in trouble if I let Boomer tear things up."

"I'm surprised how few people are using the park today. It's gorgeous out." She turned her face toward the sun and closed her eyes. "I love warm, sunny days like this."

"I remember."

His soft reply made her heart flutter a second time. Hoping she wouldn't give herself away, she turned her attention to the dog. "You love the weather, too, don't you, Boomer?"

"Do you want to throw the Frisbee for him?" Nick held the disc toward her.

"I'm not very good at throwing."

He laughed softly. "Some things I forget, but I remember that too." His tone seemed filled with affection.

"Do you also remember that line from the movie *The Sandlot*?" She smiled back at him, wanting to prolong the moment. "I really do 'throw like a girl.'"

His laughter faded, but he continued to hold out the Frisbee. "Go ahead, Sam. Give it a try."

She was unable to resist his urging. "All right." She took the Frisbee. "But Boomer's going to hold this against you since it's your idea."

"Nah. Not Boomer. He's very forgiving." He grinned. "At least he is of me."

Samantha tried to feign irritation, but it was a hopeless attempt. Laughing again, she turned to throw the Frisbee. Boomer started running before Samantha straightened her arm.

"Come back, Boomer. I'll never throw it that far."

With all of her strength, she tossed the floppy disk into the air. But she was right. The dog had far outdistanced her effort. In fact, the Frisbee made a sharp turn to the right and collided with a tree. Then it bounced and cartwheeled across the grass.

Boomer's expression seemed to say, *What was that?*

"Sorry, fella," she called to him.

Nick pointed. "It's over there, boy. Get it, Boomer."

Wisely, when the dog retrieved the Frisbee, he took it to his master rather than to Samantha.

"I told you so," she said.

"Can't have you throwing like that for all of Thunder Creek to see." He tossed the disk through the air. "I guess we're going to have to work on that arm of yours this summer."

A shiver of pleasure coursed through Samantha at his words. She had to fight the urge to ask when they could start.

Chapter 19

*A*s Nick stepped outside of the church following the Sunday service, he heard someone call his name. He turned and watched as Craig Hasslebeck—one of the guys who attended the study on Tuesday evenings—approached, drawing a young woman along with him.

"Nick, I want you to meet my sister. She recently moved back to Idaho and is staying with me and my wife for a while." Craig looked at his sister. "Leanna, this is Nick Chastain. Nick, Leanna Hasslebeck."

"Nice to meet you." Nick offered his hand.

Leanna looked a lot like her brother, only her features

were more delicate. Except for her brown eyes. They were larger and more expressive than Craig's. "Nice to meet you too," she returned, shaking his hand.

"Nick's pretty new to Thunder Creek," Craig continued. "He works for a company that does irrigation work for farmers in the area."

"Oh." It was a bland response.

Nick grinned. "Not very interesting, is it?"

Leanna blushed. "Sorry."

"Hey, listen." Craig motioned toward his wife, who was talking to two women near the church steps. "Bethany didn't want to cook today, so we're taking Leanna to the Moonlight. Why don't you join us?"

Nick and Craig were close to the same age and shared similar interests, including outdoor sports like cycling and river kayaking. Accepting the invitation seemed natural. Besides, all he had waiting for him at home were leftovers in the fridge.

"Sounds good. Are you going straight to the diner?"

"Yes. As soon as I can get Bethany away from her friends. That usually takes a while."

Nick nodded, as if he knew what that was like. But he didn't. He'd never done much waiting for anyone. Certainly not for a wife. Not even for a girlfriend. He winced internally, remembering more than one occasion when he'd left Samantha behind because he hadn't been willing to wait. Where was his faulty memory when he needed it?

"I'll try to hurry her along." Craig headed toward Bethany.

"How long have you been in Thunder Creek?" Leanna asked, drawing Nick's gaze back to her.

"A few months."

"But you're from Idaho?"

"No. Wyoming is where I grew up, but I lived in Oregon for many years."

"Did you like it there?"

"Oregon?" Nick had the impression Leanna was trying to fill the silence with her questions, not that she cared about his answers. "I loved it there. What about you? Where did you move back from?"

"I've been working in Washington, DC. But I . . . I decided to come home for a while." Sadness flickered in her eyes.

A broken heart, Nick suspected. Uncomfortable, he glanced in her brother's direction. But his gaze stopped when he saw Samantha and her grandmother exiting the church. They took the sloped ramp down to the sidewalk, Ruth leading the way. Nick watched them. Or more precisely, watched Samantha. She wore an apple-green dress with a full skirt that ended about two inches above her knees. A different look from yesterday when they were in the park. Both unforgettable.

Samantha saw him, smiled, spoke to her grandmother, then walked in his direction. Halfway to him, she noticed Leanna at his side, and he thought he detected a falter in her step. Or maybe he'd only imagined it.

"Good morning," she said when she reached them. "Another great sermon, wasn't it?" Her eyes flicked to Leanna and back.

"Sure was." He wondered if he needed to introduce the two women. Just in case, he said, "Do you know Leanna Hasslebeck?"

It was Leanna who answered. "Yes, we've met once before. Do you remember me, Sam? It was the summer you came to stay with your grandmother, and we met up in McCall at the church campout. I was still in high school at the time."

"Oh, that's right." Recognition lit Samantha's face. "I remember."

"That was the weekend I learned to slalom ski. And you kept shouting encouragements from the boat, telling me I could do it."

Samantha nodded, then looked at Nick, a question in her eyes—although one he couldn't decipher. Feeling a need to break the silence, he said, "Leanna's brother and I know each other from the men's group. They've asked me to go eat with them at the diner."

"No, don't go to the diner." She put her hand on his arm but looked at Leanna. "Gran sent me over to invite you to Sunday dinner. It's her first one since the accident. I suppose you've heard that her Sunday dinners are famous hereabouts. Anyway, there's room for all of you at Gran's table. Seriously. She hasn't asked anyone else except for Derek and his family."

Nick began, "That's nice, but it isn't up to me. I don't know if—"

"Are you kidding?" Leanna interrupted. "We'd *love* to come to Mrs. Johnson's. I'll tell Craig and Bethany."

Nick looked back at Samantha. "Uh . . . I guess the answer is yes."

"Gran will be pleased." Her smile seemed to say that she was pleased too. "I'd better get her home so that she can start fussing over the food." She gave him a parting wave. "See you soon."

If not for the scooter and large black boot on Gran's foot and lower leg, no one would know she was recuperating from anything. She wheeled herself around the kitchen, checking this, stirring that, sometimes humming to herself. Gran was in her glory, and Samantha tried not to spoil it by helping too much. She stuck to setting the dining room table, putting ice cubes in the water glasses, and adding chopped celery and carrots to a vegetable tray.

Derek, Brooklyn, and Alycia were the first to arrive. Alycia stayed with the adults only long enough to be courteous, then slipped away to the den with a tablet in hand, whether to play games or read, Samantha didn't know. Derek settled onto the sofa with the Sunday edition of the *Idaho Statesman*. Brooklyn offered to help in the kitchen, but the offer was declined.

"Not today, dear," Gran sang out. "I'm having far too much fun. But you and Sam can sit at the table and visit with me while I put on the finishing touches. Our other guests will be here soon."

The two younger women exchanged smiles. But before they took their seats, Samantha thought she noticed something different about Brooklyn. What was it? Her shoulder-length hair was up in a ponytail. Not unusual; she often wore it that way. Her peach-colored, oversized top over gray leggings and comfortable walking shoes were casual but stylish. Not unusual either. So what looked different about her?

As if reading her mind, Brooklyn asked, "Do I look fat?"

"What? No. Why would you say that?"

"Because I can't get into most of my regular clothes. It happened so much faster than with Alycia." She shook her head, amusement dancing in her eyes. "But that was nearly fourteen years ago. My body has changed a lot since then."

Brooklyn didn't look fat, but she did seem to glow. That's what Samantha had noticed. That's what was different. She said so to Brooklyn, and her friend's responding smile revealed complete and utter joy. That small voice of envy whispered in Samantha's ear again. She pushed it away as she had before.

"Being pregnant obviously agrees with you," she said.

Brooklyn nodded. "When I was expecting Alycia, I was alone in a strange city. Having a loving husband beside me this time makes being pregnant so much more fun."

From the other side of the kitchen, Gran said, "You have much more than a husband by your side, Brooklyn, dear. This time you have that proverbial village. Not to mention a great-grandmother who can't wait to babysit. Thank goodness I'll be rid of this contraption on my foot well before then."

Samantha almost said that she would be glad to babysit

as well. Then she remembered she wouldn't be in Thunder Creek by the time the baby was born. She would be back in Oregon and would miss the baby shower and the birth and the christening and the babysitting.

The doorbell rang, intruding on her thoughts. She rose from her chair, but before she could leave the kitchen, she heard Derek call, "I've got it." Moments later, multiple voices were heard from the front of the house.

"Go greet our guests," Gran said. "Both of you. I won't be but a few minutes longer."

"Come on, Brooklyn. We'd better do as she says."

"I've learned that," her friend answered with a laugh.

As the two women entered the living room, they heard Derek say, "I don't think it'll be long before we eat. But does anybody need something to drink?"

The response was negative all around.

Derek saw Brooklyn and Samantha. "Hey, honey. Come here and meet Craig's sister, Leanna. She's recently moved back to Thunder Creek. Leanna, this is Brooklyn, my wife."

"All right, everyone," Gran's voice called from the dining room. "Take your places. Dinner is ready."

Without being asked, Samantha and Brooklyn went straight to the kitchen and brought the platters and serving bowls to the dining room table. By the time they were finished, everyone else was seated, Gran in her usual place at one end of the table and Derek at the other. Samantha couldn't help noticing that Nick was seated between Craig and Leanna. His idea? Something uncomfortable niggled in her chest.

Samantha took the open chair across from Leanna while Brooklyn sat at Derek's right hand, opposite Bethany Hasslebeck, and Alycia took the chair between them.

The blessing was said, then serving dishes began to move around the table in a clockwise direction. Samantha had missed these lively Sunday dinners. They'd been a fundamental part of her life the summer she lived with Gran. Back then, she'd made the acquaintance of so many of Gran's friends and neighbors while seated at this table. Laughter and voices from the past mingled with those of the present, increasing her pleasure.

She heard Nick ask Leanna about her years in the nation's capital and felt a second twinge of irritation. But before she could examine the feeling, Nick looked in her direction and smiled, something tender in his eyes. At once the room seemed to empty of everyone except for the two of them. Pleasure loosened the tightness in her chest.

No longer holding Nick's attention, Leanna looked at Gran. "Mrs. Johnson, thanks so much for inviting us to join you today."

"I'm delighted you could come." Gran's gaze circled the guests at her table. "The meal wasn't anything fancy. I haven't spent much time in the kitchen lately." She glanced toward the scooter off to the side.

Bethany said, "Everything was delicious, Mrs. Johnson. And you were so gracious to include us at the last minute."

"That's what I love most about Sunday dinners. Seeing who God will have join me."

Her gaze still on Nick, Samantha found herself wishing she were more like her grandmother. She wanted to open her heart to the unexpected, to let go of her need to control all the small details of her life.

In a setting like this one, she almost believed the change was possible.

Chapter 20

The following Saturday Samantha drove Gran out to Derek and Brooklyn's place. While her grandmother and Brooklyn planned a bridal shower for Sandra Dooley, Thunder Creek's postmistress—the entire town was in amazement that the woman had finally said yes to a proposal of marriage—Samantha and Alycia were going for a horseback ride.

Glancing over the saddle at her young cousin, Samantha said, "I've been in Thunder Creek for a month and a half. Why haven't I borrowed one of your horses before now?"

"I don't know. But I'm glad you wanted to come riding today. Mom's decided she won't do it anymore until after the baby comes."

"That's probably smart of her after what happened to Gran. Nobody plans to take a fall. It just happens."

"Yeah, and Mom's not confident in the saddle. She was never around horses until after we moved into the house next door. You know, before it was the inn. I'd never been around horses either, but I always loved 'em."

The girl talked so fast that Samantha almost couldn't keep up with what she said.

"I'm gonna start doing o-mok-see this summer. Did you ever compete like that? I'm not very good yet, but I'm getting better. My friend's got an arena where we can practice. She's gonna help me train Pegasus. I plan to ride over there a lot once school's out."

Swallowing a smile, Samantha gave the cinch a final tug. "I used to compete when I was your age. I prefer trail riding now. It relaxes me."

"Do you have a horse where you live? Who's taking care of it?"

"No, I haven't owned a horse for years. I've been too busy working. Plus, I live in the city, so it isn't convenient."

Alycia gave her a look that said she was crazy. She thought the girl might be right.

The two of them swung into their respective saddles, and they rode out of the barnyard, following a trail that took them first to the banks of Thunder Creek and then in the direction of the Snake River. The weather was glorious, the sky a sharp blue, the temperature warm but not yet hot. Leaves were thick on the trees that lined both sides of the creek, and moved by a gentle breeze, they seemed to applaud the passing horses.

Alycia wasn't content to simply enjoy the serenity of the day. Without encouragement, she talked about her other plans for the summer, in addition to training her horse. She had recently acquired a weekly babysitting job and had opened a savings account for her earnings. She was also participating in a summer reading challenge, which excited her; she loved to read. And to top it all off, two weeks of camp up in McCall awaited her in August. "Do you like to camp, Sam?" Finally, she drew a breath.

"Yes." Samantha smiled, memories of camping with her dad and mom flitting through her head.

"I'd never been camping until I was ten. Can you believe that? I even got lost in the mountains the first time I went. Dad found me the next morning. Of course, when that happened he wasn't my dad yet."

Samantha glanced over at Alycia. "You're a lucky young lady."

"I know." The reply, though simple, revealed the depth of the girl's feelings for the man who had become her father.

Unexpected tears burned the back of Samantha's eyes, and a lump formed in her throat. What an amazing experience it would be to watch Alycia flower into adulthood. Derek and Brooklyn were blessed to have her for a daughter. Would Samantha ever be that lucky? Would she ever find love and have children of her own?

"You okay, Sam?"

She looked at Alycia, who wore a frown of puzzlement. "Yes. But I'm tired of walking. Let's give the horses their heads." The words were scarcely out of Samantha's mouth before Alycia's horse burst into a canter. "Hey!" Samantha shouted, then pressed her heels against Blue Boy's sides and took off after them.

⁂

When Nick turned his bike into Derek's driveway and saw the familiar car, he grinned. He hadn't known Samantha would be at the farm, but it brightened his day to discover her vehicle there. They'd begun text messaging each other on a semi-regular basis, which made the days when he didn't see her pass more quickly. He'd seen something amusing in Caldwell and shared it, along with a photo. She'd responded with some goofy emojis. She'd heard something funny from a customer at Sips and Scentimentals and told him about it. He'd replied with a wry comment of his own. Those easy exchanges had brightened his day and increased the hope for the future that had recently blossomed in his heart.

He stopped his bicycle off to one side of her automobile and dismounted, then leaned it against a tree and hung his helmet from one handlebar. Boomer trotted along beside Nick as he headed to the front door. His knock was answered by Brooklyn.

She smiled in greeting. "Hey, Nick."

"Hey, Brooklyn. I'm not interrupting anything, am I?" He glanced in the direction of the living room, but his view was blocked.

"Not really. Come on in." She glanced down. "You can come in, too, Boomer."

A few steps inside allowed Nick full view of the living room. Ruth Johnson was on the sofa, her broken ankle propped on a footstool topped with a pillow. But Samantha wasn't with her. "Hi, Mrs. Johnson. Are you able to drive now?"

"Heavens, no."

"I saw Sam's car out in the driveway."

"Oh, she brought me. But she's off horseback riding with Alycia. They've been gone a few hours now."

"Did you want to see Sam?" Brooklyn asked.

"Uh . . . no. No, I was out for a bike ride and thought I'd stop in to see Derek. Is he around?"

"Yes. He's mending fence. I'll point you in his direction."

Brooklyn led him through the kitchen and out the door. Once on the porch, she indicated where he could find Derek. Nick and Boomer set off in that direction.

Beyond trees, shrubs, fencing, and a length of pasture, Derek came into view. He stopped work when he saw Nick's approach. "Didn't expect to see you today."

"Yeah. The weather's great for a bike ride, and as long as I was out this way, I thought I'd stop by." He motioned toward the fence. "Need any help?"

"Wouldn't turn it down if it were offered."

"Okay. I'm offering. Just tell me what to do."

Derek grinned, then pointed to a post lying on the ground near a hole. No further instructions were necessary.

The two men worked in companionable silence for twenty minutes or more. But when Nick heard laughter in the distance—a woman's laugh, as familiar to him as his own—he stopped and looked. He saw two horses with riders coming toward them. Even from a distance, he recognized Samantha's hair. He raised an arm, hailing the pair. Woman and girl waved back.

"You know," Derek said, "you're welcome to ride one of our horses anytime you wish."

He was more at home on a road bike than a horse, but if Samantha wanted to go with him, he would do it in a heartbeat. "Thanks. Maybe I'll do that sometime."

Samantha and Alycia stopped their mounts a short ways off.

"Have a good ride?" Derek asked.

"We did." Samantha dismounted.

Nick noticed she moved a little stiffly.

As if reading his thoughts, she said, "It's been too long since I was in a saddle." She rubbed her backside with one hand.

There was something adorable about her action, and he felt like laughing. He glanced away, swallowing the sound, afraid she might think he was making fun of her.

Alycia hopped down from her horse. No stiffness in sight. "We went all the way to the Young place. Dad, you should see it. It looks so sad with nobody living there."

"Is there a *For Sale* sign up yet?"

"I don't know." The girl shook her head. "I didn't look."

Samantha answered. "Yes, there was a sign. I noticed one out near the road."

"You did?" Alycia shrugged. "All I looked at was the house."

Curious, Nick asked, "Has it been empty long?"

"Over a year." Derek removed his work gloves. "There was a family dispute after Harvey Young, the owner, died. All the kids and grandkids have long since moved away from the area, and his wife passed on about a decade ago. I don't know all the details, but rumor has it there was more than one attorney involved. If it's up for sale, I guess something got resolved. Too bad nobody in the family wanted it. The house isn't big, but it's in a great location. Got a beautiful view of the creek and isn't too far from the river. The trail goes right by the property and all the way to the Snake."

Nick glanced toward the west. "Sounds like it shouldn't be on the market long." He felt an unmistakable desire to go look at the place. Odd, since he wasn't in the market to buy and had no need to move from his rental. And yet . . .

"We'd better put the horses up," Samantha said, bringing Nick's attention back to her. "See you later."

He nodded. "Later." His gaze followed her and Alycia as they led their horses away.

"How are things going between you two?" Derek asked in a low voice.

"Good, I think, but I'm taking it slow. We're friends again, and that may have to be enough. I don't know. I care about her, more than I thought possible. But there are still lots of unknowns." He touched his temple with an index finger. "More than just this faulty head of mine." He returned to the post-hole digger.

Derek stepped closer to him. "Nick, do you think Brooklyn and I know what tomorrow will bring? We don't. No one does. We got married and we're having a baby and we make plans for our future as a family. But there aren't any guarantees in this life. That's where trust comes in. Where faith comes in." His eyes narrowed. "If you care for Sam, don't you think she should have something to say about it too?"

It was a question Nick would ponder long after it was posed to him.

Chapter 21

*A*fter a rainy Memorial Day that ranged from drizzle to downpour and back again, Nick was glad to see Tuesday dawn with clear skies. Still, the ground was drenched, and his crew collected enough mud on their boots to make walking the worksite miserable and sometimes impossible. At noon Nick released his men for the remainder of the day.

His intent was to head home, but somehow his truck turned in the opposite direction. A few miles down the road, a *For Sale* sign came into view on the right side of the road, and he realized that was what he was looking for: the Young property. He slowed and turned into the driveway.

The house was a split-entry-style home. Probably three bedrooms, by the look of it, and about eighteen hundred to two thousand square feet. The two-car garage was detached, connected by a short, covered walkway. The back of the house, both upper and lower levels, had good views of the creek and the tall trees growing on both banks. From what he could tell, the property was around two acres. A fenced pasture took up about three-quarters of the land. There was an unkempt look about the place, as Alycia had intimated on Saturday, but nothing that appeared too serious. It wouldn't take much to get it back into shape. A bit of paint for the house. Some landscaping and reseeding of the lawn. A little fence work. Not much else.

Of course, there wasn't any way of knowing the shape of things inside without a key to the lock.

He got out of his truck and began to walk around, looking through the windows of the lower level, opening the unlocked side door to the garage, testing the sturdiness of the pasture fencing.

"Look, Boomer. A kennel."

The dog wagged his tail, as if pleased with the discovery.

Finally, Nick walked out to the *For Sale* sign near the road and took a flyer from a box on the post. It gave some details, including the asking price. He was surprised how low it was. Were there problems he couldn't see, or did the remaining family members simply want to unload it in a hurry?

He looked at the house again. At this price he could manage twenty percent down, and unless his math skills had completely abandoned him, the house payments wouldn't be much more than the rent he paid now. Perhaps an additional fifty dollars a month, he guessed.

Do it. Don't think about it too much. Just do it.

He glanced down at the flyer again, at the same time pulling his phone from his pocket. He punched in the number and then listened. It rang twice before being answered.

"Roberta Carie. How may I help you?"

"My name's Nick Chastain. I . . . I'm out at the Young place on Homestead Road. Is it possible you could show me the inside of the house this afternoon?"

"Of course. I'd be delighted to. In fact, I'm only about ten minutes away now. Do you mind waiting for me?"

"Not at all."

"All right. See you in a few." The call ended abruptly.

Nick looked down at Boomer. "What do you think, boy? Am I nuts to even consider it?"

The border collie seemed to smile at him.

"Some help you are."

The dog's tail began to wag again.

True to her word, Roberta Carie arrived in ten minutes. By that time, Nick had walked back to the house. He stood on the front stoop as the white Lexus rolled to a stop beside his truck.

The real estate agent was a tall woman in her mid-forties. She wore a pastel pantsuit that looked out of place in this country setting and an excess of silver jewelry on wrists, rings, ears, and throat. "Mr. Chastain." She held out her hand as she approached, her many bracelets jangling. "A pleasure to meet you. I'm Roberta."

"Nice to meet you. Call me Nick."

Her smile was dazzling. "Let's go inside, shall we?"

Nick told Boomer to sit and stay.

Roberta unlocked the door, then motioned Nick through ahead of her. "The house only went on the market a few days ago. You are the first person I've shown it to. But with this location and price, I don't expect it to be available for long."

They climbed the stairs to the upper level.

Roberta rattled off statistics regarding the measurements of the rooms. Nick listened and nodded. Downstairs she did the same, as well as telling him about recent improvements—new carpet, new furnace and water heater, and a five-year-old roof.

Nick's place in Oregon had been a bachelor pad with style. The price of it had been staggering. In contrast, this house had an old-fashioned, homey feel to it. It was the kind of place where families lived. Despite it being summer, he could imagine a Christmas tree in front of the large living room window, like the Chastain family had had when he and his brothers were kids.

But it was something even more than a sense of home and family about the place that appealed to him. He felt a nudge in his heart. No, more like a firm shove. For no reason he understood right then, it felt like God was speaking to his spirit.

"Let's write up an offer," he said as he faced Roberta.

There was a flicker of surprise before she schooled her face into a smile once again. "Wonderful. Wonderful." She walked to the kitchen counter, set down her oversized purse, then withdrew papers, clipboard, and a pen from inside of it.

Nick didn't question his decision. Not even for an instant. For the first time in a long while, he was dead certain that he was doing the right thing.

◎

"Sam, dear, you haven't let the grass grow under your feet."

Ruth rolled her scooter to the center of the gift shop, her gaze scanning the mostly bare shelves that lined two walls. The abundance of scented candles had been narrowed down to one small area in a center-room display, and the arrangement of the shop was dramatically changed from the last time Ruth had been in it.

Excitement sparkled in Samantha's eyes as she detailed where the different merchandise would go as it arrived. "And this," she finished with a hand flourish, "is going to be the book corner. Your customers are going to love it, Gran. We'll highlight books about Idaho and books written by Idaho authors, but we'll have other choices too."

Ruth glanced toward the counter where Camila stood, observing them.

Her friend nodded. "She's got good business sense, that one."

"So I see."

Samantha continued, "Brooklyn's working on some sort of promotion for the bed-and-breakfast, along with specials for the summer concerts at Dubois Vineyards. I thought we would feature her items near the checkout counter."

"I cannot believe what you've accomplished in such a short time, Sam. It's amazing."

"Thanks." Her granddaughter beamed. "I hoped you would approve. I know you said you trusted me, but still . . ." She allowed her words to drift into silence, almost as if she held her breath.

Ruth reached out and took hold of Samantha's hand. "I more than approve, dear. I think it's wonderful." She wondered if her granddaughter was aware how much her demeanor had brightened over her weeks in Thunder Creek. Especially the last one or two. There was an aura of happiness that had been missing before. A look of the girl she'd once been, the one with a zest for life.

More customers arrived, and while Gina Evans, the part-time server, took their orders, Camila left the gift shop so she could prepare the beverages.

"I know it looks a little empty now," Samantha said, "but it's going to fill up fast. Marked-down items"—she pointed—"are over there. Brooklyn said she could put some sale items in her gift shop too."

"I think I should hire you to be my manager."

"I might take the job if you offered it."

Ruth felt her eyes widen. Samantha's did the same.

"Well," Ruth said after what seemed a lengthy silence, "that's something to think about. Isn't it?"

Samantha *did* think about it. Time and again as she sat in Gran's office, staring at the computer screen without seeing anything except the shadow of her reflection, she heard her grandmother suggest making her the manager of Sips and Scentimentals. Crazy, right? A long visit, sure. But beyond that? She rubbed her eyelids with the pads of her fingers.

"Hey." A rap sounded. "Can I intrude?"

She looked up to see Nick standing in the office doorway.

He jerked his head toward the coffee shop. "I can wait out there until you're free."

"I'm free." As she stood, her gaze shot to the clock on the wall. "You aren't working today?"

"The ground was so muddy, we quit early. It'll be dry by tomorrow."

"Mmm. It looks like it's beautiful out now."

"It is." Nick shoved his fingertips into the back pockets of his jeans, looking as if he had something more to say but didn't know how to begin. The look made nerves inexplicably whirl in Samantha's stomach.

"Care to have coffee with me?" he asked after a short silence.

"Sure."

He stepped back, leaving room for her to pass through the doorway. She did so, then led the way to the counter.

Camila smiled as she observed their approach. "Did you work up a thirst?"

Nick answered before Samantha could. "She needed a break." He looked at her. "What would you like?"

"Just a regular coffee."

"Two please," Nick told Camila.

It didn't take the older woman long to fill their order.

"Shall we sit outside?" Nick took the coffees, one in each hand.

Samantha smiled. She hadn't stepped outside once today, and nothing sounded better to her than a breath of fresh air.

The outdoor seating at Sips and Scentimentals—three sets of black wrought-iron tables with three matching chairs each—faced the town park and was shielded from street view by thick climbing vines on latticework. At this hour of the day, she and Nick were the only customers sitting there.

"The gift shop looks kind of bare." Nick set both coffees on a table. "What's up?"

It pleased her that he'd noticed. "We're changing things up a bit. New stock will start arriving this week."

"Can't wait to see what you've got in mind." He took a sip of his coffee, then set the cup on the table again, his hand still around the rim. "I'm changing things up a bit myself."

She raised her eyebrows and waited for him to go on.

"You know the Young place you and Alycia mentioned on Saturday?"

She nodded.

"Well, I made an offer to buy it, and the seller accepted."

For a moment surprise struck her dumb. But at last she said, "You're going to stay in Thunder Creek? I mean, I know you like your job, but . . ." She let the words drift off.

"I'm planning to stay for the long term." His grin widened. "God willing and the creeks don't rise."

She shook her head. "I didn't think you would. I didn't picture you here for good."

"Why not?"

"I don't know. Maybe because you . . . you always lived your life so . . . large." She gave a slight shrug. "Isn't Thunder Creek going to feel small to you after a while?"

He considered her question before answering, "No. I don't think it will. It suits me. It suits who I am now."

"Who I am now." His words reverberated inside of her. Nick *was* different. She'd recognized many of the changes before, but she hadn't expected them to last any more than she'd expected him to stay in Thunder Creek.

"It's kind of hard to explain, even to myself. But when I looked at the house and land, I sensed that it was an answer to something I've been praying about for a while." He gave a slight shrug. "I've asked God to somehow use what happened to me, my injuries and my recovery and everything about my life, for a good purpose. And today it felt like God was setting my feet on a path that would make it happen."

She wished she would hear God speaking in her own heart, to show her clearly what path she should follow.

"Would you like to see the house?" Nick asked, drawing her from her thoughts. "Maybe you can give me some decorating tips. You know how lousy I am at that."

She laughed softly. "Yes, I do know."

"How about Saturday morning we take a bike ride out there and I could show you around?"

"I don't have a bike."

"Not a problem. I can find you something to ride. Maybe Brooklyn or Alycia has one you could borrow. Don't worry. I'll take care of it."

There was an eagerness in his voice that made it impossible for her to refuse his request. She smiled. "All right. I'll go."

"Great. Let's plan for me to be here about ten o'clock. I'll pack us a lunch, and we can eat it by the creek. Somebody built a nice little picnic area there. Needs some work, but it'll do for us this time."

Chapter 22

On Saturday morning Samantha found it almost impossible to decide what to wear. The morning air was cool, but by the time they rode back to town after their picnic, the temperature was supposed to warm a good fifteen to twenty degrees. Should she wear leggings or jeans? Should she wear a top with sleeves or wear something summery and add a sweater to it? And what to do with her hair? Down or up? Baseball cap for a sporty look or bare headed?

Is this a date or two friends spending a few hours together?

She held her breath as she stared at her reflection in the mirror. The question, she realized, had been swirling around in her head since he'd issued the invitation, but she hadn't allowed it to take conscious shape until now. More troublesome was not knowing what she *wanted* the antic-ipated excursion to be. Why did it feel like something . . . *more*? And did she want it to be more?

"Sam," her grandmother called up the stairs. "Nick just pulled up."

"Be right there."

She hurried to finish dressing, grabbing a short-brimmed baseball cap at the last second. Carrying it in her right hand, she descended the stairs. By the time she reached the entry hall, Gran was opening the front door.

Nick stood on the sidewalk at the foot of the stoop. Beside him, resting on its kickstand, was a cream-colored bicycle with accents of lime green on its step-through frame. It had upright handlebars with a bell and a silver metal bas-ket on the front. Although obviously new, it had an antique appearance that appealed to her. Artificial flowers had been woven into the mesh of the basket, a girly-girl addition that she loved on sight. A yellow-and-cream helmet, accented with a touch of green, hung by a strap from one bar.

"What do you think?" Nick motioned to the bike with both hands.

"I like it. Is it Brooklyn's?"

"No." He grinned. "It's yours."

"Mine?" She stepped out of the house.

"Yours. It's a gift. From me to you."

"But, Nick, I—"

"Don't say you can't accept it. We'll call it a belated birthday present if we have to."

She shook her head. "You already gave me a birthday present. Remember? A bracelet."

"Fine." His smile was gone now. "Then it's belated from a couple of years ago."

"We weren't together on my birthday two years ago."

"No, we weren't. But if we had been, maybe this is what I would have given you." He shrugged. "Guess we'll never know."

What are you doing, Nick? What are we doing? But she didn't have the courage to ask the question aloud.

He didn't seem to be bothered by similar thoughts. "Are you ready to go?"

She swallowed, then nodded.

From behind her Gran said, "You two be careful. The country roads aren't wide, and you have to share them with cars."

"Don't worry," Nick answered. "I'll take good care of Sam."

"And of yourself."

He smiled again. "And of myself."

For some reason the brief exchange between her grandmother and Nick eased Samantha's nerves. She dropped the baseball cap she'd carried into the basket, then put on the helmet. It fit perfectly, as if Nick knew even this detail about her. Warmth rose in her cheeks.

He gave her an approving look. "I'll get my bike."

She followed him with her gaze. His bike, waiting at the curb near his pickup, was black and silver. No basket on the front, but it had saddlebags on the back. No doubt that's where their lunch was kept. While he put on his helmet, she grabbed the handlebars, pushed up the kickstand with her foot, and walked her bike toward him.

"Where's Boomer?" she asked, looking toward the bed of the truck.

"It's just you and me today. It doesn't kill him to be left in his kennel every now and then."

After waving good-bye to Gran, they rode off. Nick set a leisurely pace as they followed Sharp Street to Lewis, then turned left onto River, which would take them out of town and eventually past the Inn at Thunder Creek and Derek's organic farm. They passed a young couple walking on the sidewalk and returned waves, even though she had no clue who they were. Did Nick know them? It seemed he did.

Beyond the town limits, he glanced at her. "If you want, we can stop to see Derek and Brooklyn on the way back. But let's keep going for now."

"Okay."

He looked over his shoulder to check for traffic. "I think we'd better go single file now, in case any cars come up behind us. Want me to lead?"

She nodded. "Yes, please."

Between the helmet and the self-made breeze in her face, sounds faded away. She felt the morning sun on her back. Water from irrigation sprinklers caught the sunlight and reflected it in a glittering spray. The air smelled of rich earth and growing things. No exhaust from heavy traffic here.

"It's a beautiful day," she said, not needing to be heard, just needing to say it aloud.

Every so often, Nick glanced over his shoulder. Each time their eyes met she smiled, wanting him to know she was enjoying herself. Like the horseback ride last weekend, she wondered why she'd allowed so much time to pass without getting on a bike. Neither served a purpose other than simple, pure enjoyment. Why had she removed so many pleasures from her life in recent years? It was a part of her personality that troubled her, and something told her she wouldn't find real peace in either her personal or professional life until she figured it out.

When Nick motioned that they were about to turn, it surprised her. She'd taken little notice of the passing time and could scarcely believe they'd arrived at their destination. And yet there it was. Nick's soon-to-be home.

The house had looked sad to Samantha a week ago. But it didn't look that way today. Almost as if it understood what the *Sale Pending* sign at the end of the driveway meant.

They left their bikes next to the garage and walked to the front entrance. Nick pulled a key from his pocket and unlocked the door. The interior of the split-entry home was cool and shadowed. Nick motioned for Samantha to precede him up the stairs, which she did.

"I had my parents sell the furniture from my old place," he said. "At the time I didn't think I'd need it again. I'll have to buy quite a bit to replace it. Right now I don't have much more than a bed, a small sofa, and a kitchen table and chairs."

With both of them standing near the living room window, she turned to look at him. "Do you miss it, Nick?" she asked impulsively.

"What?"

"The life you had before?"

He seemed to consider her question before answering, "Not the house, if that's what you're asking. I definitely miss my students. That was the hardest part to give up. It hurt knowing I couldn't go back to teaching."

"Maybe someday you'll be able to."

"Maybe." He shrugged. "There's a verse in Philippians that's helped me come to terms with it. It's the one where Paul said that he'd learned to be content, whether he had an abundance or was suffering a need. I've learned to be content with the way things are. Or at least I'm in the process of learning to be."

It was her turn to pause and consider. Then she said, "I believe that's true about you, Nick."

Scarcely aware of what he was about to do, Nick leaned toward Samantha and kissed her. It was a little like coming home, but also new and unexpected. Somehow he resisted the urge to pull her into a close embrace, to deepen the kiss, to force her to remain where she was even one moment longer than she wished.

When she drew her head back, her gaze met his, and he

saw a host of emotions in her green eyes, all of them unreadable. What was she thinking? What was she feeling? Was she glad he'd kissed her? Was she unhappy about it? What would she think if he—

His brain turned fuzzy. Uncertainty flared in his chest. He took a step back and looked around the room, forcing his breathing to remain even and regular. The threatening panic receded as his thoughts cleared. But the episode, brief as it had been, left him chilled. Drawing a quick breath, he faced Samantha again. "Sorry. Maybe we should forget I did that."

She didn't reply.

Derek's advice whispered in his mind: *If you care for Sam, don't you think she should have something to say about it too?*

He should explain. He should tell her what just happened, why he'd reacted the way he had.

"Yes. Let's forget it." He saw her mouth the words more than he heard them. Hurt flickered in her eyes.

"Sam?"

"What?"

"Don't misunderstand why I said I was sorry."

Her eyes widened a fraction.

"I *wanted* to kiss you. You can't know how much I wanted it. But . . . but I don't think I should have given in to what I wanted. It isn't fair to you." Frustration welled. He could curse himself for ruining what had been a perfect day up until then. And on the heels of that thought came the need to curse himself for ruining what might have been before that ill-fated trip to Colorado. He'd hurt her. He shouldn't risk hurting her again.

"Just friends," she said. "Right?"

It made him want to take her in his arms again. Instead, he nodded.

Her shoulders rose and fell as she drew in a deep breath and released it slowly. "Well, *friend*." She emphasized the word. "I guess you'd better show me the rest of the house. I'm starting to get hungry, and you promised me lunch beside the creek."

"You're right." He tried to sound lighthearted. He was anything but. "Come with me to the kitchen."

Twenty minutes later, after completing a tour of the house, Nick led the way down a path to the creek. The water was clear enough to see the smooth stones, large and small, that lined the bottom. Someone had built a wooden deck amidst the cottonwoods, complete with picnic table and benches and a railing on three sides. The red stain had long ago faded, and a board or two needed replacing. But all things considered, it wasn't in bad shape.

Nick set the saddlebags he carried on the table and pulled out sandwiches, chips, cans of diet soda, a bag of cookies, and some paper towels. He slid one of the sandwiches in Samantha's direction. "Chicken salad."

"Thanks."

He'd remembered that she liked chicken-salad sandwiches. That's why he'd made them. But he kept that information to himself. There'd been an awkwardness between them ever since the kiss, an awkwardness all his own fault, and he didn't want it to worsen.

With the sun directly overhead, warming the deck, Samantha removed the light sweater she'd worn all morning. A breeze caused wisps of hair to dance against the sides of her face. He wished he had the freedom to reach out and brush them back. Instead, he unwrapped his sandwich and took a bite.

"If you care for Sam, don't you think she should have something to say about it too?"

He should explain. Instead, he kept silent. For her sake, he told himself. He did it for her sake.

Although neither Nick nor Samantha spoke as they ate, the day was not silent. Leaves rustled and the creek gurgled and splashed. On the neighboring farm, hidden from view by the trees lining the stream, a cow mooed and a calf bawled an answer. Nick imagined himself relaxing in this spot at the end of a workday, throwing the Frisbee for Boomer or reading a book or the newspaper, cooled by the flowing water.

But when he imagined the scene, he pictured Samantha with him.

∞

The feel of Nick's lips on hers had lingered while he gave Samantha a tour of the house, while they'd eaten their picnic lunch in silence, and during the bike ride home again. The feel of the kiss lingered still as she lay in bed that night, sleepless, staring upward in the darkness.

"Maybe we should forget I did that."

She couldn't forget it. How could she? She felt like a drowning woman getting her first gasp of air after an eternity. She hadn't known how much she'd longed for a kiss—how much she'd longed for *his* kiss—until it happened.

"I wanted to kiss you. You can't know how much I wanted it."

Couldn't she know? Was it as much as her own longing?

"I don't think I should have given into what I wanted."

Why not?

"Because we're only friends," she answered herself aloud. "That's why."

Then he answered in her memory. *"It isn't fair to you."*

Nick was right, of course. It wasn't fair to her. It wasn't fair to either of them. Once upon a time there had been the possibility they could find long-term love. That time had passed.

She touched her lips with her fingertips. Warm, as if the kiss had just ended.

Maybe the time hadn't passed. Perhaps it wasn't an impossibility. Maybe she could change his mind.

Maybe . . .

Chapter 23

$\mathcal{N}$ick caught up with Samantha and Ruth on their way to the church parking lot following the Sunday service. He greeted them both, then addressed his question to the older woman, afraid if he asked Samantha, he would be refused. "Would you mind if I stole Sam for the rest of the afternoon? I'm taking a drive up into the mountains and was hoping for her company."

"That's a grand idea," Ruth answered.

"Gran. You've got people coming for Sunday dinner. I should be there to help."

Ruth shook her head. "Only Camila and Emilio are my

guests today. We'll fend for ourselves quite nicely. You go with Nick."

Samantha looked at him, and his pulse leapt. For he didn't see the expected reluctance. Her eyes said she wanted to go with him. Relief flooded through him.

He'd thought a lot about what had happened the previous day. Somewhere along the way, he'd determined to explain his reaction to Samantha. He'd decided he would, at last, follow Derek's advice, that he would put aside the last remnants of his tattered pride and tell all.

"What exactly are we doing besides driving?" Samantha asked, adding, "so I'll know what to wear."

"We'll grab something to eat on the way. And if we find the right spot up in the forest, we'll walk a bit. Let Boomer chase a stick or chipmunks or whatever. No strenuous hiking. Just a nice stroll. Sound okay?"

She nodded. "Sounds okay." Her smile was tentative. And perhaps hopeful?

"Can you be ready in about twenty minutes?"

"Yes."

Determination shot through him. If the chance came to kiss her today, he wouldn't apologize.

"Great. I'll be there."

Half an hour later, the two of them, along with Boomer, drove out of town. The wind whistling through the open windows made it hard to have a conversation without shouting, so they traveled in silence until they stopped at a drive-through to order burgers, fries, and milkshakes. Even Boomer got to indulge, although his quarter-pound burger was plain with no bun. Nick tore the meat into pieces, and they disappeared in a few bites.

Samantha laughed as the dog turned a pleading look in her direction. "You're not starving. You eat too fast." She ruffled his ears.

Nick grinned. "I've told him and told him not to scarf down his food, but he doesn't listen to me."

"Silly dog." She looked up. "I guess you can't complain. He minds you in every other way."

"Yeah, he does."

She stroked Boomer's head but kept looking at Nick, happiness sparking in her eyes. His mouth went dry and his breath caught in his chest. He loved her. Loved her more than he'd thought possible.

He'd danced around that word—*love*—even when he'd admitted he wanted to share the future with Samantha. He'd danced around it for weeks. Since his brother's wedding. Maybe even longer than that. He couldn't dance around it now. He loved her. Deeply loved her. Sure, there were difficulties to be overcome. Location. His health. Even hurts from the past. But if it was in his power to overcome them, he would.

Samantha breathed in the pine-scented air as Nick steered the truck along the winding highway. Sunlight and deep shadows alternated in the canyon forged by the river. The changing light was almost blinding, and she was thankful she wasn't driving. She would much rather enjoy the beauty of nature all around them than pay attention to the road.

The pickup rounded a curve and slowed when a bridge came into view. "Here we are," Nick said. "That's got to be the south fork of the Payette." He turned onto the connecting road right after crossing the bridge.

Both the shadows and the forest deepened. The river beyond Samantha's door now thundered and foamed.

"That's something to see, isn't it?" Nick steered the pickup into a parking area. "Let's get out and walk awhile."

"All right."

Boomer seemed delighted with the idea. He dashed around the trees, sniffing the blanket of pine needles that covered the ground. A chipmunk scolded him from a high branch, and the dog barked his annoyance.

"Come on, boy." Nick turned toward Samantha. "I saw a trail down closer to the river. Let's see how far up it goes." He held out his hand for her to take.

It seemed such a natural thing to do, and she smiled as his fingers closed around hers.

"Have you been up here before?" he asked.

"No. I've been past the junction on the way to McCall but never turned this way."

They crossed the highway and descended to the trail along the riverbank. When they got there, Nick stopped and pointed up river.

"Look!"

She did so in time to see a large yellow raft buck its way across rough rapids. The four passengers inside the raft hooted and hollered, oars held above the water.

Her heart rose into her throat, and she had trouble breathing.

"Amazing!" Nick cried as he waved at the rafters with his free hand.

Amazing? More like terrifying.

As if in answer to the thought, the raft crashed down hard and one of the passengers—a woman, by the high-pitched sound of her scream—was thrown into the water. She disappeared for an instant, then rose to the surface.

Nick released Samantha's hand and hurried to the river's edge. He grabbed hold of a shrub and gave it a hard tug, then leaned forward, ready to grab the woman, who was bobbing and flailing her way toward him.

Boomer barked a warning but stayed beside Samantha, as if sensing he would be in the way.

"Nick!" Samantha cried. "Be careful!"

If he heard her, he gave no indication. His focus was completely on the woman in the water. At least she wore a helmet and a bright-yellow life jacket, making it easier to see her.

Samantha lifted her gaze to the raft. The remaining people were paddling toward the bank; they shouted but she couldn't understand them. She looked back at Nick in time to see him lean out as far as the shrub and his arm would allow. He caught hold of the life jacket above the woman's shoulder. The rush of the water and weight of the woman

---

jerked him downward, and for a moment Samantha thought he would lose his grip and be pulled downstream with her. But instead, he managed to drag her onto the bank. He collapsed beside her, breathing hard.

Samantha moved forward, heart hammering.

"Are you all right?" Nick asked the woman as she struggled to sit up.

She coughed and nodded, then coughed some more.

"Nick?"

He glanced over his shoulder. "She's okay."

But it wasn't the stranger Samantha had been worried about. It was Nick.

Shouts came from behind her, and she turned to see the other rafters running toward them from down river. She moved out of their way and observed the hugs and heard their joyous laughter. She watched as each one of them, in turn, shook Nick's hand and thanked him for what he'd done. The celebration went on and on.

Finally, Nick broke away from the little group and stepped toward Samantha.

"You're wet," she told him.

"I'll dry." Excitement filled his voice.

"You took quite a risk."

He shrugged. "I made sure I had a good hold."

Samantha wished she could say the same, but watching him had left her feeling as if she were the one caught in the swift current of a river, bobbing up and down and in danger of drowning.

"Come on." He reached for her hand. "Let's keep walking. I'll dry off faster that way."

She didn't think he cared about his wet clothes or the danger he'd been in. All he looked was pleased with himself. Begrudgingly, she admitted the rescue might have been necessary. But the woman had worn a helmet and life preserver. She might have made it to the riverbank without his help. Someone who hadn't nearly died in a different river could have gone to her aid.

The lively sparkle in Nick's eyes as he waited for her to take his hand seemed to say he hadn't felt this good in a long time. In fact, it seemed to say that he would give just about anything to have been in that raft with the others.

"Hey." His smile faded. "Where'd you go?"

He hadn't changed as much as she'd hoped. He was still a risk-taker.

"Sam?"

"I think we should head back."

He lowered his hand. "What's wrong?"

"Nothing." It was a lie, and she was certain he knew it.

"I was hoping we could find a place to sit and . . . and to talk."

They should talk. He was right about that. She should tell him how his recklessness made her feel. But she was too rattled to discuss it. All she could do now was shake her head and say, "Let's go home."

Frustration set his jaw. "Okay, Sam. I'll take you home."

Chapter 24

*A*few days later, Ruth had a follow-up appointment with her orthopedist. Afterward, she and Samantha stopped for lunch.

"The doctor says I'll be out of this boot and into a splint in another five weeks." Ruth slid onto the seat of the booth. "And that means I'll be able to drive again. I am *so* ready for that."

"Gran, you're going to make me feel unwanted." There was a teasing glint in her granddaughter's eyes.

Ruth was glad to see it. Samantha hadn't seemed herself lately. Ruth longed to ask why, but something in her granddaughter's demeanor kept her from posing any personal questions.

"The next five weeks will go by in no time," Samantha said.

"I confess I'll be happy when I can get in the car and go someplace whenever I want. I'm used to more independence than this injury has allowed."

Samantha picked up the menu from the table. "Mom says we come from a long line of strong, independent women."

"Very true." Ruth smiled, images of her mother, grandmothers, and aunts flooding her memory. "But not so independent that we haven't loved our families with our whole hearts." She touched the back of Samantha's hand. "Just as I love you."

"Thanks, Gran. I love you too."

Ruth saw the tinge of sadness in her granddaughter's eyes. She'd seen it there for the last several days. She could only guess at its cause, although fear and lack of confidence were almost always at the root of Samantha's unhappiness. This much she had become aware of through the years.

The server came to take their orders. Both Ruth and Samantha ordered salads, although different kinds.

Alone once more, Ruth was about to pick up the conversation where they'd left off, but Samantha's phone rang, stopping her. Her granddaughter looked at the screen, hesitated, then tapped Accept. "Daniel."

Ruth heard the male voice of the caller but not the words.

"No, that hasn't changed. End of July." Samantha looked down at the table. "Sorry, Daniel."

Pretending disinterest, Ruth unwrapped the napkin from around the table service and carefully smoothed it flat before placing it on her lap.

"You're joking. When exactly?"

Ruth glanced up and tried to read Samantha's expression.

"I see . . . No, I don't think so . . . Yes, I could manage that . . . Of course. I'll let you know . . . All right. Good-bye." Her granddaughter lowered the cell phone from her ear and tapped the screen to end the call.

Ruth sensed an internal struggle and held her breath.

Samantha dropped the phone into her purse before meeting Ruth's gaze. "That was my boss."

"It sounded important."

She shrugged. "Maybe. He says I'm being considered for a promotion. In fact, he's certain it will happen this time."

"When will you know?"

"He wants me to fly to Portland on Friday to attend some meetings."

"That's not much notice."

"I know. But I could go and come back on the same day. As long as there are still seats available, I can catch a flight at six in the morning and land back in Boise before eight at night."

"You know the airline schedule off the top of your head?"

"No. Daniel checked before calling me."

"That was thoughtful of him."

"Thoughtful? Maybe. But that's not usually a term I apply to Daniel." She drew a deep breath as she lowered her eyes again. "This might be the best thing for everybody," she said softly.

Ruth wondered if she'd been meant to hear the comment and waited for an explanation. She didn't get one.

"You'll be all right if I decide to go for the day?"

"You know I'll be fine. And Camila is right out in the shop if I need anything. You go do what you need to do and don't worry about me."

❦

Marti Barbera—a casual friend, as well as a colleague—awaited Samantha at the curb outside the Portland terminal, where she'd texted she would be. Samantha dropped her briefcase into the backseat before joining the other woman in the front.

"You look good," Marti said before merging into the busy airport traffic. "Time away has been good for you."

"Thanks. How's it going for you at the office?"

"All right, I think. Daniel doesn't like me much, but I don't think he can complain about my work any longer."

"Daniel doesn't like anybody." Samantha released a humorless laugh.

Marti didn't join in. "He likes you."

"Me? No. He *depends* on me is more like it. He's been my boss almost from the start of my employment at Whitewater. He's used to me."

They fell silent for a while, allowing Marti to negotiate the rush-hour traffic without distraction. Once they were safely on the freeway and into the flow of weekday commuters, Marti took up the conversation as if they'd never left off. "I think you might be wrong about Daniel. He does like you. I heard he put your name forward for that new position and has been pressing the big bosses to approve you for the promotion."

That would be a change, Samantha thought as she stared out at the drizzly morning.

The closer they got to their destination, the more she felt like an old-fashioned alarm clock that had been wound too tightly. It wasn't nerves about the scheduled meetings. It wasn't even anxiety over whether or not she would get the promotion. But what was the cause of this crazy feeling?

Whitewater Business Solutions was located in a three-story brick building on several acres of land. Flowers bloomed on all sides as well as in planters and beds scattered throughout the parking area and the perimeter of the property. The interior design, especially the lobby and meeting rooms, had an understated, yet elegant appearance.

"Welcome back, Sam," the receptionist said with a smile.

"Thanks, Theresa, but I'm not back yet. Just visiting for the day."

She and Marti headed for the elevator and rode up to the third floor. Once there, Samantha received more words of welcome from various coworkers.

"Samantha." Daniel stepped out of his office as he spoke. "Glad you made it."

She gave him a smile and a nod. Marti excused herself before heading in the opposite direction.

Daniel looked at his watch. "We've got half an hour before the first meeting." He motioned toward the desk behind him. "I've got a few calls to make. You might as well look over things in your office, see what hasn't been done while you were away, and then we can go to the board room together."

"Sure."

But she had no intention of looking over things in her office. She *wasn't* back yet. She was on leave, and she trusted Marti. Instead, she walked to the break room to get herself another cup of coffee. When it was ready, she settled onto a chair and took her first sips of the strong brew—a drink that couldn't compare to her grandmother's.

It took a few moments of sitting in silence for Samantha to realize how unusual her response to her boss had been. In the past she would have done his bidding almost before he let it be known. She not only would have looked things over, she would have squeezed in as much work as possible before the meeting. Being on leave wouldn't have made a difference to her. For that matter, she'd worked more than once while on vacation. But not today.

A smile tugged at the corners of her mouth, and the tightness that had begun inside of her on the commute released. She felt confident. No, more than that. She felt unafraid.

It was a good feeling.

Nick left the office in Caldwell shortly after four o'clock. He'd spent the last few hours untangling a supply snafu. Thankfully, he didn't need to go out to the worksite again. He could call it a day.

But instead of driving straight home, he went into Thunder Creek to Sips and Scentimentals. He didn't try to pretend that he needed caffeine after the type of afternoon he'd had. He wanted to see Samantha. Needed to see her. Their outing on Sunday had ended badly. Whatever upset her had left her uncommunicative, starting then and continuing throughout the week. He'd done his best to break down the barrier she'd thrown up, without success. He was sick of trying to solve things over the phone and via text messages. He was determined to talk things out today, to tell her how he felt and give her a more thorough understanding of his potential health issues. Then, if she still wanted to push him away or shut him out, fine. He'd have to live with it. But he wasn't going down without a fight.

The only customers inside the beverage and gift shop were three teenage girls, one on a tablet and the other two totally engrossed in their smartphones. He glanced toward the gift shop, making note of the changes made since the last time he'd been in. But what he really wanted to do was to walk to the closed office door and knock.

"What can I get for you, Nick?" Camila called to him.

"I'll grab myself one of those bottles of Diet Coke." He moved toward the refrigerated display.

"Anything else?"

"No." He walked to the counter, pulling his wallet from his pocket on the way.

Camila rang up the purchase. "She isn't in the office."

"What?"

"Sam. She isn't here."

Was he that transparent? Apparently so. He tipped his head toward the door that led into the house. "Is she with Ruth?"

"No. Sam's in Portland."

"Portland?" She hadn't mentioned it.

"Yes. Something to do with her job. She might be getting a big promotion, Ruth said."

His heart sank. "A promotion. That's great. Tell her I wish her luck with it."

A promotion. Was that why she'd been reticent to talk to him? She hadn't wanted him to know about a possible promotion? Maybe she'd guessed what he had to tell her, and she'd thought it better not to give him the chance to do so.

"When will she know if she's got it?"

Camila shook her head. "Ruth didn't say."

"How long is she staying in Oregon?"

"It was a day trip. She gets home tonight."

He opened the bottle of soda. "Well, like I said. Give her my best. Ruth too."

He left the shop, got into his truck, and drove home. Once there, engine off again, he pulled out his phone, opened the messaging app, and—against his better judgement—began typing:

Just heard news about promotion. Hoping for best. Have
safe trip back to Idaho.

He stared at the screen for a few moments, then pressed Send. A whooshing sound indicated the text was on its way. He dropped the phone back into his pocket and got out of the truck.

"Come on, boy," he said to Boomer. "I need to pack some more boxes. We move next weekend."

As if in response to his comment, his phone rang. He hoped it would be a call from Samantha, even though he knew he shouldn't want it, but a quick glance gave him his answer.

"Hey, Dad."

"Hi, Nick. Your mom said I needed to let you know right away what we've decided. Instead of shipping the things you have in storage, she and I are going to bring it in a U-Haul. We want to see your new place. Then we'll fly home after we've helped you with your move."

"Dad, that's a lot to ask."

"Nonsense. It gives us another excuse for a visit. The wedding was kind of crazy, and we'd like to see more of Thunder Creek than the quick tour we got last month. You won't mind putting us up for two or three days, will you?"

"Are you kidding?"

"Yes, as a matter of fact. I am kidding. I know you better than that, son."

Nick gripped the phone between ear and shoulder as he unlocked the door to the house. "What day will you arrive? I'll arrange for you to stay at the Inn at Thunder Creek for a couple of nights. That'll be better than you sleeping at the new house, and you won't have to put up with the chaos."

"You've got a spare bed in storage. We can assemble it and—"

"No, Dad. You and Mom are going to stay at the inn. You'll love it there, and you'll get a good night's sleep and eat good food too. Neither of those will be available at my place during the move."

His dad laughed. "All right, all right. I'm sure your mother will approve of that decision."

"Great. When do you expect to arrive?"

"On Friday evening. We'll get an early-morning start. Hopefully by four. If we don't have to make too many stops, we should roll into Thunder Creek no later than eight that night."

"That's a long trip in a miserable truck."

"We'll be fine. If it takes us longer, it takes us longer."

"It'll be good to see you again, Dad."

"Same for us. And before you ask, yes, we've got lots of help to get the stuff out of storage and into the truck. A bunch of guys from church volunteered to get it done on Thursday."

"I've got the same kind of volunteers on this end. My friend Derek began organizing help for the move before I could ask anybody myself."

"Great. Sounds like it's all in hand. We'll let you know when we're on our way on Friday. Forecast is for sunny and warm. Should be perfect for moving."

"I hope so. Thanks again, Dad. Give Mom my love."

"Will do. Love you back."

After saying good-bye and ending the call, Nick paused long enough to thank God for his parents. Then, Boomer following him from room to room, he set to work filling more boxes.

Chapter 25

The only people at Gran's Sunday dinner were family members. Gran and Samantha, plus Derek, Brooklyn, and Alycia. Others had been invited, but it seemed half the congregation was out of town for the weekend and the other half had plans of their own. Gran did not seem disappointed. If anything, she was pleased with the intimacy of the meal.

"Sam, tell us what happened in Portland." Brooklyn passed the platter of pork chops to her left. "I've been dying to know, but the inn was so busy yesterday I didn't have time to think, let alone make a phone call."

"It's great that you're so busy."

Brooklyn laughed. "Don't prevaricate."

"Prevaricate?" Samantha raised her eyebrows.

"Do I sound pretentious?" Her friend laughed again. "It was the word for the day on my dictionary app. Now, spill about your job."

Samantha did as requested, filling in as much detail as she thought necessary about the meetings and the people involved, finishing with, "It sounds as if a promotion will come through within six months of my return to work."

"With a healthy raise, I hope," Derek interjected. "Because even I understand how lucky they are to have you in their employ."

She sent a smile of appreciation across the table. "Yes, I'll get a nice raise when it happens."

Unfortunately—and she didn't mention this part aloud—Daniel would still be her boss. She'd hoped she would move to a new department when a promotion came. That wasn't going to happen.

All of a sudden tears pricked the backs of her eyes, and she knew it had nothing to do with Daniel remaining her boss. It was the thought of leaving Thunder Creek—and perhaps the thought of leaving Nick, although she didn't want to admit that part, not even to herself. Thankfully, in the silence that followed her answer, everyone had turned their attention to their dinner plates. She had enough time to blink away the moisture before anyone looked up again.

The conversation, when it resumed, moved to other topics. Gran shared Sandra Dooley's latest wedding plans. Alycia talked about the new filly that had been born to a neighbor's mare. Derek detailed his plans to expand the greenhouse.

"Oh," Brooklyn said when there was a lull, "guess who's going to stay at the inn this coming weekend." She didn't wait for anyone to guess. "Nick Chastain's parents."

Samantha lowered her fork. Nick had texted her on Friday, wishing her well on the promotion. She'd texted back her thanks that evening. But he hadn't replied again. He certainly hadn't told her his parents were returning to Thunder Creek. Why not? Didn't he want her to know?

If not, it's your own fault. She cringed at the thought.

"They're bringing down the rest of his furniture and whatever else he had in storage in a U-Haul. I think Nick said it was more than a twelve-hour drive. They're going to be exhausted by the time they pull into town."

Derek said, "Nick plans to spend Friday night in his new place so he'll be ready when the rest of the guys show up on Saturday morning. Shouldn't take us long to unload the U-Haul and move the rest of his stuff out of the rental."

Should she offer to take over food for the men helping Nick?

Gran had a similar idea. "Sam, we'll send you over first thing in the morning with hot sticky buns and coffee. And if the men are there through the morning, you can take sandwiches and sodas for lunch. Derek, how many do you expect?"

"Counting me and Nick, probably six. Maybe eight. Plus his parents."

"I suppose the move is why we didn't see Nick in church this morning," Gran added.

Derek shook his head. "No, his boss had him drive down to Salt Lake to pick up some equipment. He left yesterday morning and is driving back today."

Again, something Samantha hadn't known. She felt shut out and wanted to be hurt by it. But what else could she expect? She'd kept Nick at arm's length ever since he'd rescued that woman from the river, ever since she'd watched him put himself in danger. She'd convinced herself that he was as reckless and careless as ever, and she'd refused to talk with him, even when he'd tried.

And I was wrong, wasn't I? I was unfair to him. I didn't even tell him what I thought. I just shut him out.

She felt a shudder of shame in her heart and prayed that God would give her a chance to make things right with Nick.

The sound of tires spinning on the freeway hummed in the truck cab. Boomer sat in the passenger seat, mouth open, tongue hanging out one side. His ears were up, and he wore a look of canine contentment as he watched the passing countryside. The dog didn't care how long the trip back to Thunder Creek took. He knew how to enjoy the moment.

Nick didn't feel the same. He wanted to be home again.

He wanted to see Samantha again.

"But she doesn't want that. So where does that leave me?"

Boomer looked over at him, smiling that doggy smile of his.

"Yeah. Some help you are. You never offer advice, even when I need it."

A rest stop sign appeared on the side of the freeway. A mile later, Nick pulled off the road and went to a parking space near a designated pet area. He snapped the leash onto Boomer's collar, and dog and master got out and walked around, Boomer marking bushes and sniffing the ground. When the dog was done, Nick filled a travel bowl with water and watched as Boomer lapped it up.

"You should be good for another hundred miles."

The dog wagged his tail in apparent agreement.

"We'll grab a bite in Twin Falls."

In another ten minutes, they were back in the truck and on their way. It wasn't long before Nick's thoughts returned to Samantha. He wondered if it was for the best that she hadn't given him the chance to tell her he loved her. Maybe the right thing was for him to remain silent, to not ask her to step into that uncertain future with him.

"For I know the plans that I have for you," a voice whispered in his heart. *"Plans for welfare and not for calamity to give you a future and a hope."*

A future and a hope. With Sam? That's what he wanted it to mean. Could it? Even now?

Nick: Stopped in Twin Falls on way back from Salt Lake. Any
chance you could meet soon for dinner at the Moonlight?
I'd like to talk.

Samantha: When?

Nick: Monday or Thursday would work best for me.

Samantha: Can't Monday. Let's make it Thursday.

Nick: Thursday great. 6:00?

Samantha: Yes. Meet you there.

Feeling the coward, Nick dropped the phone into his
pocket. He could have called her instead of texting. Maybe
he should have driven over to see her in person when he got
back tonight. But he wasn't ready yet. He needed time to
pray about all that he wanted to say to her, and he needed
assurance that he wasn't reading his own feelings into what
he thought God was telling him.

*Please, God. Don't let me blow it. Help me do and say
the right thing.*

Chapter 26

Samantha looked at the calendar on her computer screen and counted out the weeks of her remaining leave. Eight more. But Gran had insisted that, once she was out of the boot and into the splint, she could manage on her own. Staying while Gran was in physical therapy wasn't required.

"Not that I want you to leave, Sam," Gran had told her. "If I could, I would keep you here for good."

Stay for good. The words stirred a longing in her heart that wasn't wise.

She gave her head a slow shake, then clicked on Thursday in the calendar application and looked at the dinner appointment with Nick. Six o'clock at the Moonlight. Was it wise to meet and talk? Or was it foolish? Once she returned to

Oregon, her life would go back to normal. And normal was good. Wasn't it?

Not necessarily. At least she hadn't thought so when she first came to stay with Gran. Was a promotion enough to change those old feelings?

"Knock-knock."

Samantha turned toward Camila.

"There's someone here to see you. About some books you ordered."

Thankful for the distraction, she said, "Sure. I'm coming."

Out in the gift shop, she saw a tall man, his back to her, looking over the bookshelves. No one else was in the gift area, so she had to assume this was Camila's "someone."

"Hello," she said.

He turned to face her, and something about him seemed familiar. Had they met before?

"I'm Samantha. How may I help you?"

His friendly smile made his handsome features even more so. "Aaron McNulty." He offered his right hand.

No wonder he seemed familiar to her. She'd seen that face on the backs of his novels for years. "What a pleasure, Mr. McNulty. I love your books." She shook his hand while hoping she hadn't gushed or come across like a crazed fan, à la the one in *Misery*.

"Aaron, please."

"Aaron," she echoed. After a moment's hesitation, she added, "This is so unexpected."

"Sorry. Hope I didn't catch you at a bad time."

"No. Not at all."

"As I understand from my publisher, you requested a book signing when you placed an order for my books, and they got word to me. Since I was driving to Nevada and Thunder Creek isn't much out of the way, I thought I would drop in to see you in person." His gaze swept the gift shop, stopping on the eye-level shelf. "I didn't expect to see a display of so many of my titles in a coffee and gift shop."

"You *are* quite an Idaho celebrity." Thankfully, she stopped herself from reeling off some of the details she knew about him. Where he lived. How old he was. His major book awards. Even the names of his two dogs.

He chuckled. "It's kind of you to say so."

But it wasn't kindness. It was a fact.

"Well"—another quick glance around the shop—"let my publicist know when you want to have that book signing." He held out a business card. "If my schedule allows for it, I'd be happy to oblige."

"You would?" She took the card.

"Yes, I would. And it was a pleasure meeting you, Samantha."

Her pulse raced. "Sam."

"Sam." There was that smile again.

"May I get you something to drink to go?" she asked hurriedly.

"Yes, thank you. That would be great."

A short while later, Samantha watched as Aaron McNulty exited Sips and Scentimentals, an iced coffee in one hand. As the door closed, she released a held breath and sank against the counter at her back.

"What's come over you, Sam?" Camila asked.

"Didn't you hear who that was?"

Camila shook her head.

"Aaron McNulty. The author." She motioned toward the bookshelves. "We sell his books now."

"Oh." The woman was completely unimpressed.

It was clear she wasn't going to get the desired response from Camila, but she knew who would give it to her. "I've got to tell Gran." And with that, she hurried into the house.

As expected, Gran—a lover of books, like Samantha—responded with excitement. "But, Sam, that's amazing! In our little shop. Right here in Thunder Creek. I never imagined such a thing could happen." Her smile disappeared. "Does he charge for the appearance?"

"He didn't say so, and I didn't think to ask." She glanced down at the business card. "Should I call the publicist?"

"Yes, I think you should. Strike while the iron is hot, your grandfather always said. Besides, you'll want to arrange for the signing before you return to Oregon. Otherwise you would have to fly back for the event. I'm surely not going to want to handle all the arrangements. This is your brainchild."

Some of her excitement drained away at the reminder that she didn't plan to be in Thunder Creek much longer.

His work finished for the day, Nick stopped by the Johnson farm. Derek had offered the use of boxes he had in a storage shed. Brooklyn was seated on the back porch.

"Come join me," she called to Nick as she held up a glass. "Derek will be back soon."

"Love to." He gave a command to Boomer, who hopped out of the truck and made a beeline for Miss Trouble.

"Long day?" Brooklyn asked.

"Long enough." He sank onto an empty chair.

She poured tea from the pitcher into a glass. "Why don't you stay and have dinner with us? Nothing fancy. We're having leftovers."

"Are you sure?"

"I am."

"All right. I won't make you twist my arm. I saw what you did to Sam to get her to go to paint night."

She wrinkled her nose at him.

He ignored it and took a long sip of the cold tea. "Mmm. I needed that."

"I can't believe you'll be moving into your new place in only a few more days. It happened so fast."

"Yeah, it did. I sign the papers at the bank on Thursday morning, and then it's mine. Mortgage and all."

"Bet you're excited to have your parents here again. I'm looking forward to meeting them."

"And they're looking forward to staying at the inn. Especially my mom. She's done her share of camping, what with raising four boys, but she still thinks roughing it is a Motel 6."

She laughed at his joke. Only it wasn't a joke. He'd spoken the truth.

A brief silence followed as they each sipped their tea. Sunset wouldn't arrive for hours, and yet the look of evening had fallen over the countryside. It drew the last of the tension of the workday from Nick's shoulders.

Brooklyn was the first to speak. "Hey, I don't suppose you heard what happened to Samantha at Gran's shop today."

Nick shook his head. But anything Brooklyn might say about Samantha was of interest to him.

"She got a visit from Aaron McNulty."

This time he frowned.

"The *author*."

Now he recognized the name. He'd seen the man's books on Samantha's shelves in her Beaverton apartment years ago. As he recalled, she owned every single one of them in hardcover editions. And she'd never been shy about sharing a favorite passage or turn of phrase from one of those novels. "How does Sam know him?"

"She doesn't. Or she didn't until today. I'm not sure of all the details. All that matters is he's agreed to do a book signing at Sips and Scentimentals. If we can arrange it, we hope to do something that also includes one of the summer concerts at Dubois Vineyards and will maybe bring guests to the inn for the weekend. You should have heard her on the phone. She's bubbling over with ideas."

It was easy for him to imagine Samantha's enthusiasm.

"We're going to try to pull it all together before Sam goes

back to Oregon, but we don't have a clue if that will be too soon for Mr. McNulty. Sam's checking with his publicist to see what's possible."

If Aaron McNulty could make Samantha excited about staying in Thunder Creek, Nick was all for whatever she and Brooklyn concocted. He would be even happier if *he* was the reason she wanted to stay.

Chapter 27

*N*ick left the jobsite earlier than usual on Thursday. At the rental he took a quick shower, washing away sweat and grime from the workday. Most everything in the small house was boxed up and ready for the move that would begin the next afternoon. But he'd kept enough clothes and toiletries out to get him through until he was settled in his new home.

After feeding Boomer and giving him a bit of exercise, Nick put the dog in the kennel. "Sorry, fella. Can't go with me this time."

He arrived at the Moonlight Diner at ten minutes before

the appointed time. He told Lucca he was early and would wait for the rest of his party, but she said it wasn't a problem and seated him anyway. He ordered a Diet Coke to drink while he waited.

Those extra ten minutes crawled by.

But at last Nick saw Samantha cross Main Street, having walked the short distance from her grandmother's house. She wore a pale-yellow dress, sleeveless and with a short skirt, and she carried a sweater of the same color in one hand. Her long hair was pulled back on the sides, then fell loosely down her back. The red strands caught and reflected the early-evening sunlight.

His pulse quickened as he watched her enter the diner. He stood, and when she looked around and saw him, he gave her a brief wave and a smile.

"You walked over." Internally, he winced. His nerves were showing.

"Yes. It's only two blocks."

"Yeah."

She slid into the booth across from him.

Lucca arrived to take Samantha's beverage order, but before she walked away, she said, "I hear something exciting's going on to do with Ruth's shop. I tried to get Brooklyn to tell me, but she clammed up."

"She knows how to keep a secret."

"So, will you tell me?"

Samantha's smile was radiant. "Nope. Not a chance."

"You rat." Lucca shook her head. "I'm usually better at

getting people to spill the beans. You know. Similar to telling a bartender your woes."

"Sorry." Samantha didn't look the least bit sorry.

Lucca released an irritated huff, but her quick smile said it was all for show.

Nick leaned against the booth and waited until the server was gone. "She didn't even try to get the information out of me."

"What could you tell her?" Samantha gave him a narrow glance.

"If it has to do with a guy whose initials are A. M., then I could have been of some use to her."

Now her eyes widened. "Who let the cat out of the bag?"

"The same person you said knew how to keep a secret."

"Brooklyn! How did you weasel it out of her?"

He shrugged. "Just sat on the back porch, sipped iced tea, and let her talk."

She was silent for a few moments and then laughed, that light, airy sound Nick loved so much.

Suddenly he couldn't think straight. All he wanted to do was look at her. He blinked, grasping for a thread of their conversation so he could continue where he left off. Oh yeah. He remembered. "I hope you'll tell me more about it."

Still smiling, she shook her head.

"You can trust me, Sam." And he meant far more than keeping a secret about a book signing by a popular author. Would she realize that?

"Hey, Nick."

He looked up to see Craig Hasslebeck approaching their booth from the back of the diner. "Hey, Craig." He liked the guy, but now wasn't the time for interruptions.

"How's it going, Sam?" Craig added.

"Good."

Craig looked at Nick again. "You sure you don't need any extra help tomorrow night?"

"I'm sure. Derek and I have it covered."

"All right. Then I'll see you bright and early on Saturday." He pointed with his thumb toward the cash register. "Better go. Enjoy your dinner."

As Craig walked away, Samantha said, "You've made a lot of friends in Thunder Creek."

He looked across the table. "You're right. I have. I knew more people in Corvallis, between the university and my sports activities, but I don't think I could have called most of them friends. Not real friends. Not the kind Derek and Craig have become." He leaned slightly forward. "Not friends like you and Ruth are to me."

"I'm glad we can be friends, Nick."

"Me too." Only he wanted more than friendship. And before this evening was through, he was determined he would tell her so.

Samantha's gaze slipped to Nick's mouth as he acknowledged their friendship, and desire coiled inside of her. Emotional desire. Physical desire. She couldn't separate them. Memories flared, memories of when he'd kissed her in that empty new home of his, memories of years ago when he'd kissed her a hundred other times.

She drew in a breath, trying to push those unwelcome memories away before they could overwhelm her, and said the first thing that came to mind. "Brooklyn told me your parents are staying at the inn this weekend."

"She told you *my* secret?" Nick looked surprised.

For a few moments, she thought he was truly taken aback. But then she caught the amused glint in his eyes. Her tension eased. "Tit for tat, as Gran would say."

"Or all's fair in love and war."

At his choice of comeback, that strange sensation coiled in her belly a second time.

He seemed to sense her reaction. His gaze became more intense, his amusement gone. "Seriously, Sam."

Seriously what?

He glanced around the diner, every booth and table filled with customers, then back at her. "Do you mind if we eat later?"

She shook her head. Her hunger had vanished before entering the diner.

"Could we walk to the park? There's something I'd like to tell you, but it's hard for me to think in here. It got kind of noisy."

After Nick paid for their beverages, the two of them walked out into the soft summer evening. Their steps were unhurried as they crossed Main Street. It wasn't until they reached the corner of Orchard and Sharp that he spoke. "I'm glad you agreed to meet me, Sam." They crossed the street and entered the park, following a path toward the footbridge. "I know things got strange between us last week. I'm not quite sure why."

Tell him. Tell him what you thought. Tell him why you were scared.

Nick jammed his fingertips into the front pockets of his jeans. "There's so much I want to say to you. I've been rehearsing it in my head so I wouldn't forget."

"Oh, Nick."

"But the thing is—" He stopped walking.

She took a couple of steps before realizing it, then turned to face him.

"The thing is, Sam . . ." One hand came out of his pocket and he raked his fingers through his hair. "I want— No. I have to tell you something else first. I need you to know more about . . . about my accident."

Those weren't the words she'd expected him to say.

"No, not the accident itself," he continued. "The effects of it."

"You told me."

"I didn't tell you everything."

What more could there be? And what did it matter?

"I've kept it from most everyone. I told myself it was 'cause I didn't want anybody to feel sorry for me. That's not true. It's pride, pure and simple. I think I told you I'm learning to be content. But I'm not there yet. Not completely. Not all the time."

"That's understandable."

He didn't seem to hear her. "A few weeks ago I got lost on my way to the jobsite. My brain just shut off. I didn't know where I was or where I was going. I panicked. It's why I didn't call you all that week after the wedding." He released a sound of frustration. "Getting lost and panicking happened to me a lot while I was staying with my parents. Almost every time I left the house alone. But it hadn't happened to me in a while. I thought it was a thing of the past, despite my physicians warning me I can never be sure of that."

Samantha's chest tightened, making it difficult to breathe.

"What if it happens again—and it could—and when it does I put someone at risk? Not just me being late somewhere. What if I was supposed to pick up a little kid after school and forgot? Not for a few minutes but completely forgot. What if it was five degrees out and that kid was left standing out in the cold because of me?"

She didn't know what to say. He didn't want her pity. She knew that much.

"Wondering that scared me, Sam. Really scared me. It filled me with doubt. I decided the best thing to do was to never be responsible for or to anybody. I told myself I would be okay that way, just me and my dog. Only the trouble is that's not what I wanted." He took a breath. "It *isn't* what I want."

"Nick—"

He held up a hand, stopping whatever she might have said. "When I was driving back from Salt Lake last weekend, I felt like God promised that He had a better future in store for me, that I needed to forget all the reasons why I don't think I can have the life I want. That I can't be afraid. That I have to trust Him with tomorrow."

Samantha knew more than she cared to admit about what it meant to be afraid. She'd lived that way most of her adult life. She only had to think back a couple of weekends for an example: the terror she'd felt as Nick had leaned over that churning, foaming river.

"This is the part where you come in." Nick took a step toward her.

She caught a whiff of the fragrance of his shower soap or shampoo. She saw the warmth in his gaze.

"Sam, I love you, and I want us to be much more than friends."

He loves me?

A second step brought him to her. His hands closed on her bare arms below her shoulders. She seemed to melt on the inside at the touch. The sweater she'd held in one hand dropped to the ground. Nick lowered his head, and instinctively she tipped hers back so their lips could meet.

He loves me.

Nick Chastain had kissed her many times during those months they'd been a couple. He'd kissed her again less than two weeks ago. But none of those kisses affected her the way this one did. Perhaps it was cliché, but she went weak in the knees. If he hadn't held her, she would have crumpled to the ground.

He loves me.

But was love enough? He'd broken her heart before, even if some of the fault was hers, and now he'd explained to her one more reason why she should be afraid to be with him. Strength returned to her legs. She put her hands on his chest and ended the kiss by stepping back. He didn't release his hold on her arms at once. Instead, he looked intently into her eyes, as if he would see into her soul.

"Nick, I . . . I'm only here for a couple more months." The words came out in a whisper.

"I know. But is going back to Oregon what you want?"

Her heart wanted her to return to his embrace, and it forced an honest reply. "I don't know."

"Do you think you could come to love me?"

The answer came out a whisper this time. "I don't know." Which wasn't as honest as before. Because she already cared for him. Perhaps more than she wanted. Perhaps more than was wise. She drew in a breath and released it. "Nick, do you remember what it was like between us before?"

A frown creased his forehead. "Yeah. Mostly."

"We were attracted to each other. There's no doubt about that. But what we wanted in life was different. What we wanted from each other was different. I always wanted more than you were willing to give. You . . . you put yourself first." She drew a breath. "You hurt me." She thought of him leaning over that rushing river, with no thought for her. "How can I trust you now?" Surprise flickered in her chest. Those weren't the words she'd meant to say to him. And yet, she realized, she'd needed to say them. She probably should have said them the day he'd asked for her forgiveness.

He was silent a long while before answering, "Maybe you're right, Sam. Maybe you don't have a good reason to trust me. But I'm asking you to give me a chance to prove I'm different. We've got eight weeks. Right? Give me a chance to prove that I'm the man I should have been before. If I do that, if I prove it to you, we can work through everything else. Whether it's here or in Oregon. But if you find you can't love me, if you find you still can't trust me, then I'll send you off with my best wishes. I promise. No anger. No harsh words like before. Because I love you, and I want your happiness."

Fear warred with hope inside Samantha, and she wondered which one would win, even as she answered, "All right, Nick."

Chapter 28

$\mathcal{N}$ick and Derek had completed the unloading of their pickup trucks and set up his bed in the master bedroom by the time Nick's dad drove the U-Haul into the driveway. Nick hurried out of the house as his dad helped his mom from the cab. He gave each a quick hug and didn't say they looked exhausted. He figured they knew that.

"Did you stop to get something to eat?" he asked as he stepped back from his mom.

"Yes. Around Twin Falls."

Hearing footsteps on gravel, he glanced over his shoulder. "This is my friend Derek Johnson. Derek, my parents, Rocky and Tricia."

Derek shook hands with Nick's father and greeted his mother warmly.

"Let's get you over to the inn." Nick gestured toward his truck. "You can get a good night's sleep and be rested before tomorrow."

"Are you sure you don't need any help before we go?" his mom asked. "We've hardly said hello."

He heard the dread in her voice. She wanted nothing so much as a hot bath and an early night. He couldn't blame her. "I'm sure, Mom. We'll spend plenty of time with each other tomorrow."

Relief washed over her face.

"Where's your luggage? We'll get it into my pickup and have you to the inn in no time."

He was as good as his word. In less than ten minutes, he was on the road, driving toward the Inn at Thunder Creek, Derek about five minutes ahead of him. By the time he and his parents arrived, Derek and Brooklyn awaited them on the front porch of the inn. More introductions were exchanged, then Brooklyn escorted Nick's mom inside, the three men following behind.

Nick waited until his parents had been shown to their guest room, then gave them both another hug and said he would see them in the morning. "It doesn't have to be early. Just call when you're ready. I've got lots of help coming to unload the truck, so you aren't needed for that. And if I can't come get you when you're ready, I'll have someone else come on my behalf."

"I'm looking forward to meeting all your friends," his mom said.

Nick nodded. "Me too."

Downstairs, he thanked Derek for his help, then headed out to his pickup. Leaving the inn, he almost turned the wrong direction, preparing to drive toward the rental rather than the house that now belonged to him. At least he didn't have to blame the almost-wrong-turn on his head injury. This time it was because he was tired and muscle memory had kicked in. Normal, all things considered.

When he arrived home, he let Boomer out of the kennel and threw the ball for him, hoping to burn off some of the dog's energy before bedtime—which was going to be earlier than usual. As he watched Boomer sail across the yard, his thoughts went to yesterday and his conversation with Samantha as they'd walked in the park.

"Give me a chance to prove that I'm the man I should have been before," he'd asked of her. And she had answered, *"All right, Nick."*

That's where they'd left it when he escorted her back to her grandmother's house. While her reply had encouraged him, it also felt . . . tenuous. He was ready for certainty. She wasn't in a similar place. Maybe she never would be.

Something Adrian had said from the pulpit a few Sundays ago returned to him. Something about the job of the Christian disciple being obedient to God and leaving the results to Him. Something about obedience being the blessing. What if Nick did everything right and Samantha still didn't want to stay, still couldn't love him? He wanted to resist that as a possible outcome, although life had taught him people didn't always get what they wanted. Could he be obedient no matter what?

Boomer's tail moved faster as he looked at his master, waiting for another throw. Nick obliged, but his thoughts were far from the dog or this backyard. He was facing the harsh truth about who he used to be. More so than he'd done in the past. Before the accident, he'd never given serious thought to marriage. His relationship with Samantha had lasted longer than most, but it had lasted because of her, not because of him. She'd held them together as a couple. She'd hoped for more than he'd been willing to give. Now it was his turn to hope for more. Would she be able to want the same a second time? Or had he destroyed his chances long before his accident?

He set his jaw. He wouldn't give up. He was different, and he would prove it to her. Somehow.

"Come on," he said when Boomer returned, ball in mouth. "Let's call it a night."

Although there were a few pieces of furniture in the living room and bedroom, the house felt empty. There was an echo when he spoke to the dog, his voice bouncing off the walls. He went into his bedroom and managed to find sheets for the bed after looking in a couple of boxes. Boomer stayed on the alert, moving from one side of the room to the other, watching Nick's every action as he made up the bed.

"This is home, boy. You can relax."

Boomer didn't seem inclined to obey that suggestion, and

he kept a close watch while Nick went into the bathroom to complete his nighttime routine. It was only after Nick had returned to the bedroom that Boomer sniffed at the plush dog bed, turned in several circles, and flopped down with a groan.

Nick chuckled softly, then groaned himself as he turned off the light and closed his eyes. He half expected more thoughts to churn and keep him awake. But he was asleep before that could happen.

Thirty-six hours had passed since Samantha and Nick walked in the park and he'd told her he loved her. Thirty-six hours, but the words he'd spoken hadn't left her, not even in her sleep. They'd replayed in her dreams, greeted her first thing in the morning, and echoed in her memory the last thing at night. And they were with Samantha on Saturday morning as she drove toward Nick's new home, a box of fresh-from-the-oven sticky buns and several thermoses filled with hot coffee on the passenger seat beside her.

Two trucks were parked well off the side of the road, one before and one after the driveway. When she turned in, she saw two more pickups parked on the grass. A U-Haul sat near the front door of the house, and Nick's pickup was inside the garage, the door open. Men carried items from the moving truck into the house and came back empty-handed.

Samantha parked her car in the grass beside the other

vehicles. Then, holding the box of pastries with one arm and gripping the handles of the thermoses in her opposite hand, she headed for the house. Her nerves churned faster with each step she took.

"Hey, Sam." Derek stopped as he came out the front door. "Is that Gran's coffee and goodies she promised to send over?" His grin said he knew the answer.

"Of course."

Her cousin stopped, then gave a whistle to the men at the truck. "Sam's brought coffee and something to eat from our grandmother." He took the thermoses from her hand and motioned with his head for her to follow him. "You probably know it, but the kitchen is this way."

She followed right behind.

The first person she saw was Nick's mother. Tricia Chastain, wearing jeans and a sleeveless top, moved around putting plates and other dishes into one of the cabinets.

"Here's Sam," Derek announced as he set the thermoses on the counter.

Tricia smiled. "Hello, Sam. Derek told us we would see you this morning. And he promised that your grandmother's pastries are the best."

"They are." She set the box on the counter next to the coffee.

As if to prove the reputation of Gran's coffee and confectionaries, all of the men began to fill the kitchen and dining room. Samantha's nerves quieted, and she laughed at the eagerness in their eyes and smiles.

"We've got napkins and paper plates." Tricia opened a cupboard door. "And here are mugs for the coffee." She set them on the counter, two by two.

Samantha stepped out of the way, and it was then she saw Nick, standing in the doorway between the kitchen and hall. He smiled, and her stomach flip-flopped. It shouldn't surprise her that he could do that to her so easily, yet it did.

"How else can I help?" She moved toward him.

His smile remained, but it changed somehow. "I'll bet Mom would like your company once all the guys get out of the kitchen again. Is that all right?"

"Sure."

"I'm glad you came," he added, his voice lower.

"It's what friends and neighbors do for one another." It was true, yet the words felt false as they passed her lips. There were other reasons why she'd come. Trying to figure out what she wanted, as he'd suggested, was one of them.

"Yeah," he answered. "It's what they do." But the look in his eyes said he was glad it was more than that for her.

When the crew of men—including Nick—had downed both pastries and coffee and headed back to their moving duties, the kitchen felt twice the size it had moments before. Samantha drew a breath, then asked Tricia, "What can I do to help you?"

Nick's mom smiled as she pointed. "Those two boxes have food items that should go in the pantry. And don't worry about where you put things. Nick doesn't care if peaches are mixed in with cans of green beans."

Samantha laughed softly. "I remember."

Tricia didn't say anything, but there seemed to be new understanding in her gaze.

Ducking her head, Samantha went to retrieve the first box and began to set its contents on the eye-level shelf. Cans of fruit, vegetables, and soups. A few boxes of prepared foods. A sealed bottle of ketchup.

As she worked, she remembered the first time she'd looked for something in Nick's Corvallis kitchen. They hadn't been dating long at that point, but she'd believed the man was organized and meticulous. Until she saw his pantry. It had been a disaster. When she commented on it, he'd responded that he never gave much thought to what he ate.

Understatement. Nick had lived too large to care about a neat pantry. His home decorating had been minimal too. Just enough for basic comfort and occasional entertaining. His garage, on the other hand, had been a work of art. Three kayaks. Two bikes. A couple of tents. There had been outdoor supplies beyond anything she could comprehend, and everything had been stored in its proper place.

A strange feeling tugged at her insides. It took a moment to realize what it was.

"Excuse me, Tricia." She stepped out of the pantry and turned. "I'll be right back." Then she headed outside.

The men who were emptying the moving truck paid her little attention as she walked to the detached garage. One of the two doors was still open. She moved to it, stepping to one side of Nick's truck so that she could see the other side of the building's interior. She noted the bike he'd ridden when he brought her to see the property. Other boxes cluttered the cement floor, all with handwriting on the tops, indicating the contents. A few large tools—shovel, rake, post-hole digger—leaned against the far wall. And near them, raised by two sawhorses, was a familiar red kayak.

She moved farther into the garage. As she got closer to the kayak, she saw that it was damaged. Was it the one he'd used on that ill-fated trip? She thought it must be. Could it be used again? Fear surged through her. It must be usable. Why else would it be there? He hadn't changed. He wasn't different. He still wanted the danger, the risk, the thrills. The realization terrified her and broke her heart at the same time.

"I'll put it in the garage for now."

She turned at the sound of Nick's voice. A moment later, the door to the second bay of the garage opened. Nick carried a pair of snowshoes. Two other men held large boxes.

Nick's eyes widened. "Hey, I didn't know you were in here." He grinned.

"I . . . uh . . . I was going to head back to Gran's. Looks like you've got the truck about empty."

"Almost." He leaned the snowshoes against one of the sawhorses. "I'm taking my mom and dad out to dinner tonight. Could you and Ruth join us?"

"I don't know. Wouldn't they rather spend their time with you?"

His smile dimmed a little. "I'd like them to know you better, Sam."

"I'll have to check with Gran. She might have plans." Her gaze flicked to the kayak and snowshoes—painful reminders—then back to him. "I'll call you."

"Okay." A frown furrowed his brow, and he lowered his voice, even though the other men had put down the boxes and left. "Is something wrong?"

She shook her head, not sure if she was lying to herself or to him. "I'll call you," she repeated, then turned and hurried to her car, not caring that she'd left the thermoses behind.

Tears began to fall the moment she left his driveway. "God, help me. I don't want to be afraid all the time. I'm tired of it. So tired of it."

You don't have to be afraid.

She hiccupped on a sob, wanting the whisper in her heart to be true.

Chapter 29

Ruth knew something was amiss the instant she saw Samantha's face. It was set like stone. Her granddaughter barely said hello before hurrying to her upstairs bedroom. At that moment Ruth despised her broken ankle more than ever. She wanted nothing so much as to climb those stairs and get to the bottom of things, but she was trapped on this lower level. She would have to wait until Samantha came downstairs again.

To help pass the time, she rolled her scooter into the kitchen and began to make salads for lunch. She washed and tore the lettuce. She mixed in fresh spinach leaves. She sliced cherry tomatoes in half. She added slivers of cucumber. All the while her thoughts roiled. She had plenty of questions and no answers. She wanted answers.

After setting the serving bowl on the table, she added a bottle of Samantha's favorite salad dressing and a container holding homemade croutons right next to it. Two plastic tumblers filled with ice and water followed. Her last trip from cupboard to table brought salad plates and utensils.

With still no sign of Samantha, she decided the next move was up to her. She rolled to the stairs. "Sam? Lunch is ready."

Silence.

"Sam?"

"I'm not hungry, Gran."

"Well, come sit with me while I eat. I need company."

Another lengthy silence.

"Samantha, please."

Ruth took a deep breath, her gaze focused on the top of the stairs. She was about to give up when she heard movement from the floor above. A moment later, Samantha stepped into view. Her expression hadn't changed much. Or perhaps it looked even sadder.

What on earth had happened?

Ruth glided her scooter into the kitchen, with Samantha not far behind. Once both were seated at the table, Ruth said the blessing, then slid the serving bowl toward her granddaughter. Dutifully, Samantha used the tongs to move a small amount of salad to her plate.

The silence chafed at Ruth. "How was everyone over at Nick's?"

"Fine. Very busy. The men almost had the truck emptied by the time I left."

"You weren't gone long. I thought you would stay and help awhile."

"I . . . I helped a little." She speared some lettuce. "I left the thermoses. I hope that's okay."

"Of course. Nick or Derek will make sure they're returned."

Samantha put down her fork and reached for the bottle of dressing. "Nick wanted us to go to dinner with him and his parents tonight. But I said I would have to check with you."

"Oh, I would love to go. I want to meet his parents."

"Okay." Her shoulders rose and fell with a breath, a look of defeat on her face. "I'll call him and find out the time and place."

"Sam." Ruth gave her granddaughter a stern look. "What's wrong?"

She shrugged.

"No. Don't put me off, dear. Tell me."

"I guess," Samantha began, "that I'm still afraid."

"Afraid of what?"

"Of falling in love with him again."

The confession didn't take Ruth by surprise, but the war going on inside of her granddaughter made her heart ache. *How can I help her?*

"He's different, Gran, but I don't know if he's changed enough for it to work between us. As much as I wish it could." Samantha placed her napkin next to her plate and stood. "I'll go call him now."

"Sam, wait—"

But her granddaughter was already out of the kitchen, having said everything she intended to say for now.

❧

Nick grabbed his cell phone off the counter and answered it. "Sam."

"Hi. I talked to Gran. She would love to go to dinner with you and your parents."

He noticed she didn't say the same was true for herself. "Great."

"Where should we meet you and what time?"

"There's room in my truck. We could swing by to get you."

"No, thanks. We'll meet you wherever you say."

Frustration welled inside him. Only a couple of days had passed since he'd asked her to give him a chance to win her love. Only a couple of days since she'd agreed to give him that chance. And already she was pulling back. If only he knew why. How could he fix it if he didn't know the reason why?

"Nick?"

"Yeah. I'm here. I thought we should try out Delaney's. It's a new restaurant Brooklyn told me about. The food's supposed to be excellent." He reached for a slip of paper and read aloud the directions Brooklyn had given him. "I made the reservation for six thirty. Does that work for you?"

"Yes. Six thirty is fine."

He heard her take a breath, sensed her desire for the call to end.

"Okay," he said. "See you then."

He lowered the phone from his ear, staring at the screen before it went dark.

"That was Sam?" his mother asked.

"Yeah." He met her gaze. "She and her grandmother are able to join us for dinner."

"Oh, good. I'm glad I'll get to meet Ruth and spend more time with Sam."

"Me too."

"I hope to know her better over time." His mom cocked an eyebrow.

There was no point denying it. "That's what I'm hoping, too, Mom."

"I thought as much."

He gave her a wan smile.

"Doesn't she return your feelings?"

"It's complicated."

His mom laughed. "When isn't love complicated." It was a statement rather than a question.

"I wouldn't know. This is the first time I've been in love. And it's the real deal."

"I'm glad for you, Nick. I've wanted you to find someone special. Even when you didn't think you needed anyone, I've prayed for it to happen."

"I hope God answers your prayers, Mom. I really do."

Before his mom could reply to that, his dad entered the

house through the sliding doorway to the deck. Boomer followed right behind, tongue lagging out one side of his mouth.

"Your dog would chase a ball from dawn to dusk if anybody could keep throwing it." His dad leaned over and ruffled Boomer's ears. When he straightened, he tossed the slobber-soaked tennis ball to Nick.

After catching it, Nick grimaced. "Thanks, Dad." He laughed as he shook his hand, as if to flick off the moisture. More symbolic than anything else. And he was thankful for the distraction. He needed answers from Samantha before he tried to respond to more of his mom's questions.

Delaney's was located in a converted 1940s home not far outside the Nampa city limits. It had what could only be described as "character," complete with curved archways, rounded corners, and pastoral wallpaper with shepherdesses in billowing green skirts holding crooked staffs. The wood floors were new. Or looked new after old carpeting had been ripped out and the wood refinished. Either way, the rich tone added an overall warm glow to the establishment.

As the five guests were led to a table near a window overlooking an emerald green lawn, shadowed by two giant weeping willows, Samantha tried to imagine how the home had originally looked. Walls had been removed to open up the space, and yet the architect had somehow managed to keep the homey feel.

Gran must have thought much the same thing. "This place is charming. I'd never even heard of Delaney's until Sam told me where we were going."

Nick answered, "Brooklyn promised we would love it."

They took their places around a large round table. Nick sat on Samantha's left, Gran on her right.

Looking at Gran, Tricia said, "Brooklyn should know. Her inn is utter perfection."

"I'm glad you're finding it so."

Tricia glanced at her husband. "I may be able to convince Rocky to spend an extra night or two before we fly home so we can enjoy it a little longer."

"Not sure we've had a chance to enjoy it at all," he replied with a wry smile. "I think we were so tired last night we could have slept on a slab of wood and thought it wonderful."

"Rocky," Tricia said beneath her breath, her look both chastising and tolerant at the same time.

Samantha felt a tug of increasing affection for Nick's parents. Especially for his mom. And it wasn't a feeling she welcomed. It only complicated her emotions when it came to Nick.

"Sam." He leaned close, his voice low. "Would you take a walk with me in the garden?"

She looked at him, surprise and suspicion mingling inside her.

"Please."

"Wouldn't that be rude? To leave everyone here?"

"Please."

"We haven't ordered yet."

"Tell your grandmother what you want. That way we'll have longer in the garden."

She hadn't a clue why she agreed to his request, but after a quick perusal of the menu, she told Gran what she wanted.

Nick stood. "Sam and I are going to have a look around outside."

He slid Samantha's chair back from the table and motioned for her to lead the way to the rear exit. From there a pathway wound between the trees. The summer air was heavy with the aroma of flowers.

Samantha followed the path, not stopping until she reached the back fence. There, she turned and looked at Nick, questioning him with her eyes.

"We need to talk, Sam."

"About what?"

"About whatever happened this morning. You've pulled away from me again."

"I don't know what you—" She stopped. That wasn't honest. "I saw the kayak in your garage."

"My kayak?"

You don't have to be afraid, the voice whispered in her heart. She ignored it. "Why is it there?"

"I always kept the kayaks in my garage."

She folded her arms over her chest. "Do you intend to use it again? Is that why you kept it? Is that why you moved it here with your other belongings?" She imagined him in it, flipping over, hitting his head, drowning.

Understanding replaced confusion. "No, Sam. I don't intend to use it again."

You don't have to be afraid. "Then why did you keep it?"

"Because"—tenderly, he touched her cheek with his fingertips—"it's a good reminder to me of God's mercy."

Her heart tumbled at the unexpected reply.

"Sam, I'm not a fool. You might argue with that, given my past. I admit I miss some of my old adventures. I loved them. But I have no intention of risking my health or my life unnecessarily. I told you the doctors cautioned me about what another head injury could do. I mean to listen to them."

She wanted to believe him. Could she? Should she?

You don't have to be afraid.

"And if none of that was enough to stop me, Sam, I wouldn't do it again because you don't want me to."

"You didn't care enough to stop before."

He shook his head. "No. You're right. I didn't care enough back then. For anybody. I did whatever I wanted." He held a hand toward her, silently inviting her to take it. "But that isn't how I want to live my life today or in the future. If you'll give me a chance, I want to put God first and you first."

Was he proposing? Her heart nearly stopped beating.

"I love you, Sam. Don't pull away from me. Don't be afraid. Talk to me. Ask me whatever you want."

She opened her mouth as if to ask something, then closed it as she realized God had already told her the only thing she needed to know. She didn't have to be afraid. She didn't have to try to control everything in her life. She could let go and trust Him.

The discovery must have shown on her face, for Nick's own broke into a grin. "Is that a yes?"

Was it a yes? There were so many reasons she should say no. Good reasons. Sensible reasons. Her job. His new home in Idaho. Her home in Oregon. And yet . . . she didn't have to be afraid. She loved him, and she didn't have to be afraid.

"Will you marry me, Samantha Winters?"

Certainty rushed in, replacing fear and lingering doubts and even what she would consider common sense. "Yes, Nick Chastain. I'll marry you."

Gently but firmly, he pulled her into his arms and kissed her. A long, slow kiss that made her heart soar. When he drew back his head, he stared down into her eyes, and she felt the warmth of his love all the way to her toes.

It was going to work out. No obstacles would be too much for them to overcome together. Somehow, someway, they were going to be okay.

Chapter 30

If Nick enjoyed the impromptu celebration that happened after he and Samantha announced their engagement to Ruth and his parents at the restaurant, it paled beside what he felt at church the next morning, with all the congratulations and back slapping and good-natured ribbing from friends. By the time he and his parents got into Nick's pickup for the drive to Ruth's house for Sunday dinner, he felt as if his face might crack from all the grinning.

It was obvious, upon entering the Johnson house—the front door stood open, inviting them to enter on their own—that Ruth's plans for this Sunday dinner had begun early.

Probably while she'd still been at Delaney's last night. Women's voices carried to the entry hall from the kitchen. Delicious odors wafted from the same direction.

"It sounds like that's where the fun is." His mom pointed toward the kitchen. She patted Nick's cheek. "See you later," she said and hurried off.

A moment later, Samantha appeared. "You made it."

"Even on my worst day I can find my way for a block and a bit." He reached for her and drew her close, feeling as if it had been ages instead of minutes since he'd held her.

She kissed him lightly. "I missed you too."

"When this is over"—he pressed his forehead against hers—"let's go for a drive. Just the two of us."

"I'd like that."

Although he didn't say it aloud, they had lots to talk about. That morning at church he'd lost count of the number of times he answered a question with, "I don't know" or "We haven't decided." It was okay not to know, but he would at least like to have the discussion.

Samantha turned to Nick's dad and gave him a welcoming hug. "I think you met everybody at church, but come with me and I'll make sure."

Before Nick could follow them, he heard sounds of others arriving and turned to see Derek and his family entering through the front door. As had his mom, Brooklyn made a beeline for the kitchen after saying a quick hello.

"Do you ever feel superfluous?" Derek asked wryly, then chuckled.

Nick laughed with him.

Derek looked toward the living room, then into the dining room. "Looks like Gran invited a lot of people for this Sunday dinner."

"I haven't counted, but I think you're right."

"She's more than a little excited. You've earned her seal of approval."

"I hope so."

"If it matters, you've got mine too." Derek patted Nick's shoulder.

"Thanks. And yeah, it matters."

Derek motioned with a tip of his head toward the living room. "Let's get comfortable. Doesn't look like there's any help needed by the likes of us."

Alycia had already made her way to the living room. She sat in an easy chair, her thumbs tapping away on an iPad. She didn't bother to look up when her dad and Nick entered. Two other men had found refuge there too. They were strangers to Nick. Derek took care of that with quick introductions.

"Nick, this is Camila's husband, Emilio."

Emilio stood and Nick shook his hand.

"And this is Chuck Babcock."

More hand shaking.

"Have you met Sandra Dooley, Chuck's fiancée?"

"I don't think so."

Derek glanced toward the kitchen. "I imagine she's in there."

Chuck nodded as he settled onto the sofa.

"Well, you'll meet at dinner."

Women's voices seemed to wash from kitchen to dining room, swelling in volume. Nick looked over his shoulder in time to see his dad walk toward him, and the expression on his face made Nick laugh. He looked as if he'd escaped a fate worse than death.

"You okay, Dad?"

"I think so." He rubbed the back of his neck.

Nick was about to suggest they sit down when the pastor and his wife arrived. Moments later, Ruth's voice sang out. "Come find yourself a spot at the tables."

In short order all fourteen people were seated in chairs, ten at the large table and four at a smaller one that had been added to a corner of the dining room. Ruth asked Adrian Vinton to say the blessing and then platters and serving bowls began to circle the tables.

Silently Nick added his thanks to God for bringing him to Thunder Creek and making him a part of this community. And not only of the community. He was thankful to be a part of his own family and, soon, a part of Samantha's family. It had taken a rough patch to bring him to this place and time, but it had been worth it. Who could have guessed that a near-fatal accident would bring him into a closer relationship with God and then give him a second chance with Samantha?

He prayed he would never fail to be worthy of her.

℞

Nick drove his pickup out of Thunder Creek and followed the highway to the south. Not that Samantha cared which direction he took. It was enough to finally have him to herself again. They'd been surrounded by others almost from the moment she accepted his proposal.

The weather was warm but not hot, and they chose to roll down the windows instead of running the truck's air-conditioner. Samantha wore her hair in a ponytail at the nape of her neck, loose hairs whipping around her face. It made her feel free and happy.

"I'd give a lot for a truck without bucket seats," Nick said, speaking over the wind.

"I was thinking the same thing."

He took hold of her hand and squeezed.

Samantha leaned her head back on the seat and closed her eyes, contentment flowing over her . . .

It was the silence, the stillness, that awakened her. She blinked as she straightened away from the seat.

"Hey, Sleeping Beauty." Laughter filled Nick's voice.

"How long was I asleep?"

"Not sure. Close to two hours."

She rubbed her eyes. "You're kidding."

"Nope. I figured you were tired, so I just kept driving so you could keep sleeping."

"Where are we?" She looked out the window.

"The Bruneau Canyon."

"Where?"

"Come on. There's an overlook. It promises to be spectacular." He opened the driver's side door. "But keep a lookout for rattlesnakes."

Samantha sat a little straighter. "What?" Was he kidding?

He laughed as he hopped out and closed the door behind him. She watched as he rounded the front of the truck and came to open the passenger door.

"Come on. It'll be worth it." He held out his hand for her to take.

Nick was right. It was worth it. In the midst of nothing but sand and rock and sagebrush, rushing water had carved a gash in the land that sank to an impressive depth. Lava cliffs fell abruptly away to the river far below.

"How deep is the canyon?" She took a step back from the railing at the edge of the outlook.

Nick didn't seem the least bit troubled by the sheer drop. Instead of stepping back, he leaned forward. "Oh, I'd say a good seven or eight hundred feet. Maybe a bit more." He looked up. "And I'd guess the canyon is well over a thousand feet across."

Samantha was no fan of heights, but she was a fan of the beauty of nature. The view made her tingle on the inside. The mixture of purples, reds, greens, browns, yellows, and blues was almost more than her eyes could take in.

"Looks like there's a hiking trail." Nick pointed off to his left. "Maybe sometime we can return and see where it goes."

"Sounds fun."

He turned to face her. "I've got beverages and a snack in a cooler in the back. I'll go get it. Wait here."

A short while later, he was back with more than the cooler. He had a couple of blankets over one arm and a camera slung around his neck. As Samantha recalled, he'd used to own several nice cameras, including one that was waterproof.

Nick made a spot for them well back from the edge of the canyon but still with a magnificent view. For a short while after they were seated on the blankets, he snapped photographs of the canyon and the horizon and even nearby sagebrush. And eventually he turned the camera on her.

"Don't." She laughed as she put up a hand to block the shot. "I must be a sight."

He lowered the camera. "You are a sight. A beautiful one." He leaned in and kissed her.

"Mmm," she moaned when he drew away at last.

"I agree."

She heard desire in the husky tone of his voice and knew it matched her own.

As if reading her mind, he said, "Which makes me want to ask the same question we've been asked all day. When's the wedding?"

Soon, her heart answered. But common sense forced her to say, "Maybe we should discuss where we're going to live first."

"Okay."

"There's my job. It's in Oregon."

"There is your job," he agreed, revealing nothing.

"I have that promotion coming."

"Yes."

"I've been with Whitewater a long time."

"A long time."

"Nick, if I didn't want to leave the firm . . ." She let the question drift into silence.

But he didn't hesitate. "Then I'll move to Oregon."

"You would? Just like that, you would go."

His smile was tender. "If your job is important to you, Sam, then you keeping it is important to me. I can get irrigation work in Oregon or find something else to do. I'm not completely without skills, and my boss will give me a good reference." He leaned closer for a second time. "Did you think we would get married and then live in separate states?"

"No." But she had expected him to make this more difficult for her.

"Well then, that's settled."

Only it wasn't settled. At least not the way Nick thought. Because Samantha had been happier and more content in the last couple of months in Thunder Creek than she'd been for years elsewhere. Even before she'd fallen in love with Nick for the second time, she'd been happier. Why on earth would she want to throw that away?

"What?" he asked, his eyes narrowing.

"I think I'd rather live on an acreage in Idaho."

"Really?" He grinned.

"Gran likes what I'm doing at Sips and Scentimentals. I think she would welcome my help even after she's walking again."

"And if working there isn't enough?"

Thoughts started to tumble in her mind, discoveries newly made. "Remember the day you told me you thought God was setting your feet on a path that would make something good come out of your accident? And you thought your new house was part of that?"

He nodded.

"I felt envious of your certainty. I wanted to know as clearly as you what path I should follow."

"Really? You were envious?"

"And just now I realized that maybe the best path for me is to walk beside you on yours. Does that make sense?"

He grabbed the camera and snapped another photo of her.

"What was that for?"

"I want to record the moment," he answered with a grin. "I don't want either of us to ever forget it."

"You're crazy."

"Crazy for you." He sobered. "So. Back to my first question. When's the wedding?"

Chapter 31

Nick could almost see the calendar pages flipping in Samantha's head as she considered all that would need to be done before a wedding took place. Was there a chance he could talk her into an elopement? Nah. He wouldn't want to do that either. He wanted to see her walk down the aisle in a white wedding gown, smiling at him, making him feel as if he ruled the world or hung the moon.

"Help!"

The faint voice almost failed to penetrate his happy imaginings.

"Help us!"

He twisted on the blanket. "Somebody's in trouble." He stood, his gaze searching the terrain.

"Help!"

He caught sight of movement in the distance near the canyon rim. A woman waving both arms in the air. He took several steps away from the blanket.

"Nick, wait!"

He broke into a run.

"Nick!"

He raced along the rough path toward the frantic young woman. A black lab hopped and bounced around her, obviously as distressed as its mistress. As Nick got closer, he called, "What happened?"

"It's my husband. He's fallen over the side."

Dread caused Nick's gut to clench. He slowed to a walk and approached the open rim of the canyon. Looking over the side, he saw the fellow on a narrow ledge about fifty feet below. He lay on his back, eyes closed. He appeared to be unconscious. Dressed in shorts and a T-shirt, his knees and arms were scraped and bleeding, but nothing lay at odd angles. Hopefully it meant no bones were broken. What wasn't good was how narrow the ledge was where he'd landed. If he rolled over . . .

Nick stepped back and turned. "What's his name?"

"Brandon."

"And yours?"

"Kayla."

"Okay, Kayla. I need you to be calm."

She nodded, her eyes wide.

"I've got rope in my truck. I'm going to see if I can get down to him and make sure he's secure."

Samantha arrived in time to hear what he said. "Nick, shouldn't we go for help instead?"

He looked at her. "I don't think there's time for that." His gaze dropped to his cell phone, now in his right hand. No bars. No service. "But we should get help as soon as possible." He looked from one woman to the other. "Do either of you have cell phone service?"

Samantha looked at her phone and shook her head.

Kayla said, "I didn't bring mine. I didn't think I'd need one." Her voice rose in panic.

"It's all right." He held his phone toward her. "Is that your SUV in the parking area?"

"Yes."

"Do you have keys or does Brandon have them?"

"I have keys."

He felt momentary relief. "Great. I want you to take my phone and drive toward Bruneau. Keep going until you have service. When you get it, call for help."

Kayla hesitated only a moment, then grabbed the phone from him and took off, her dog at her heels.

"Wait, Kayla!"

She stopped and turned.

"You'll need my code to unlock the phone." He gave it to her.

She repeated the six numbers, then took off again.

"Nick, you can't mean to try to go down that cliff." Samantha's voice held almost as much panic as Kayla's had.

"I have to."

"You could fall."

"I know what I'm doing, Sam."

"This is even worse than when you pulled that woman out of the river. At least there you weren't hundreds of feet above it." She stiffened and her lips thinned. "You promised you wouldn't be foolish. You promised me."

"This isn't being foolish, Sam. It's being expedient." Frustration deepened his voice.

"You can't risk it, Nick. What if you fall? Or what if you bump your head on the way down to that boy?"

"Sam." He took a step toward her. "I won't fall. I won't hit my head. I promise."

She took a matching step backward. "You can't promise that. You don't know what will happen."

He sighed. "I know this much. I can't let that guy just lie there and risk rolling off that ledge. Not when I have the training and ability to help him." He stared at her for a few torturous moments, hoping for a sign that she agreed. It never came, so he turned and ran toward his truck.

It wasn't long before he'd driven over the rough terrain and parked his rig within a reasonable distance from the rim, his front wheels tight against a large boulder. From the storage box behind his cab, he withdrew a couple of ropes, each of suitable length for the task before him. What he wouldn't give for more rock climbing equipment and another experienced climber or two to help him. But the ropes would have to do. When they were secured to the winch on the front of his truck, he carried the opposite ends with him toward the rim.

"Nick, please," Samantha whispered.

He stopped and looked at her. "I'm sorry, Sam. I'll always want to do what you ask of me. Always, with one exception: I've got to do what God asks of me first. If you can't trust me, Sam, then at least trust Him."

She sucked in a breath, as if his words had hit a vulnerable spot.

Nick took another step closer to the rim. "Pray that Kayla is able to call for help soon. Until rescuers get here, Brandon and I are going to wait it out on that ledge."

❧

Terror gripped Samantha as she watched Nick go over the edge, one rope tied around his waist. God had told her not to be afraid, and look where it had brought her. She moved backward until she leaned against the truck.

How could Nick do this to her? How could he leave her standing there, all alone, the desert wind whistling around her? Her and the rattlesnakes. She knew the poisonous reptiles were there, waiting to strike. He'd warned her that they would be.

She was scared. Not only that, she was stuck. She couldn't leave. She couldn't run away.

Run away.

The words reverberated through her, followed by a deep sense of regret. Running away was her first instinct, wasn't it? It had been for years. Gran had urged her to stop living in fear. Nick had asked her to trust him, and if she couldn't trust him, to trust God. Why couldn't she seem to do that? She wanted to. She wanted to more than anything.

Help me, God, to trust You more. Change me, please.

Samantha and her dad glided off the ski lift and out of the way of other skiers doing the same behind them.

"What a great day," he said, excitement in his voice.

As far as Samantha was concerned, any day she got to spend with her dad was a great day. She wasn't a fan of snow and cold—she much preferred the beach and warmth—but she was her daddy's girl. If he wanted to ski, she would go.

"Last run." He moved his goggles down from his helmet to cover his eyes. "I'll race you to the bottom."

"You always beat me, Dad."

His laugh trailed after him as he pushed off with his poles.

She set off right behind, not concerned with winning. It didn't matter to her. But she at least wanted to stay close.

Her dad led the way out of the wide clearing at the top of the mountain, sailing along as the trail narrowed and the pines thickened. Cold beat Samantha's cheeks as she bent her knees and leaned forward, gaining on him. She smiled to herself. Maybe she could beat him after all.

The trail turned to the right. Her dad rounded it with ease. She slowed a little, not quite as confident, but completed the turn. Several images immediately flashed in her eyes . . .

A skier on the ground in the middle of the trail.

Another kneeling beside him.

And her dad, veering off to avoid them, crashing through the trees before coming to a hard, fatal stop.

And in that instant, Samantha's life was forever changed.

Samantha closed her eyes against the memory, but still she came face-to-face with a hard truth. The fear that had taken root in her heart the day her dad died had tainted her relationship with Nick from the beginning. Yes, he had been selfish and reckless at times. But she had been intent on trying to change him, trying to mold him into someone else.

"I can't ask him to be less than he is just because I'm afraid."

Fear didn't evaporate with those words the way she wanted it to. It remained, crushing her chest, squeezing her heart. But even so, her mind cleared. And in that moment of clarity, she discovered another truth she couldn't deny: she couldn't love a man who would leave someone in danger the way she'd asked Nick to leave Brandon.

Samantha pushed off the truck and inched her way toward the canyon rim. When she was a yard or so away, she lowered herself to her hands and knees, ignoring the grains of sand, dirt, and pebbles that pressed into her flesh. Then she moved forward again. As her head neared the rim, she lowered herself onto her belly, heart hammering.

The canyon seemed to swim beneath her. The sight stole her breath, and it took all the strength within her not to shimmy backward. Instead, she closed her eyes and said another prayer for help. When she opened them again, she forced her gaze to focus on Nick.

He had arrived at the ledge and was kneeling beside the young man. He'd already begun to work the second rope beneath Brandon's torso. She felt a tug of relief when she noticed the young man's eyes open. Her relief surged once the rope was secured around him. As if he felt her watching, Nick looked up. Their gazes met and held before he gave her a thumbs-up to let her know they were fine.

"I can't ask him to be less than he is," she repeated. And this time she felt herself let go of fear and take hold of trust.

Dusk had begun to fall over the earth by the time the last vehicle left the canyon overlook. There had been a great deal of activity from the moment the first rescuers arrived. Nick hadn't had time to give Samantha more than a few quick glances after he was pulled to the rim of the canyon again. He'd been too busy answering questions and doing whatever he could to see Brandon and Kayla on their way, calamity diverted.

But finally, only the two of them remained. Samantha waited for Nick by his pickup, the setting sun casting a soft glow on her face, the shadows deep behind her.

"You okay?" he asked as he approached.

"I'm okay."

"Your grandmother's probably getting worried."

"She knows I'm with you."

Her words gave him a flicker of hope. "Sam—"

"Nick . . . I'm sorry."

He gave his head a slow shake.

"You were right."

"Was I?"

"Yes. I realized something while you were down there. I shouldn't have asked you to be less than you are. I was wrong to ask it. Even worse, I shouldn't have asked you to be less than God calls you to be." She lowered her gaze to a spot on the ground between them. "There was a young man on that ledge who could have died, and all I wanted was to stop you from doing anything I thought was reckless. And it wasn't because I love you, even though I do. It was because I was afraid. I've been afraid for far too long." She looked up again. "I don't want to be that way anymore."

He waited, heart hammering, sensing that she had more yet to say.

"I'm done running away. From now on I'm going to run toward what I want, not away from what scares me."

He saw it then, the change in her, the absence of the fear he'd seen in her eyes so often in the past, the fear he'd seen again a few hours ago before he'd descended the canyon wall. He stepped closer and drew her into his embrace. He didn't know for certain what the future held, but he did know God held that future.

"Run to me, Sam," he whispered, his cheek laying against her hair.

"I already have, Nick. I'm already here."

Epilogue

ingertips slid over Samantha's eyes, and Nick whispered, "Guess who?"

She turned from the sink, easily moving into his arms. "I haven't a clue. Just who are you?"

"Maybe this will help." His mouth pressed against hers, gentle yet possessive. It caused heat to flow through her veins.

She drew her head back, looking into his eyes. "Nope. Sorry. Still don't know. Try again."

He obliged. One of those long, slow kisses that could curl her toes. When the kiss ended at last, he said, "Happy anniversary."

Three years. They'd been married for three years. It felt

as if she'd been with him always. It felt as if the wedding had happened yesterday.

"I've got a surprise for you." Nick took her by the hand and drew her from the kitchen to the living room sofa.

"Nick. We said no gifts this year."

A year ago Nick and Samantha had opened a recovery and retreat center—Jeremiah's Hope—on a parcel of land next to their home. It had taken courage, a healthy bank loan, numerous investors, and a giant leap of faith, but they had done it. Nick worked closely with the physicians and counselors, helping clients and patients on the road back to health—physical, mental, emotional, even spiritual. Samantha managed the accounting side of things. And as the business manager, she kept a tight rein on finances. They were doing well after their first year, all things considered, but new businesses were a risk.

Risk. The word caused her to smile. Risk meant something quite different to her than it used to. She no longer ran from it. No fear! Never once had she regretted her decision to leave her job with Whitewater Business Solutions. Never once had she feared the many changes or challenges that had followed.

"It isn't a gift," Nick said, drawing her down onto the sofa. "It's a surprise."

She shook her head, laughing softly. "I hope you aren't going to be in trouble over this."

"Be in trouble with who?"

"With your accountant."

"I'll take my chances."

She leaned forward and brushed her lips across his. "You still like to take risks, don't you? But you do it for all the right reasons."

"What are you talking about?"

"Never mind. Tell me your surprise."

"Jeremiah's Hope is receiving a commendation from the governor." Nick beamed. "There's going to be a ceremony and reporters and everything."

"Nick! Really? That's amazing. I can't believe it."

"Believe it."

"I'm so proud of you."

"I didn't do it alone."

She lay her head against his chest. "God gave us a future and a hope," she whispered.

"He sure did." Nick stroked her hair.

"Our lives look very different from what I once expected."

"That's what makes it an adventure, Sam."

She swallowed a laugh as she straightened. "I'm glad you still like adventures."

He cocked an eyebrow.

"Because we're about to go on a big one."

Confusion spread across his face.

This time she gave into the laughter as she took his hand and moved it to her belly. "You'd better be ready to jump in with both feet, Mr. Chastain, because our next adventure should arrive in about six months."

Confusion changed to disbelief. "Are you sure?"

"I'm sure."

"Wow." His look was reverent as he gazed at her abdomen. His hand pressed tighter against her before he looked up again, a huge grin spreading across his face. "That *will* be an adventure."

"Are you ready?" she whispered, knowing that the idea of being responsible for a child had once caused him anxiety.

"More than ready." Confidence laced each word. "Because God's got this."

She met his loving gaze. *No fear*, she thought. *For either of us.* And then she kissed him.

Discussion Questions

1. Returning to Thunder Creek was fun for me as an author. A little like going home again. Do you still live in your home town? If so, what keeps you there? If not, do you enjoy going home again?
2. Due to her broken ankle, Ruth required lots of help. Have you ever been dependent upon others for things you once took for granted, like driving a car or climbing the stairs? Were you able to accept help graciously?
3. Samantha is restless and unhappy at the start of the book and doesn't seem to know the reason(s) why. How did she evolve over the course of the story?

4. The death of Samantha's dad left her a fearful person. Time and again, Jesus told His followers not to be afraid. Are you able to follow that command? How do you let go of fear, especially when it surprises you?

5. Nick lost a former way of life that he loved because of a serious head injury. Have you had to start over again for any reason (in your profession, where you live, etc.)? In what ways did you succeed? In what ways did you struggle?

6. Nick prayed that God would bring something good out of his accident. Do you trust God to cause all things to work together for good to those who love Him and are called according to His purpose (Romans 8:28)? How did God answer Nick's prayer? How has God answered your prayers?

7. Was Samantha right to think that Nick's love of sports like whitewater rafting and rock climbing were reckless? Is there anyone in your life who you feel walks too close to the edge or lives too large? How do you deal with it?

8. Do you have a favorite scene or line in the book? Why is it a favorite?

Acknowledgments

$\mathcal{M}$ any, many thanks to the entire fiction team at HarperCollins Christian Fiction for helping to birth another of my stories, from conception through editing and cover design through marketing and publicity and sales. It's hard to believe that nearly seventeen years have passed since my first title for HCCP was released (under the Zondervan imprint). I appreciate you all more than you know.

Special thanks to my editor Leslie who is always a joy to work with and who knows my writer's voice so well. You never fail to make my work better.

I can't imagine my writing career without my terrific agent of twenty-eight plus years, Natasha Kern. Natasha, you are a friend, confidante, sounding board, brainstormer, and so very much more. Thanks!

Of course, my husband, Jerry, deserves a boatload of thanks for holding down the fort when my writing keeps me tied to the chair in my office.

Finally, to the Author of life, who created me to create, who gave me a passion for storytelling and put a love for His Word in my heart.

Read Brooklyn and Derek's story in *You'll Think of Me*!

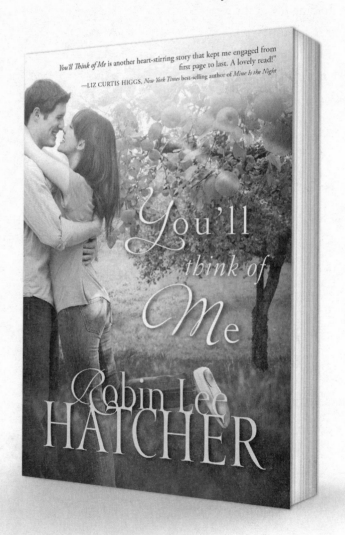

About the Author

*B*estselling novelist Robin Lee Hatcher is known for her heartwarming and emotionally charged stories of faith, courage, and love. The recipient of Lifetime Achievement Awards from both RWA and ACFW and winner of the Christy, RITA, and numerous other awards, Robin has authored over 75 books. She and her husband make their home in Idaho where she enjoys spending time with her family, her high-maintenance Papillon, Poppet, and Princess Pinky, the DC (demon cat).

For more information, visit www.robinleehatcher.com
Facebook: robinleehatcher
Twitter: @robinleehatcher